Conquered

NCP

GOLDIE MCBRIDE

Be sure to check out our website for the very best in fiction at fantastic prices!

When you visit our webpage, you can:

* Read excerpts of currently available books
* View cover art of upcoming books and current releases
* Find out more about the talented artists who capture the magic of the writer's imagination on the covers
* Order books from our backlist
* Find out the latest NCP and author news--including any upcoming booksignings by your favorite NCP author
* Read author bios and reviews of our books
* Get NCP submission guidelines
* And so much more!

We offer a 20% discount on all new ebook releases! (Sorry, but short stories are not included in this offer.)

We also have contests and sales regularly, so be sure to visit our webpage to find the best deals in ebooks and paperbacks! To find out about our new releases as soon as they are available, please be sure to sign up for our newsletter!

The newsletter is available by double opt in only and our customer information is never shared!

Visit our webpage at:
www.newconceptspublishing.com

CONQUERED

Conquered is an original publication of NCP. This work has never before appeared in book form. This work is a novel. Any similarity to actual persons or events is purely coincidental.

New Concepts Publishing
5202 Humphreys Rd.
Lake Park, GA 31636

ISBN 1-58608-687-1
Conquered (c) copyright by Goldie McBride, 2003

Cover art (c) copyright 2004 Jenny Dixon

NCP books are available at special quantity discounts for bulk purchases for sales promotions, premiums, fund raising, or educational use. For details, write, email, or phone New Concepts Publishing, 5202Humphreys Rd., Lake Park, GA 31636, ncp@newconceptspublishing.com, Ph. 229-257-0367, Fax 229-219-1097.

First NCP Paperback Printing: July 2004
10 9 8 7 6 5 4 3 2 1

Printed in the United States of America

Conquest

of the

White Rose

❧

GOLDIE
MCBRIDE

Historical Romance

New Concepts   Georgia

GOLDIE MCBRIDE

Other Books Available from NCP by
Goldie McBride

Chapter One

The first roar of fury barely penetrated Elspeth's semi-conscious haze, although it generated a spark of fear and the vague thought that the Normans, who'd taken over Rasgarth, her family's holdings, were embroiled once more in a drunken brawl among themselves. The second was punctuated by a kick that lifted the man she was trapped under. Elspeth peered up at the man who stood above her through one eye. Her other eye was swollen nearly shut.

Her heart nearly stopped when the blurry visage looming above her swam into focus.

A demon!

She knew it must be, for it could be no man—this dark giant, his perfectly chiseled face twisted in fury, his eyes as black as sin.

Renard belched a gaseous cloud of soured wine in her face at the blow, but gathered himself and rolled off of her.

Elspeth made a feeble attempt to cover herself, but

Renard had lain upon her so long that she could not seem to command her limbs to move. It was some relief that the dark lord's rage seemed to be focused upon Renard. A flicker of hope went through her. Perhaps he'd come to take the vile Normans instead of the women they had despoiled?

Renard lifted his head groggily, focusing with obvious difficulty. When he finally did manage the feat, his eyes all but bulged from their sockets, which seemed to lend a good deal of credence to Elspeth's fears.

Renard had led the band of ruffians that had descended upon them like demons from hell after William the bastard's army had defeated the forces gathered to repel him from Saxony, and had lain waste to the lands her father had spent a lifetime building to fruitfulness. They had slain all who opposed them and many who had only tried to flee—and those had been the fortunate ones. Those who'd survived had endured a reign of terror such as they could never have imagined.

Her own life had become such a nightmare since Renard had first fastened his lascivious gaze upon her that she had longed for death to end her suffering and would have sought it if he had not watched her so assiduously as to remove all opportunity of a quick and painless end.

"Guillume—my Lord Arnaud! We did not expect you for at least another fortnight!"

"That much is obvious!" Arnaud of Valognes said in a voice that was deadly cold. "Else you and your guard might have been on watch instead of rolling about on the floor with your laymen." He glanced toward the doorway and Elspeth saw two men at arms stood at attention there. "Take him."

"But … Guill—my Lord!"

The two soldiers strode forward at the command.

Each grasped an arm. Hauling Renard to his feet, they marched him from the room between them. The man he had called Lord Arnaud watched their departure through narrowed eyes. When he turned at last, his gaze focused upon her and Elspeth's blood ran cold.

"Out!"

Elspeth stared at him blankly. She had made it a point to pretend she didn't understand a word of their language. She wasn't certain if it would transpire that there was any sort of advantage to it, but she had thought it possible it would. At the very least, she knew they would speak more freely around her and she might be warned of any evil intent toward herself or their people in time to prevent more bloodshed.

She was in no condition at the moment, however, to recall the dangerous charade she had been playing. She looked at him blankly because she simply could not fathom what he wanted.

After studying her a moment, he strode toward her impatiently. Reaching down, he grasped her by one arm and hauled her to her feet. Renard had shredded her gown when he'd fallen upon her. Trying vainly to cover herself, Elspeth grasped the tatters of her clothing as he pulled her to her feet.

The abruptness of being dragged up so quickly sent a wave of dizziness through her and worse, her body was still numb and uncooperative from being pinned to the cold floor beneath Renard so long. Her knees refused to hold her. The moment his hand loosened, she began to sink toward the floor despite her best efforts to brace herself upright. With a sound of impatience, he hauled her up once more. This time, he caught her face in one hand, jerking it up for his inspection. "Are you too drunk to walk?"

Elspeth stared back at him fearfully, but she'd had time to consider her situation. It seemed unlikely, despite his irritation, that he had it in mind to kill her on the spot. As tempting as it was to respond immediately and try to spare herself yet another beating, her knowledge of their language, pitiful as it was, was her only weapon. Instead of answering, therefore, she merely met his gaze as steadily as she could manage, swallowing her terror.

His frown turned thoughtful as he scanned her face and then looked her over more carefully. She would've given much to know what was going through his mind, but the dark eyes typical of the Norman devils made them nigh impossible to fathom. Finally, apparently satisfied that he had discovered what he sought, he released the bruising grip on her cheeks and turned, dragging her from the room.

She did her best to keep up, unwilling to test his temper further by deliberately provoking him, but her legs still felt strange and uncooperative and it was difficult to hold her gown together with one hand. His long stride was impossible to match in any case.

She stumbled. He glanced down at her frowningly several times and finally slowed his angry stride.

She saw when they reached the great hall that it was overflowing with Normans. The servants were gathered in frightened knots, watching while those, apparently, who'd arrived with Lord Arnaud, lay about them with the flat of their swords, and fists, and booted feet, rousing Renard's drunken men from the floor.

Even as she reached the hall with Lord Arnaud, they began to push the revelers toward the door.

From the knot of frightened servants, an elderly woman detached herself and Elspeth recognized her old nurse, Griselda. "Lady! Lady! What has that monster done to you?" she wailed, falling to her knees beside Elspeth.

10

Elspeth stared down at her in horror as Lord Arnaud came to an abrupt halt. "Shh! Are you mad, woman! Do you want me to join my ancestors? I've survived nigh two weeks of that pig of a Norman. I've taken no serious hurt, not near so much as I'm likely to take if they learn who I am."

Griselda scrambled to her feet abruptly, wringing her hands and casting fearful glances toward Lord Arnaud.

Elspeth didn't dare look at him. She knew few of the Normans had any grasp of the Saxon tongue, but it would take no great intellect to figure out who she was if Griselda was determined to treat her as her lady in front of them. With the exception of her mother, who had passed on many years ago, the Normans had slain the rest of her family—her father and brothers had all fallen beneath Norman blades when they'd gone to protect the realm from the invaders from across the sea. She had no protector and no way of knowing whether the Normans would be satisfied with the blood already spilled or if they were bent upon wiping out the last of her father's seed. It seemed to her, though, that the possibility was great that they would prefer not to harbor the daughter of the old lord.

After a moment, Lord Arnaud tugged her into motion once more and strode toward the servants purposefully, releasing her at last when they reached them. Elspeth cast an uneasy glance at him, but he seemed to have dismissed her. With an effort, she hobbled over to join them. They stared at her fearfully, but parted, allowing her to find her way to the back where she would be less noticeable.

"Who among you speaks French?"

Everyone shifted, exchanging nervous glances when he addressed them. Finally, Jean, the young man who'd come into her father's household as a troubadour and

11

remained as her tutor, stepped forward cautiously and bowed. "I do, my lord."

Lord Arnaud looked him over, assessing him. "You are not Saxon."

"I am a troubadour, originally from Vereins. I joined Lord Odolf's household last spring."

Lord Arnaud's brows rose. "And stayed to entertain so long?"

Jean blushed but didn't glance in Elspeth's direction. "I made myself useful."

Lord Arnaud studied him for so long that Jean shifted restlessly. "Then you may stay and make yourself useful to me, as well. I've need of someone who can speak their crude tongue and pass my orders along until I can master the language myself."

Jean bowed again. "I am happy to be of service, my lord."

Lord Arnaud nodded. "Then set them to work cleaning this pig sty. Remove anything that can be fixed for the craftsmen to repair. The rest should be piled far enough from this tender box so that it can be burned without setting the house ablaze, as well."

Jean looked at him uncomfortably.

"Is there ought about the order that you do not understand?" Lord Arnaud demanded impatiently.

Jean swallowed with an effort. "The carpenter and his apprentice were killed when the … uh … others arrived," he said weakly.

Lord Arnaud's lips tightened with barely suppressed fury. After a moment, he nodded. "The order stands. Use your best judgment. Dispose only of those things that appear beyond redeeming."

Battered as they were, everyone was so relieved that they were expected to do no more than perform the tasks familiar to them that they nigh fell over themselves to show their willingness to comply. Elspeth knotted her gown together the best she could and set to work with them.

The first of the servants to venture outside to begin the task of disposing of broken furnishings returned fearfully. Lord Arnaud, they said, had rounded up Lord Renard's men and had lined them up at the whipping posts. The news sent a ripple of unease through everyone as the thought occurred that they might be next, and everyone bent to their tasks with renewed vigor, despairing, but hopeful their efforts might please Lord Arnaud enough that he would consider showing some leniency.

Elspeth would have preferred to remain inside and as unobtrusive as possible, but she was as fearful as the others and presently gathered an armful of refuse and went out to see what she might learn of Lord Arnaud's plans. She made Griselda walk with her, hopeful it would make her less conspicuous, but when she nerved herself to glance toward the proceedings, she saw that Lord Arnaud was watching the progress of the servants to and from the growing pile of refuse. His dark gaze so unnerved her that she stumbled. Griselda steadied her, preventing her from falling on her face, and she concentrated thereafter on listening rather than watching.

When she returned to the hall, she was able to report that Lord Arnaud had ordered twenty lashes for each of the men he'd charged with the task of securing his holdings, including Lord Renard, who was his bastard half brother.

They were certain she must be wrong. Twenty lashes hardly seemed like any punishment at all if he truly was displeased about their behavior. When Jean confirmed her report, they became excited with the no tion that it seemed to indicate Lord Arnaud was not nearly so much to be feared as they'd thought.

It was a dangerous misconception, Elspeth thought, and pointed out to them that Lord Renard, whom they were so certain was far more to be feared, had quailed before his half brother. "I think it's far more likely he doesn't wish to render them completely useless. It would be a mistake we might all come to regret to perceive him as weak only because he seems to have shown mercy to his men. There seems to be some hope, however, that so long as we do as we are told, we need not be overly fearful."

They scattered and hurried about their tasks when they saw that Lord Arnaud had returned to check their progress. Unfortunately, no one noticed his arrival until Elspeth had finished speaking, including Elspeth, and she couldn't forebear sending a panicked, and she didn't doubt, guilty, glance in his direction before she hurried to join the servants and, hopefully, vanish among them.

When she finally nerved herself to glance at him again, she saw that his gaze was on her still and the uneasy feeling that he had realized she was the old lord's daughter could not be shaken.

To her relief, he seemed reasonably satisfied with their progress, however, and left again after he'd thoroughly frightened everyone out of the little wit that remained to them by watching their progress with his cold, assessing gaze. Mid morning, Jean was summoned and disappeared for a while. When he returned it was to inform them that they were to prepare a meal for the men. Ordinarily, that wouldn't have been cause for great alarm, but there was little left in the larder to appease fighting men. Her father had taken much of their supplies with him when he'd gone off to make war, and Renard's men had made great inroads into what

14

had been left in the two weeks since their arrival. To make matters worse, much had been destroyed when they'd seized Rasgarth.

Renewed fear swelled among them. It didn't matter that they were not responsible. They would be held responsible and bring Lord Arnaud's wrath down upon their heads.

Assuring them that something could be managed, Elspeth directed them to return to their work, sent the kitchen folk to the kitchen to set it to rights and went off with Jean to check the larder to see if it was possible to keep her word. Her mother had died at her birth. She had been chatelaine of her father's household for years and there had been many lean ones in her time when the crops had failed or a particularly bad winter and late spring had required a good deal of skill to keep the folk fed. She felt—hoped—she could come up with something that would at least be filling if not particularly elegant.

The condition of the larder dismayed her, however. There was no fresh meat since Renard and his men had seemed more inclined to drink and whore than pursue anything useful, and very little smoked meat. The bread was virtually non-existent and most of the cheese was gone, as well.

"We are going to starve," Elspeth said with conviction once she'd assessed the situation, "if Lord Arnaud doesn't slay us first. How many Normans would you guess there are, Jean?"

Even as she glanced toward Jean, the larder grew dark as someone stepped into the doorway, blocking the light. She glanced quickly toward the door.

"What did she ask you?" Lord Arnaud asked coolly.

Jean glanced at Elspeth nervously before he an

15

swered. "We were trying to calculate how much we would need to feed everyone, my lord."

Lord Arnaud studied him piercingly for several moments and finally turned to survey the larder, his face hardening. "By what name is she called?" he asked as his gaze settled at last upon Elspeth.

"La—Elspeth."

Lord Arnaud's gaze zeroed in upon Jean once more. One dark brow arched upward. Instead of commenting on Jean's near slip, however, he informed Jean to see to unpacking the supplies he'd brought with him.

Elspeth sagged with relief when he'd left with Jean following at his heels. She found that she was shaking with reaction. She had never considered herself a coward, but the reign of terror they'd experienced at the hands of the Normans had done more than instill a healthy respect of them. It had made her long to flee to some place safe from their merciless tempers. She would have except that she had no where to run to—any family she might have that had survived the invasion would not be in any position to lend her aid. She was certain in any case that the Normans would only hunt down anyone who tried to flee—Lord Renard had made great sport of doing so.

She'd hoped to escape notice, however, and with the best will in the world, she could not make herself believe that she had. Somehow, most likely because he believed she was his brother's whore, Lord Arnaud had focused his attention upon her—with suspicion she feared, but she did not want his attention for any reason.

That thought provoked a wry glance at herself. She had once been considered comely, but she need not look upon her reflection to know that she could have no appeal now for any man. Lord Renard had battered her face into a grotesque, misshapen mask. She was filthy from having been thrown on the floor like a common doxy at any time Lord Renard had been sober enough to spy her, and she had been slow enough for him to catch. Her hair was filthy as well, and scarcely half of it still contained within its braid since they had ransacked her apartments and she no longer even had so much as a comb to her name.

She wasn't certain why Lord Arnaud was interested, but she thought she needn't fear that he would take his brother's place. Unlike his pig of a brother, Lord Arnaud seemed a fastidious man. He wore the grime of the road, of course, but he had not the look of someone careless about their person, and his determination to see that the manor was cleaned seemed to support that assessment.

Very likely it was only that he suspected that she was not a servant at all, but that was hardly reassuring.

Despite her anxieties, Lord Arnaud concentrated on securing his new holdings and setting it to rights. He and the men he'd brought with him spent most of their days hunting for fresh meat for the larder, patrolling, and making certain the serfs were tending the fields that had not been destroyed. The men he'd had whipped were given the additional punishment of having to supply the labor they'd deprived their lord of by slaying so many of his serfs and were put to work preparing the foundation for a stone wall that was to surround the manor in the style of a European fortification.

Little more than a week after his arrival, just as they'd begun to relax and the workings of the manor had begun to resume some semblance of normalcy, they learned why Lord Arnaud had set about seeing that the household was put to rights as quickly as possible. His bride arrived from Normandy.

Chapter Two

Elspeth and Griselda had found shelter for them-selves in one of the tiny cottages near the manor that had belonged to one of the craftsmen killed in the ini-tial raid. Lord Renard had been kept far too busy to turn his unwanted attentions upon her since Lord Arnaud's arrival, and the lord himself had been preoc-cupied with trying to set his estate in order. Yet, Elspeth knew the peace would not last.

Her bruises had faded. Sooner or later, if she was too available, Renard would notice her again and life would once more become the nightmare it had been before Lord Arnaud's arrival.

The cottage provided the most that she could hope for in avoiding Renard.

Little escaped the new lord of the manor, however, as Elspeth discovered when she opened the door to Jean one evening after she and Griselda had finished their duties and been allowed to seek their rest.

He looked uneasy and Elspeth was immediately

alarmed. "What has happened?" she asked a little breathlessly.

Jean twisted his cap uncomfortably. "Might I come in for a word with you, Lady?"

Elspeth gripped his arm and dragged him inside. "I wish you would not call me that! I am lady no more, and I would as soon our enemies did not know that I am the daughter of Odolf."

He flushed but looked even more uncomfortable. "I am not so certain he has not figured it out. He sent me to find you. I am to tell you that he expects you to serve his lady and you must make yourself present-able."

Griselda was more outraged than Elspeth, if possible. "Our lady to serve as maid to that Norman whore!" She turned to look at Elspeth. "I told you, my lady! You should have told him who you are and demanded that you be treated according to your station!"

Elspeth flushed angrily. "He said that I was to make myself presentable!" she demanded furiously. It was insulting, even though she was obliged to admit that she was a disreputable creature, as bad or worse than the lowest scullery maid. It was hardly her fault, however, that she dared not even allow herself the comfort of decent grooming for fear that Renard would assault her yet again.

"Nay! He did not say that. He said only that he had need of a woman to serve his lady. I thought it would be easier for you, my lady! He asked me about you and I told him that you had been maid to the old lord's daughter.... I could think of nothing else to say once he had remarked that you did not seem to be a common peasant." He stopped, blushing furiously. "And I know that you have tried to hide yourself among the servants and have no wish to draw attention to yourself, but you can not expect to be accepted as lady's maid when you.... It is not at all a wise idea to challenge him by appearing...."

"Like a filthy Saxon peasant?" Elspeth finished for him.

"She is too good to serve such a one as that devil's whore, even if she looked like a swine maiden ... which she most assuredly does not!"

Elspeth glanced at Griselda uncomfortably. In truth, she could pass for one now and it irked her no end that she must go about soiled and untidy, wearing nothing but the mended rags that remained from the gown Renard had torn from her when she had struggled with him.

"You should have thought of something else to tell him. I will not suffer being mauled by that pig of a brother of his!"

Jean frowned. "You have no protection here. If he decides to seek you out, you will be at his mercy. At least if you serve his lady, you will have some protection. You would sleep on a pallet in her room to be close for her call. Renard would not dare to enter there—and you would spend your days in her company."

Elspeth studied him, wavering. As repugnant as the idea was of serving as maid in her own home, it was surely no worse than serving as a lower servant in her own home, and she couldn't deny that the lure of protection was nigh irresistible.

Jean mangled his hat nervously. "I don't think Lord Arnaud would take a rejection kindly, lady."

Elspeth's lips tightened, but she was not such a fool as to think that she could defy the new lord with impunity. Finally, she nodded. "When am I to present my self?"

* * * *

She had nigh forgotten how good it felt to be fresh and well groomed, Elspeth reflected as she made her way to the great hall the following morning at sunrise. The gown Lord Arnaud had sent to her had been one of her own, which had caused her more than a pang or two. It was an older gown and well worn—Renard had taken her better gowns and sold them at the market to put a few coins in his pockets—but it was far better than the one she'd mended and worn for so long.

It made her feel hopeful of a future free from fear. It made her incautious.

She had already passed the men working on the wall when someone caught her arm, jerking her to a halt. Whirling, she found herself face to face with Renard. Terror closed her throat instantly.

"I have missed you, my pale Saxon rose."

Elspeth blinked at him rapidly, trying to force her mind to work. She didn't think to respond in his own language or she might well have done so, even knowing that she would not be able to reason with him regardless. All she could think was that Jean had told her she would be safe. "Unhand me," she said, her voice cold, but shaking with the terror that gripped her.

He grinned. "Fortunately for you, I can not understand your guttural tongue, or I might know that for the insult I suspect it was."

She tried to pry his fingers loose but to no avail. "Lord Arnaud summoned me to serve his lady," she said desperately.

Renard's eyes narrowed at the only two words that needed no translation. "Lord Arnaud?" He stepped back to survey her from head to foot. "He'd have no interest in taking my leavings, chere, even if not for the fact that he expects his bride this very day."

Elspeth licked her lips and turned to look at the manor, so near, and yet so far away. "Jean! Please come! Jean!" she screamed, tugging at her arm again in an attempt to free herself.

Renard laughed, glancing around at his men, who'd gathered closer to watch, their gazes avid as if they had been promised a special treat. "Do you hear that? She summons the scrawny boy to her aid! I am quaking in my boots!"

"You should be," Guillume growled from directly beside them.

Renard's head snapped around so quickly that he met the fist Lord Arnaud slung at him head on. The impact laid him on the ground. Blood spurted from his nose and ran down his face. Arnaud moved to stand over him, waiting to see if he would rise to challenge him. When Renard merely remained where he'd fallen, holding his nose and gaping up at his brother stupidly, he stepped back and surveyed the men who'd gathered around them.

"Know this—the war has ended. This is my home and I will have peace in it. No man will take an unwilling maid. Slake your needs on the willing, or take your coin and pay for the services of a whore." He glanced down at Renard, his face tight with suppressed fury. "That includes you, brother."

Renard picked himself up and dusted his clothes off. He was angry but trying hard to hide it. He laughed unconvincingly. "She is willing. She likes to play coy, but she was more than willing until she set her sights a little higher. If you want her for yourself, though, brother, who am I to deny you?"

Lord Arnaud's eyes narrowed. "She was summoned

22

to serve my lady. Lady Rosabel has been sheltered and would be distressed to see her maids misused. I saw nothing to indicate that she was willing, and much to indicate otherwise—but if you want it verified, I will send for Jean to interpret for you."

Renard glared at him. "If you do not want her for herself, then why not give her to me as a reward for securing Rasgarth for you?"

Lord Arnaud gave him a look. "Do not draw me into a discussion, here, regarding what you have done for me, brother. She will serve my lady and you will look elsewhere for a layman. I suggest, this time, that you use gentle persuasion. It will take you further with the woman you choose to bestow your favors upon."

Lord Arnaud had already turned to leave when Renard spoke again. "Your gentle bride will not be pleased to learn that she is being waited upon by a Saxon whore."

Lord Arnaud turned to survey his brother coldly. "I would be … very displeased if Rosabel were to hear anything that might distress her."

With that, he turned and strode toward the manor once more. Elspeth stared after him for several moments, glanced at Renard, and hurried to catch up to him. She was so busy trying to set herself to rights that she nearly plowed into him when he stopped just inside the door.

She looked up at him when he turned to study her, swallowing her residual fear with an effort. "Merci, my lord," she said shakily and bobbed a nervous curtsey.

He surveyed her with keen interest, his gaze missing nothing. After a moment, his face hardened. Lifting a hand, he caught the thick braid that lay across her shoulder, stroking his thumb over her smoothly bound hair almost absently. "It is as I

23

thought—hair the color of sunlight; eyes as cool as a placid lake under a summer sky; skin like cream; and lips like ripe berries—you are clever as well as beautiful, chere—a dangerous combination. But do not thank me so quickly." Releasing her braid, he ran the back of his hand lightly down her cheek. "If I were not forsworn, I would have you for myself—and I am not at all certain that it would sway me if you were unwilling. If you are as wise as you seem, you will take care not to tempt me to forsake my vows."

Chapter Three

As he left her and strode away, Elspeth wondered uneasily if Lord Arnaud had known that she could understand him. Or had he said those things because he believed she could not understand?

She frowned thoughtfully. Either way, it was surely a warning, but if he had thought that she could understand, or might, then he had intended that she know. That must surely mean that he was a man who considered his vows sacred, and his honor was not a thing which he took lightly.

Perhaps he had believed his brother when Renard had accused her of setting her sights on becoming the lord's layman?

It was unreasonable. She had done nothing more than make herself presentable. She had not tried to make herself pretty to entice. She had washed and combed her hair when she had bathed the filth from herself, but she had bound her hair. She had not perfumed herself, nor sought artifice to enhance the smoothness of her skin or the color of her lips.

Renard's male conceit was such, however, that she need only suffer the misfortune of coming within sight and he was convinced that she wished to entice him.

Perhaps the Normans were all like that?

She could not recall that any Saxon had ever looked upon her as if she was his for the taking—but of course she had had the protection of her father and brothers before.

Mayhap men were all like that, believing it was enough that they should desire, and any female who did not run fast enough wished to be caught?

She shuddered. She did not want to be any man's layman, whatever they thought. In the days before, when she had thought about the time when she would take a husband, she had looked forward with excitement to becoming a woman. Renard's brutality had cured her of that. She thought coupling might not be as repulsive if it were someone other than Renard rutting her, and it was not nearly so painful as it had been in the beginning, but she could no longer imagine deriving any enjoyment out of it for herself.

After a time, she shook her wayward thoughts and went off to find Jean to discover which room was to be the Lady Rosabel's. Jean had seemed to indicate that it would not be the same room as her husband— which seemed oddly cold to her mind, but then the Normans were almost as different from her own people as night to day.

She found to her relief that she had not misunderstood Jean. Lady Rosabel was to have a room adjoining her husband's and she would be allowed to make a pallet for herself near the door, where she would be at hand for the Lady Rosabel's call, and yet not underfoot, and might come and go in her service without disturbing the lady overmuch.

She had not given much thought to what the lady, herself, might be like, but she knew that pleasing Lady Rosabel would be paramount to her own comfort and happiness and she immediately set her mind to thinking of how she might make herself welcome. She had only a vague idea of how far away Normandy was, but she knew that it was across the sea, for the Normans had come in ships. Most likely Lady Rosabel would be weary from travel, she thought, and would wish to bathe the dust of the road from herself and rest.

She immediately set about preparing for a bath. She had two of the menservants clean the tub thoroughly and then carry it up to the room and set it before the hearth, then sent them to fetch water until they had the tub half filled. When that was done, she had buckets brought up and set in a line along the hearth so that the fire she'd built would take the chill from it.

She had thought that she would fetch a tray of refreshment, but she had scarcely finished the preparations for the bath when she heard the sounds of an arrival. She bit her lip, wondering if she should go out to meet the lady, or remain where she was.

Finally, she decided that she should go out. It was certainly not the place of a servant to greet arrivals, but she would not be intrusive and she would not like to be summoned and reprimanded if it transpired that Lady Isabel wanted something upon her arrival and she was not there to see it done.

She was breathless by the time she had raced down the stairs and across the great room to the stout oaken doors that was the main entrance to the manor. By the time she had pulled the door open and slipped outside, the carriage had already drawn up before the manor and Lord Arnaud was leaning inside. She hovered in the shadows near the door, worried now that she'd come that perhaps she should not have. Before she had decided whether to remain where she was or dart inside, she saw that it was too late to change her mind as Lord Arnaud helped his lady from the carriage.

Her first impression was that the lady was very young.

Her second that her color was entirely unappealing.

She had scarcely set foot upon solid ground when she immediately threw up.

Repulsed, for several moments Elspeth could only stare in revulsion as the woman bent over and emptied the contents of her stomach on the ground. Even as Lord Arnaud threw a vaguely panicked look over his shoulder, however, she realized that the poor creature was ill—most likely from the travel—and obviously had either been ill several times before, or had been too ill to eat at all.

The woman was her enemy. She should have felt nothing at all beyond contempt, or perhaps even satisfaction that she was so pathetic a creature. Instead, pity surged through her and she moved forward to help. Pushing past Lord Arnaud, she caught the woman's hair and removed it from harm's way, slipping an arm around her waist to help hold her up. When she had ceased to gag at last, Elspeth steadied her and looked up at the manor, wondering if the woman could manage the climb to her room. Obviously, Lord Arnaud had his doubts, for he swept her into his arms and turned toward the manor.

Elspeth followed at his heels until they reached the great room and then rushed ahead and up the stairs to turn the coverlet back on the bed.

She had scarcely done so when Lord Arnaud

shouldered his way into the room and moved to the bed to settle Lady Rosabel. Rushing to one of the buckets of water, Elspeth dipped a cloth, wrung the excess water from it and hurried back to the bed to bathe the young woman's face. "She is ill?"

When Lord Arnaud didn't answer, she glanced up from her task.

He was studying her, but she found it impossible to interpret his expression. "Enceinte," he said succinctly.

Elspeth frowned in confusion, unfamiliar with the word.

"Bebe."

Enlightenment dawned and she glanced at the woman's belly, but although the woman's belly was slightly rounded, she could see little sign that a child grew there. She could not be far along. Elspeth knew very little about the process, however, since no woman that she had been close enough to to share the experience had borne a child. Griselda, however, had attended her mother through five pregnancies before her mother's death. Nodding, she studied the woman's pale face uneasily for several moments. "I should fetch Griselda. She will know what to do."

Lord Arnaud caught her arm when she would have hurried past him. "Stay. I will send for Griselda," he said in halting English, so corrupted by his Norman accent that it took her several moments to translate the words. Finally, however, she understood and nodded. Pulling her arm from his grasp, she returned to the woman, who'd done nothing thus far beyond moaning.

As Lord Arnaud went to the door and spoke with someone outside, she studied her new mistress, unable to think what else she might do to give the woman comfort.

She'd soiled her gown. Elspeth thought she would

probably be more comfortable if the gown were removed altogether and replaced with a nightgown, but she wasn't at all certain but what she would begin to retch again if she were moved. Setting the cloth aside, she slipped her arm beneath the woman to roll her over so that she could at least loosen it. As small as the woman was, however, she was heavier than Elspeth had expected. Moreover, she took exception to being disturbed, opening her eyes and slapping weakly at Elspeth.

A shriek near the door startled Elspeth and she looked up in time to see two women descending upon her, babbling so rapidly in Norman French that she could scarcely understand one word of five. Their assault required no interpretation, however.

The tallest and older of the two grabbed Elspeth by her braid and nearly snapped her neck as she yanked her away from Lady Rosabel. The second flew at her, swinging hands curled into claws. Caught off guard and off balance, Elspeth could do nothing but throw her hands up instinctively to ward off the blows, but as the first woman swung her by her braid, she abandoned that defense to catch herself as she fell. She hit the floor bruisingly, knocking over one of the buckets. The two women fell upon her before she could regain her feet. She managed to catch one woman's arms, but the woman was in a tearing rage and stronger with her fury than she might have been otherwise.

Guillume watched the scene play out before him in stunned astonishment, too surprised for several moments to react as Rosabel's maids, Yvette and Pauline, who'd only moments before seemed almost too ill from their journey even to step down from the car riage, flew into the room like harpies and fell upon Elspeth. Even as the astonishment began to wear off, however, he wasn't entirely certain of how to handle the situation. If it had been brawling men, he would have had no doubt, but he had not previously dealt with brawls involving the 'gentler' sex.

He saw, however, that Elspeth was certainly no match for the two of them and that they showed little signs of wavering in their determined attack. With a growl of irritation, he surged forward, grasped Yvette, who'd straddled Elspeth, pinning her to the floor around the waist and tossed her aside. The moment he removed the one, however, the other took her place. Grabbing Pauline by her flying hair, he dragged her off, as well.

Elspeth sat up shakily just as Yvette climbed up from the floor and, screaming, raced toward her again.

Griselda, who'd arrived at the door in time to see Yvette heading purposefully for Elspeth, screamed like a banshee and flew at the Norman woman, knocking her to the floor and locking her hands around her throat. Staring down at the writhing women with a mixture of alarm and fury, Lord Arnaud dragged the woman he still held to the door and pitched her through it, slamming the door in her face. When he'd disposed of her, he strode to the hearth, lifted a bucket of water and emptied it over Griselda and her foe. The cold water instantly dissolved their animosity. They stopped long enough to gasp for air, and he grabbed each of them by an arm, hauled them to their feet, and dragged them to the door, shoving them out one at the time and finally closing the door and barring it.

Still stunned, Elspeth remained where she was, trying to figure out what had happened. Outside, from the screams and the sound of slamming bodies, the battle still raged. Dragging in a deep breath, Elspeth got to her feet and marched purposefully toward the door. She couldn't allow Griselda to fight the two harpies off by herself.

She was halfway to the door when Lord Arnaud caught her around the waist, lifting her clean off her feet. "Put me down!" she demanded, pulling at the hand gripping her. "I have to help Griselda!"

Instead of releasing her, Lord Arnaud strode toward the door. Fully expecting to be the next one tossed out on her ear, Elspeth was stunned and indignant when, instead, he gripped her tightly and opened the door, shouting for his men at arms. They arrived breathlessly, staring in dismay at the three women rolling around in the hallway.

"Remove them and separate them until they're of a mind to settle down," Lord Arnaud said sharply.

Looking none too happy with the assignment, each man grabbed a screaming woman, slung her over their shoulder and started down the stairs again.

Lord Arnaud closed the door and looked down at Elspeth, who was still struggling for release. By that time, Lady Rosabel had sat up in the bed and was looking around the room in shock. She glanced at Lord Arnaud and asked him something in rapid French.

He nodded and finally released Elspeth.

She supposed Lord Arnaud was explaining what had happened, but she was not familiar enough with their language to understand much of it, not when they spoke so quickly. She did grasp that the two women who'd attacked her had been maids Lady Rosabel had brought with her.

She glanced from Lady Rosabel to Lord Arnaud, wondering if she was about to be dismissed and relegated to lower servant once more.

After a moment, Lady Rosabel flopped back on the

bed and began to weep loudly. Elspeth stared at her in dismay for several moments and finally turned to look at Lord Arnaud, surprising an almost identical expression on his face.

It reminded her so strongly of the way her father and her brothers had looked whenever any woman had wept around them that both sadness and amusement descended upon her at once. Biting her lip, since she knew very well that Lord Arnaud would not see the humor in the situation at all, she moved a little stiffly toward the bed and patted Lady Rosabel's shoulder consolingly. "Would you like some water? Aqua?"

Lady Rosabel lifted her head long enough to glare at her. "Non! Go away, Saxon witch!"

Elspeth felt the blood rush from her face at the woman's vehemence only to rush back in a bright red tide. Stiffly, she curtseyed, and left the room without glancing at Lord Arnaud. She wasn't quite certain of what she should do when she reached the hall. She'd been dismissed, but clearly the young woman was overwrought. If she left, would she be punished? Would she be punished if she didn't leave?

She was still trying to decide when 'Lady' Rosabel began to scream unintelligibly in French and objects began crashing against the wall and door.

Galvanized, Elspeth moved hastily down the hall to the stairs, hovering there and wondering uneasily if she should try to protect her new mistress from her brutal husband, or simply flee and allow the woman to fend for herself. Abruptly, the door to the room opened, Lord Arnaud exited, his face as dark as a thunder cloud, and he strode down the corridor in her direction, passing her without so much as a glance and taking the stairs two at the time.

The thuds and screams continued for a good ten minutes after he'd left—until, Elspeth supposed, Lady

Rosabel ran out of anything handy enough to throw, or wore herself out.

Still with no clear idea whether she'd been rejected as lady's maid or not, Elspeth dared not abandon her post and finally settled near the lady's door, wondering if Lady Rosabel was high strung in general or if it was merely her pregnancy that made her easily agitated. Quiet reigned within the room and she supposed, having vented her spleen, Lady Rosabel had lain down to rest—she sincerely hoped not to regain her strength for another round of temper, but she could not convince herself otherwise.

Perhaps an hour passed before Elspeth heard the approach of several pairs of feet up the staircase. When she looked up, she saw Yvette and Pauline, looking somewhat more subdued, coming along the upper hallway. Behind them trailed Griselda.

She watched their approach warily, but the Norman maids had apparently decided to pretend she did not exist. Without once glancing in her direction, they moved to the door, tapped softly and went in. Griselda settled beside Elspeth.

After looking her over for several moments, she apparently decided Elspeth hadn't sustained injury sufficient to comment upon. "The Norman women are worse than the men," she muttered.

Elspeth thought about Renard and his men and found she couldn't agree. Instead, she shrugged. "Lady Rosabel is with child and ill from the travel, as well."

Griselda studied her with a spark of interest. "Breeding, is she?"

Elspeth nodded. "That's why I asked for you. She seemed very ill, but I couldn't be certain if it was the child, the travel, or both—nor I'd no notion what could be done for her if it was the child. I felt sure that you would know."

A stream of agitated French interrupted their conversation, followed by a barrage of thumps against the door and wall. Yvette and Pauline hastily exited the lady's room.

Elspeth watched them dispassionately as they moved a little way along the hallway and stopped, whispering to one another. When she turned to look at Griselda, she saw that Griselda had turned her head to examine the door and wall, as if she might peer through them.

"I am only guessing, mind you, but I do not think the Lady Rosabel is very happy to be here."

Griselda snorted. "Well, she may certainly leave again and it will not disturb my rest."

Elspeth bit her lip, recalling Lord Arnaud's exit. In truth, she should not find humor in his discomfiture, but she could not help but be amused that the man who struck terror in the hearts of every man about him had been so thoroughly and quickly routed by his lady. She was surprised he had not beat the woman. Not even her father or her brothers, who were notoriously softhearted toward women, would have put up with such a temper tantrum. She was with child, however, and she had only just arrived.

She could almost feel pity for him that he had gone to such lengths to ensure her comfort only to have her throw a temper fit the moment she arrived.
"What amuses you?"

Elspeth glanced at Griselda, but as much as she would've liked to share her amusement, she knew Griselda had a loose tongue. She would almost certainly spread it about and then Lord Arnaud would be justifiably incensed. She shook her head. "Only that yon superior maids faired no better than I."

Griselda sent an evil glance their way and sniffed. "How came they to attack you?"

"I was trying to help Lady Rosabel from her gown to make her more comfortable and she did not wish me to. I suppose, to them, it appeared that she and I were struggling and they thought that they were defending her."

Griselda sent them another glance, but it was more thoughtful this time. "They did not give you the chance to explain?"

Elspeth grimaced wryly. "No, but I am not at all certain the outcome would have been very different. In any case, I can not speak, or understand, the Norman tongue as well as I had thought I could."

Griselda looked at her in surprise. "I thought you had learned their tongue from Jean."

"I had thought so, but Jean does not speak just as they do. He is not Norman, but from another duchy altogether. When they speak slowly, I understand much of what they say, but when they speak rapidly I understand very little."

"Perhaps, in time, they will all go back across the sea and we will not be forced to listen to their strange tongue."

"I do not think that at all likely, Griselda."

Chapter Four

The servants had already begun to set up the trellis tables for the evening meal in the hall below before Lord Arnaud returned. As he had left, he returned, striding purposefully toward the lady's room this time, only slightly less angry than when he had departed.

The maids all exchanged a glance as he went into the lady's room without even so much as a pause at the door, slamming it behind him. They heard the lady's high pitched, agitated voice, but Lord Arnaud's voice was too low to discern more than a deep rumble, like distant thunder.

The barrage of thrown articles did not erupt. A few minutes later, Lord Arnaud opened the door once more, fixed Elspeth and Griselda with a hard glance and summoned them inside.

Lady Rosabel, her eyes still tumultuous, was sitting up in bed. Grasping Griselda by one arm, Lord Arnaud dragged her to the bedside and explained that Rosabel was ill with her condition. Griselda, naturally, only looked at him blankly. After a moment, Elspeth moved a little closer. "Do not pretend stupidity, Griselda. You know very well what he wants," she said in a low voice.

Griselda sent her a look. "Is that what he said?"

Elspeth's lips tightened. "He has treated us well. He did not need to. He has taken this place and can do as he pleases. It is stupid to anger him needlessly."

The fight went out of Griselda, and she nodded, turning to look Lady Rosabel over. "Her color is bad."

Elspeth moved a little closer. "Their skin is darker than ours."

Griselda nodded. "Your lady mother was often ill in the first months." She touched the woman's forehead with her palm. "She has no fever. She will be better if she rests. She should only have a little goat's milk and bread when she feels ill. Otherwise it will only come up again. Most likely, if she does not feel ill she can eat most anything and it will stay."

Griselda looked Lady Rosabel over. "She should not wear her gowns so tightly. It will make it difficult for the child to grow as it should."

Elspeth shrugged. "I had thought a bath would help her feelings," she said, pointing to the tub she'd had prepared.

Lady Rosabel firmly refused their attempts to persuade her, however, demanding that Yvette and Pauline be summoned. Finally, Lord Arnaud did so, and pulled Griselda and Elspeth aside. The two maids came in, looked around a little nervously and finally hurried to Lady Rosabel at her call. After a few moments, they began tugging the bed drapes closed and, taking one of the buckets and several lengths of linen, helped Lady Rosabel to bathe and change her clothing.

Griselda gave Elspeth a look, which she chose to ignore, explaining the best she could to Lord Arnaud what Griselda had thought might help to ease Lady Rosabel's discomfort. It was more difficult than she had thought it would be. Naturally enough, the conversations that she had shared with Jean had not dealt with such subjects, and she only knew a word here and there.

Finally, he nodded however, and seemed to dismiss them, turning his attention to the proceedings on the other side of the curtains. He glanced at the tub several times and finally found a stool and began removing his boots.

Griselda studied him a moment, then, almost reluctantly moved toward him to help him disrobe. "It is our custom," she said, sending Elspeth a chiding glance, "and your duty as hostess to offer aid to your guests."

Irritated, Elspeth reluctantly joined her, helping to remove the heavy chain mail shirt that Lord Arnaud wore. He divided a speculative glance between Griselda and Elspeth, but said nothing. "I am not the lady of the house," Elspeth whispered fiercely. "And the Normans are certainly not guests."

Griselda sniffed. "I see no reason to abandon our own customs," she said haughtily.

Elspeth saw good reason to do so, however. Lord Arnaud clothed was intimidating. Lord Arnaud naked should have been less so, but in fact, was not. She did her best not to actually brush his skin, not to notice the heavy, ropy muscles that covered his arms and back and chest, and thought she succeeded fairly well.

His man root was another matter altogether. Even flaccid it was far larger than Renard's, or in fact, any of the male members of her own household that she had assisted in their baths … and it did not remain flaccid. As she helped him remove his chausses, it more than

39

doubled its size and stood erect. Without conscious volition, her gaze followed it as it lifted upward to touch his flat belly. How long she stared, she had no notion, but when Griselda cleared her throat, it instantly snapped her from her spell and she looked away, unable to prevent the color that flooded her cheeks.

She did not meet Lord Arnaud's gaze, uncertain of whether the display had been deliberate to throw her into confusion, or if it was no more than a purely instinctual reaction and beyond his control. She had never had sisters, but she had had four brothers. She knew very well that one was as possible as the other. His comments of before assailed her forcibly and her irritation with Griselda grew. She knew very well that this custom could not be practiced in Normandy, otherwise Lord Arnaud would have summoned them to help, and would not have appeared surprised when they offered to do so.

Griselda had instigated it, but that did not mean he would not see it as an attempt to 'tempt him to forsake his vows'.

She busied herself folding his clothes as he moved to the tub and climbed in. Griselda followed him, dipping her hand into the tub to test the heat of the water and then moving to the hearth and testing each of the buckets in turn. She glanced at Elspeth when she'd hefted the bucket. "You should lather his hair. I think I can manage the buckets better."

Elspeth gave her a look, tightened her lips, and finally moved behind Lord Arnaud when Griselda had dampened his hair. Lifting a bar of soap, she worked a lather into his hair. He jerked at her first touch, and she hesitated, but when he stilled she set about her task, trying to focus only on the task and not the fact that it was Lord Arnaud's hair—that seated in the tub, his head was still chest level to her, that his bare shoulders and back seemed impossibly broad and well muscled.

It was hardly surprising considering the weight of his mail, which he wore almost constantly. She and Griselda between them had struggled to lift it. She supposed the links of metal must be far more protective than the stiff leathers that her own people had worn into battle, but thought it must hamper their movements more, as well.

When she'd finished scrubbing his hair, Griselda lifted the bucket once more and poured it carefully over his scalp to rinse the soap. Elspeth put her hand beneath his chin, tipping his head back so that she could push the soap and water toward the back of his head with her other hand, brushing her palm over his broad forehead. His chin was prickly, drawing her attention. As she glanced toward his face, she saw that his eyes were upon her, his gaze moving over her face in slow, thorough, appraisal. It sent a tremor through her, demolishing the focus she'd attained in her mundane task from him to the task itself.

Shaken, she removed her hands at once, but she was far too aware of him from that moment to manage to focus purely on the task once more. Her fingers trembled as she lathered his hair once more. Heat swept through her, but she could not convince herself that it was the discomfort of embarrassment.

The soap slipped from her hand and she dove for it before she considered. The moment she touched flesh, instead of soap, she considered, and her gaze flew upward to clash with his once more. Withdrawing her arm abruptly, she stared down at the now murky water, wondering if she should simply decamp and search for another bar of soap.

He fished it from the water himself, caught her hand, and closed her fingers around it. Setting the soap

41

on the hearth, she finished scrubbing his scalp and stepped aside with a touch of relief for Griselda to rinse the lather from his hair, but she did not reach for his chin to tip his head back as she had before. She knew his gaze was upon her as he tipped his head back, however, despite her determination to ignore it and concentrate on removing the soap.

Dragging in a shaky breath, she picked up the soap when Griselda moved away again, lathered a short length of linen and, brushing his wet hair out of the way, pressed the cloth against his back until he leaned forward and then scrubbed his back thoroughly.

Feeling weak and more than a little lightheaded by the time she'd finished, she thrust the linen and soap at him and retreated to the other side of the room. Griselda sent her several admonishing glances, but she resolutely ignored the woman, settling on her pallet.

Lord Arnaud, finished his bath in frowning thoughtfulness, casting a glance toward her now and again. When he stood up at last and Griselda handed him another bucket to rinse, Elspeth stole a glance at him, watching in fascination as the water, gleaming from the firelight behind him, cascaded over his body. She glanced away the moment he began to lower the bucket, studying the puckered roughness of her hands as he stepped from the tub at last and took the length of linen Griselda held out to him.

"Merci," he murmured, his gaze settling thoughtfully on Elspeth as he rubbed the linen briskly over his body to dry himself.

Finally, he dragged his gaze from her and turned to look at Lady Rosabel and her maids, who'd watched the entire proceedings with both disapproval and curiosity, and spoke to them. The maids glanced at Lady Rosabel, who nodded, then bobbed a curtsey and departed. Elspeth got to her feet, deciding that they had been dismissed. When she glanced at Lord Arnaud questioningly, he nodded and relief flooded her. She turned to the door and went out.

Griselda joined her a few moments later, looking her over critically. "You are still fearful of men because of that pig."

It was a statement, not a question. Elspeth had no intention of answering in any case, particularly since she knew very well that it was not fear that had left her so shaken.

Griselda patted her hand. "It will pass in time, as it should. All men are not such brutes and I would not like to think that you had been deprived of one of the few joys in life only because you had been so badly used."

Elspeth reddened. "I can not see whether it makes any difference whether or not it passes. It is very unlikely that I will wed … now."

Griselda studied her a moment but let it pass. "What does mercy mean?"

Elspeth glanced at her. "Merci?"

Griselda nodded.

"Thank you."

Griselda threw her a look of surprise. After a moment, she smiled complacently. "You see! He was pleased. The Normans can not be as bad as we thought if they appreciate our customs."

* * * *

Lord Arnaud made it abundantly clear that that was one Saxon custom that he could embrace whole heartedly. Lady Rosabel made it equally clear that she considered it very unhealthful, that Saxony was damp and cold at the best of times and Lord Arnaud was bound to catch his death—but then she made no bones about the fact that she hated everything about Saxony and that she wasn't at all pleased about having been dragged here when Lord Arnaud possessed property in Normandy that was far better.

Griselda's conclusion was that the Normans were not as hearty as the Saxons, whom, long generations past, had come from an even colder clime.

Elspeth simply wished that she had strangled

Griselda instead of allowing the woman to convince her to participate in teaching their new lord their own customs, which he practiced far more regularly than she liked. He never said anything, but the way he looked at her and the tension in his body as she helped him with his bath led her to believe he found it nearly as much of an ordeal as she did.

She wasn't completely certain of why it was that he not only insisted on continuing, but objected when she tried to switch places with Griselda and bear the water while Griselda bathed him, unless mayhap he thought familiarity would breed contempt. She did not grow accustomed, far from it, and she could not see that it bothered him any less either. In point of fact, it quickly reached a point where his gaze looked almost fevered as it skated over her.

It was a relief when he was called to service, gathered more than half his men, and departed, particularly since he took his brother, Renard, with him.

Lady Rosabel's nausea vanished as she grew rounder with child. Her short temper did not grow longer, however, nor did her contempt for the Saxons abate one whit. As soon as Lord Arnaud disappeared through the newly erected gates that had been set into the growing wall around the manor, she banished both Griselda and Elspeth.

Elspeth was relieved. Griselda was torn between indignation at being considered inferior, and hopeful glee that Lord Arnaud would beat her soundly for countermanding his orders when he returned.

Elspeth thought that doubtful. It would've been obvious to a post that Lord Arnaud was looking forward to the birth of his first son. He might be tempted to beat Lady Rosabel, but it seemed highly unlikely that he would risk the health of his child.

She was far more hopeful that Lord Arnaud would relent to Lady Rosabel's wishes and allow her to return to her former position in the household. Her discomfort at assisting with Lord Arnaud's bath was only part of her reluctance. She wasn't particularly happy about Lady Rosabel's foul temper, nor especially perturbed by it, but she disliked the intimacy forced upon them by the close quarters. She did not like knowing, and quite often hearing, when Lord Arnaud bedded his wife. She also didn't like being privy to their frequent disagreements.

The marriage had been arranged. Lord Arnaud seemed satisfied with his choice, despite her temperament, which seemed to come as much a surprise to him as it did to everyone else. Lady Rosabel felt that her family had sold her short and could have arranged a better marriage. She divided her time between weeping and railing each time she was thwarted in any way, and trying to cajole 'love tokens' from him.

Sometimes Elspeth couldn't help but pity Lady Rosabel because she truly was terribly homesick, and it was obvious that she had been so spoiled and pampered by her family that she couldn't entirely grasp that her situation had changed and she was expected to behave as a wife and soon to be mother, and not her papa's spoiled darling.

Most of the time she empathized with Lord Arnaud, who was equally unhappy whenever Lady Rosabel was unhappy—which was most of the time—but better at hiding it. She might not have noticed at all, except that his relief in finding Lady Rosabel in a sunny mood was so profound as to make it impossible to ignore.

The main reason she wished for distance, however, was because she finally realized that she was with child herself. Fear and revulsion were uppermost in her mind when she reached the point where she could no longer lie to herself, for it could only be Renard's, and she despised him with a deep, abiding hatred that made her feel physically ill only to think of him. She couldn't bear the thought of having a part of him growing inside of her and the near hysterical desire to tear it from her body, or flush it with some poison, even if it killed her, gripped her for days afterward.

Griselda's reaction to the news surprised her. She merely shrugged.

"I thought as much.

"I can not bear that ... monster's child!"

"You have no choice in that, though I am sorry to see it." She shook her head. "Your mother would turn over in her grave to think you would bear a bastard child."

"But ... I can get rid of it. There are ways."

Griselda gave her a hard look. "You should not even say such things. Bad things will come of such an evil wish. Life is sacred. It is not for you to decide."

Elspeth stared at her disbelievingly. "Evil! I am evil only because I can not bear the thought of that creature's spawn in my belly?"

"The child is innocent of evil. You can not hate it."

"I do!" Elspeth said fiercely. "Only thinking of it makes my skin crawl!"

Griselda looked at her angrily. "I would never have thought to hear such talk from you!"

"I am disgraced and that is all you can say?"

"You were disgraced when that pig raped you. You are no more disgraced now."

"What you mean is that I am disgraced because I did not take my life!" Elspeth said furiously.

Griselda's eyes narrowed. "You were strong enough to bear the shame then. You are strong enough to bear the child."

"But I don't want to bear the child! I would rather die!"

Griselda slapped her soundly.

Elspeth stared at her in shock for several moments and finally burst into tears. After a moment, Griselda gathered her into her arms. "It is the fortunes of war, Elspeth, that we women must pay, but you can not blame the child. In time, you'll see that you can love it."

Elspeth shook her head. "I can not."

"Shhh! You are only thinking of that pig. Do not think about him. Your child grows in your belly. When you come to accept that it is yours, you will not think of the father, only that it is yours, and you will love it."

In her heart, Elspeth didn't believe it for one moment, but she saw that Griselda would not sympathize with her plight beyond regret that life had taken such a course for them. She would not help her to rid herself of her burden, and Elspeth realized that she would endure it because the only alternative was to take her own life and she was not prepared to do that.

Nursing the secret hope that the seed would fail and die of its own accord, she put it from her mind and worked until she could not think of anything beyond how tired she was. Even when her belly began to swell and the other servants began to glance at her knowingly, she managed not to think about it. There was not one female in the keep of breeding age that was not in the same situation and they were no happier about it than she—and no less disgraced.

The time came, however, when she could ignore it no longer. With the first fluttering of the life inside of her, her perception of it began to slowly change as Griselda had predicted. Love did not grow with it, but the hate began to slowly fade away.

Chapter Five

The pounding on the door of their shelter nigh brought it down. Unnerved, Elspeth threw a woolen shawl around her shoulders and moved quickly to answer the summons. When she snatched the door open, Lord Arnaud stood in the opening, his expression fierce.

Elspeth gaped at him, her heart hammering so wildly in her breast that she felt lightheaded. He had been gone for nigh on two months and she had grown so accustomed to her change in status that it was several moments before it occurred to her that, by Lord Arnaud's command, she and Griselda were supposed to be in attendance on Lady Rosabel.

That thought flickered through her mind, but in truth, her thoughts as she stared up at him were so chaotic she was scarcely aware of any thought at all. She had forgotten how devastating he was to her senses, how his nearness alone took her breath away, the way he could draw heat into her and make her heart pound with only his gaze.

While she was trying to gather her wits, his gaze flickered almost hungrily over her face and then traveled in a leisurely, thorough inspection of her body, fastening finally on the bulge of her belly and remaining there. The color left his face.

"Lady Rosabel sent us away," she said haltingly.

"You carry my brother's bastard," he said as if she hadn't spoken, his voice strangely without inflection. There was no surprise in his expression or his voice and she was certain that was not feigned. No doubt Lady Rosabel had informed him immediately that there was scarcely a Saxon female of child bearing age who was not with child. She had made no attempt to hide her contempt for them all.

Elspeth felt her face turning fiery red, as much with anger as embarrassment. "You can not profess to be surprised when you dragged that ... pig off of me," she snapped angrily before she thought better of it, and then fell back a step, covering her mouth with her hand, her eyes widening with fear.

His gaze moved back to hers, his gaze assessing. "You have mastered our tongue amazingly well."

Elspeth swallowed with an effort, looking down at her hands. "I beg pardon, my lord."

He caught her chin, forcing her to look up at him. "And for leaving your post? Do you beg pardon for that, as well, when I had made my wishes clear?"

Elspeth could only stare at him in consternation. She knew very well that Lady Rosabel was fully capable of lying about the entire incident if she thought it might make Lord Arnaud angry with her. He must know that she'd been reluctant to serve Lady Rosabel to begin with, which made it even more unlikely that he would believe her claim that she had been sent away.

She gathered moisture into her mouth with an effort. "Yes, my lord."

"Then why are you here?"

"Your lady said she didn't want to be attended by Saxon whores," Griselda said from behind Elspeth.

Elspeth flicked a horrified look at Griselda. "Mind your tongue!" she hissed. "We've trouble enough."

"She has … realized the error of her thinking and has changed her mind."

Elspeth's head whipped back to Lord Arnaud. His words were still thick with his native accent, but it was clear enough that he spoke, and understood, the Saxon tongue.

"Gather your things and return to the manor." He rubbed his face tiredly. "I have traveled long and hard and I need to remove the mire of the road from me."

They did as they were told, but Elspeth did so with a good deal of dread. If Lord Arnaud had returned, then Renard had also. Despite the child's presence, she had managed to put the father, mostly, from her mind. She felt ill at the thought of seeing him, of being seen by him.

He would gloat to see so obvious a sign of his possession.

As she had feared, he was in the great hall. Despite the vast number of men who had crowded inside, his gaze zeroed in upon her the moment she entered. She did her best to ignore it and move quickly through the room to the stairs, but he headed her off, blocking her path when she reached the stairs.

For several moments, he merely stared at her rounded belly. Finally, he lifted his head to leer at her. "I see my seed has found a fertile field."

He was so certain that it was his and no other's— and well he might be—but she longed that it had been otherwise, that she could wipe his smile from his face.

51

She had regretted only that he had raped her, over and over. She had neither considered the possibility of getting a child, nor how revolting it would be to know without doubt that it was his. It would have been better if he had shared her, she thought now, better if she could at least have had some doubt in her own mind.

She should have simply tried to brush past him or, failing that, turned and left, but she knew that she could not avoid a confrontation forever. Despite all her efforts to avoid him, he was determined to force it upon her.

"If I can not kill you, I will kill myself before I allow you—ever—to touch me again," she said tightly.

His eyes narrowed. After a moment, however, he withdrew his eating dagger and pressed it into her hand, flinging his arms wide.

Elspeth barely blinked. On the instant, her entire being focused on revenge and she became blind and deaf to all else, jerking away from Griselda, who'd caught her arm, trying to drag her away. Her hand clenched around the knife handle the moment he released it and she drew the dagger back, aiming for his heart. Her hand was caught before she could drive it home. She struggled briefly, but the hold tightened until her hand went numb. Finally the dagger fell from her hand and clattered to the floor. She stared down at it in consternation, dove for it, trying to grab it with her free hand, but that was caught, as well, and she was swung around to face her captor.

Lord Arnaud's expression penetrated the fog of hate for the first time since Renard had stepped into her path, and fear stabbed through her. He lowered his face to within inches of hers. "Do not allow him to goad you to your death, you little fool."

Elspeth swallowed with an effort, but the fury was still upon her and all she could think was that it would be worth it if only she could kill Renard first.

He saw it in her face and shook her until her head rocked back on her shoulders.

"She pulled a weapon upon me brother. That is enough in itself."

Lord Arnaud focused upon Renard, his eyes blazing. Catching Elspeth around the waist, he leaned down and scooped the knife from the floor, studying it. "I would not think that you would want it known that a slip of a girl overpowered you, stole your eating knife and tried to skewer you with it."

Renard shrugged, grinning. "She is jealous because I have turned my attentions upon another."

Lord Arnaud studied him a long moment. "I saw, and heard, everything Renard. If ever I catch you in another lie—if ever I catch you directly disobeying an order from me again, you will rue the day you were born," he said coldly.

Renard swallowed audibly. "I have never disobeyed an order from you, Guillume."

Lord Arnaud's eyes narrowed. After a moment, he set Elspeth on the stairs and gave her a push to urge her up them. Moving around him, Griselda caught her arm and tugged her upwards.

"You do try my patience, brother. Need I remind you of the disastrous consequences of sending you to secure my property? Did I not charge you to take it as peacefully as could be done?"

Renard reddened. "They resisted," he said through gritted teeth.

"Half the serfs are dead or have fled, and of those who remain, every female old enough to breed is heavy with child and I can expect to lose still more in child

53

bed. Nigh half the fields were burned, the manor itself was ransacked—and when I arrived you and every man under your command were lying about sot drunk. If it had been anyone other than myself that had come upon you, I would have had to lay waste to the remainder of the property in trying to take it back. You are fortunate you are my brother, else I would have slain you on the spot."

He caught the front of Renard's surcoat in his fist and leaned toward him until they were virtually nose to nose. "If you value your life, Renard, do not look upon Elspeth again."

Renard's eyes darted toward the stairs at that. "I understand you … brother."

Lord Arnaud studied him a moment and released him.

Renard straightened his clothing, smoothing it carefully with his hands as he sent his brother several resentful glares. "Since you are so displeased with my services on your behalf, I believe I will inquire about offering them elsewhere."

Lord Arnaud smiled thinly. "You are welcome to do so."

Renard flushed angrily. After a moment, he turned without another word and stalked away.

Guillume watched him until he had rejoined the group near the great hearth and then turned and ascended the stairs.

* * * *

"What possessed you to attack the Norman!" Griselda demanded in fearful anger when they had gained Lord Arnaud's quarters and closed the door behind them.

Elspeth, who had moved to the hearth to check the bath, looked at her angrily, but, in truth, the murderous desire had long since fled. "I saw only the means and the opportunity to have my revenge," she said tiredly. "I could not think beyond the gloating smile he bent upon me, his certainty that he had so cowed me that I would not dare to attempt it."

Griselda studied her in silence. "There is more to it than that."

Elspeth glanced at her sharply. "Nay, there is not."

"You endured well enough until Lord Arnaud accused you of carrying his brother's bastard."

Elspeth flushed. "I am despised for something I could not prevent. The injustice of it chafes me. In what way does that make me any different from anyone else wrongfully accused and punished?"

Griselda shook her head. "I had forgotten you were so young yet, Elspeth. It is not wrong, just unrealistic to expect fairness in this world. Experience will teach you better—But you can not gain wisdom if you are dead. Lord Arnaud was right. You should not have allowed him to goad you. If he had not stopped you…."

A cold chill ran down Elspeth's spine. She rather thought she would prefer to fall upon her own dagger than to face the executioner.

She bit her lip. "In truth, I think I have sorely misjudged the poor Lady Rosabel. There is something about being with child, particularly when one least wants to be, that induces a sort of madness."

Griselda cocked her head with interest. "Lady Rosabel is not pleased that she will bear the lord's heir?"

Elspeth sent her a look, before she could comment, however, Lord Arnaud strode into the room. His gaze went immediately to her. After a moment, he moved to the stool beside the hearth and sat, staring at the flames.

Elspeth studied him guiltily, realizing for the first time that she had been so centered upon her own problems and her fear and hatred of Renard, that she had not given any consideration to the wedge she had driven between Lord Arnaud and his brother. She knew it wasn't entirely because of her—Renard had angered him when he'd diminished the value of the property that had been awarded to him for his service to William the Bastard. Her fear and hatred of Renard were certainly justified, but she did not like being the cause of more bad blood between the two brothers.

When Griselda nudged her to gain her attention, she surged forward to help her remove Lord Arnaud's heavy mail shirt. She gasped when she looked back at him. Massive bruises covered his back and shoulders as well as a number of angry, red half healed wounds.

He glanced at her at the sharp intake of breath and she licked her lips nervously. "You have seen battle?"

He shrugged. "Skirmishes only. By and large, there is peace."

"I will go and get my medicines," Griselda said and bobbed a briefly curtsey and left.

Elspeth felt her heart squeeze painfully in her chest at the realization that Griselda had left them alone. She saw in his eyes that Lord Arnaud was acutely aware of it, as well.

After a moment, he dragged his gaze from her and finished undressing, easing himself into the tub and leaning forward to splash water over his head. Elspeth studied him hesitantly for several moments and finally grasped the soap and moved behind him, lathering his hair. He closed his eyes as she lathered the soap into his hair, massaging his scalp with her fingers.

"He will seek service elsewhere," he said, his voice sounding husky with disuse.

Elspeth glanced down at him and saw that he was

studying her. She could think of nothing to say. She could scarcely think at all beyond wondering why she had ever thought his dark eyes so cold. Finally, she managed to nod.

"Until that time, you will stay close to Lady Rosabel."

Again, Elspeth could only nod. Her throat had closed and she could not seem to force any sound past the knot there. Moving away after a moment, she went to the hearth to fetch a pail to rinse his hair.

"Leave it," he said sharply.

She desisted, moving back to the tub when he leaned forward to rinse his hair and helping him squeeze the suds from it, then lathering it a second time. When she'd finished, she took the linen she used for washing and gathered water into it to rinse as much of the soap as she could until Griselda returned to help her with the heavy pails.

He sucked in a hissing breath as she began to rub the cloth along his shoulders and she stilled. He shook his head. "Do it. It doesn't hurt nearly so much now as when I got it," he said wryly.

Still, she hesitated. Almost as if she had no will over her actions at all, she found herself reaching to smooth lightly over the ridge of healing flesh along his shoulder with a fingertip. A shudder went through him.

He caught her hand. Squeezing it almost painfully, he pulled her inexorably around the edge of the tub until she was facing him. "I would think you would rather slip a blade between my ribs than to soothe my hurts," he said hoarsely.

Elspeth swallowed with an effort, knowing that he was right. She should want nothing more than the opportunity to slay one of the conquerors who had swept through her land like some dark plague, slain her family, taken all that had once belonged to her and made her a servant in her own home. He had been a part of that. She should hate him as she did Renard.

When, she wondered, had she ceased to look upon him as her enemy?

"I do not hate you, my lord," she said hesitantly.

"Do you not? Does it not chafe you to see me, your enemy, lord in your father's home?"

Elspeth felt the color leave her face. She didn't try to deny it, however, knowing a lost cause when she saw one. She should have known that, no matter how badly he spoke Saxon, he must understand it if he could speak it, and she had not guarded her tongue as she ought. "How long have you known?"

"I suspected the moment I saw you," he said grimly. "Torn and bloodied as you were, you were not dressed like any peasant."

A pain stabbed through her chest. "You kept me here to watch me—because I am your enemy," she said with an effort.

Something flickered in his eyes, but she was too hurt to recognize it as a reflection of her own pain. All she could think of was how incredibly gullible she had been, believing that he acted out of kindness, out of concern for her welfare, when the truth was he merely wanted to make certain she did not create problems for him with the others.

Tears welled in her eyes and she dropped her gaze, trying to will them away.

"Yes," he said, his voice harsh.

The rawness of his voice drew her head up once more.

His expression hardened as he studied her face. Abruptly, he released her. "Leave me!"

Dropping the washcloth, Elspeth surged to her feet and fled. She met Griselda in the hallway. "What's this?"

Elspeth shook her head. "You should attend his wounds. There are several that look to be in need of attention."

Griselda studying her frowningly for several moments but finally left her. When she had gone, Elspeth settled on the floor beside Lady Rosabel's door. She had left her pallet when she had fled Lord Arnaud's room and she could not bring herself to return for it. She was sorely tempted to flee back to the cottage that she and Griselda had shared, but she did not want Lord Arnaud to come to fetch her back.

If Renard were not present, she might have been tempted to creep down the stairs and make her pallet with the other servants, but as upset as she was, she had no desire to encounter Renard again—whatever Lord Arnaud had said, she doubted that Renard would leave her be. He had convinced himself that she belonged to him and the fact that Lord Arnaud forbade him to claim her only seemed to have made him more obsessive about doing so.

Her swollen belly made it nigh impossible to find a comfortable position on the floor, for the heavier the child became the more pressure it placed upon her hip joints, but then neither was she comfortable pacing the floor. Finally, she merely folded her legs, dropping her head into her hands and trying to decide why she was hurt, not angry, not fearful.

She could have understood either other emotion. She had been fearful from the first of what the repercussions might be if Lord Arnaud discovered he was harboring the daughter of his enemy.

She should have been angry—with herself at least—for her clumsiness in trying to hide her identity, and her willful blindness in not realizing that she had fooled no one.

She should not be hurt that the Norman saw her as his enemy.

Chapter Six

"Did something happen whilst I was gone to fetch my herbs?"

Elspeth glanced at Griselda, but she had no desire to share her confusion, and certainly not the embarrassment that was quickly supplanting it. She forced a slight smile. "The child kicks. My belly cramped when I tried to lift one of the buckets," she lied, "but it is better now."

As she had known she would be, Griselda was immediately distracted. "It is probably nothing but it is not wise to dismiss these things. Let me check."

Elspeth refrained from rolling her eyes and allowed Griselda to place her palm over her belly.

The door to Lord Arnaud's room opened and he stepped into the hall, heading toward his lady's room purposefully.

"I do not feel it kick," Griselda said, "but I am sure there are no contractions."

Lord Arnaud checked fractionally—enough that

CONQUERED

Elspeth was in no doubt that he'd noticed Griselda's examination, and heard her assessment—before he continued, closing the door behind him.

Yvette and Pauline were evicted into the hallway and arrived carrying their pallets. Griselda and Elspeth exchanged a glance. Without a word, they collected their own pallets, which Griselda had left just outside Lord Arnaud's door when she had finished attending him. Lord Arnaud was not likely to leave his lady for many hours and they would be expected to be up and working at dawn however little sleep they might get waiting in the hall.

Lady Rosabel was not pleased to be disturbed. She complained for a while about her discomfort before the sounds in the room changed dramatically from complaints to moans of pleasure.

Obviously, servants were sticks of wood so far as she was concerned, for she'd never made any attempt to guard her tongue around them and certainly did not when they were not in sight. Worse to Elspeth's mind, she not only made no attempt to curb her enthusiasm for coupling—once Lord Arnaud had convinced her—but, Elspeth suspected, she often exaggerated.

Elspeth could readily believe that Lord Arnaud was a far better lover than Renard. He could hardly be worse, but she wasn't certain she believed the extent of Lady Rosabel's very vocal pleasure. If she enjoyed it so much, why did she always complain and try to find excuses to put him off? Merely because she enjoyed being persuaded? Because she preferred to play coy?

She was more inclined to think Lady Rosabel feigned the entire process to appeal to Lord Arnaud's male ego, for she generally ended her performance by demanding to know what trinkets he had brought for her.

Rolling onto her side, Elspeth covered her head with her blanket, squeezed her eyes closed and did her best to block out all the sounds. She did not expect to sleep. Her thoughts were still in turmoil and the drama, which she could hear far too well, beyond the Lady Rosabel's bedroom wall only added to her disturbed sensibilities. The one thing that could be said for their daily labor, however, was that it so drained them of strength and energy that only the threat of certain death could deprive them of sleep, and sometimes not even that.

When the soft click of a door being closed jerked her awake, it was nearly dawn. Barely half conscious, she sat up, glancing around to discern the threat. Lord Arnaud had paused at her movement. She blinked at him blearily and laid down again, snuggling closer to Griselda for warmth.

Her mind would not allow her to seek sleep once more, however, and as Griselda began to stir, she rose stiffly and rolled up her pallet. Leaving it in one corner, she made her way downstairs in search of a place to relieve herself and water to wash the dregs of sleep away.

In the kitchen, the servants were already busy preparing the noon meal. The cook glanced at her distractedly and pointed her toward a small mound of meat scraps, cheese and bread crusts.

Her stomach revolted at the sight of the greasy meat, but she took a crust of bread and a sliver of cheese and wandered outside to find a few moments of peace. Her confrontation with Renard was fresh on her mind, but so too was the by-play with Lord Arnaud. She thought it doubtful that Renard would so quickly dismiss the warning that Lord Arnaud had given him—but she did not wander far.

Taking a drink from the dipper in the bucket at the

well, she settled on the bench that surrounded it, pulled her shawl tightly about her shoulders and gazed off toward the sunrise, allowing her thoughts to wander to her childhood and the days before the Normans had come. She had not allowed herself the luxury before. In truth, it had been a wound so deep she thought she couldn't bear to think of it at all, but she found that the memories brought her as much solace as pain.

Her father had been a giant of a man, not quite so tall as Lord Arnaud, but broader of shoulder. She found she could not summon his face beyond the long, flowing beard that had been streaked with white and his eyes—a pale blue that had twinkled when he was amused and glinted like steal when he was angry.

It was hard, even now, to accept that she would not see her father or her brothers' faces again in this lifetime. Perhaps, when her spirit joined the mother earth, she would find them waiting? She smiled faintly to imagine them drunk and brawling, and disturbing the peace of the gods as they had so often disturbed the peace of the manor, for they had been a loud and rowdy lot, exuberant with life and as happy to indulge in a round of merrymaking as a good natured test of strength.

A flicker of movement caught her eye, distracting her from her thoughts and her heart skipped a beat as she saw Renard hesitate as he spied her and then cross the yard in her direction. She tensed, glancing toward the manner. If she were not burdened with the child, she might outrun him, but now, she knew she could not. Instead, she remained where she was, determined not to allow him to see how terrified she was of him.

To her surprise, he stopped some distance from her, studying her soberly.

"I have decided to seek service elsewhere," he said

finally.

Elspeth tilted her head, staring at him steadily, but she said nothing.

He cleared his throat. "I would be willing to take you with me as my layman."

Rage colored her cheeks. "I am supposed to be flattered by that?"

He flushed, his own temper rising. "You prefer scrubbing floors and picking up after the Lady Rosabel? Guillume will not take you as his mistress in the home of his wife. He has always been strange that way, perhaps because our father kept no fewer than three at any one time. It distressed his mother."

She knew it was unwise to provoke him, but she found she was beyond caring. "Your conceit is staggering. Do you imagine you have given me a taste for having any man rutting me? I would rather spend my days cleaning the chamber pots," she said tightly.

His hands clenched into fists. For a moment, she thought that he would surge forward and wrap them about her throat.

She felt oddly calm about it.

"There is nothing that you could do to me that would be worse than what you have done already—and no way that you will ever have me willingly. You were my hated enemy before ever I set eyes upon you and you have only taught me more hate. You can not imagine the depths of it."

His eyes narrowed, but he held himself in check with an effort. "You seemed willing enough."

That comment penetrated her calm. Elspeth gasped in outrage. "If beating a woman unconscious is your perception of 'willing' then I can well understand your confusion. No doubt every woman you have had has been as 'willing'."

He ground his teeth. "You are brave because you

think Lord Arnaud will protect you."

"I am the daughter of Odolf, late lord of this place—so long as I am useful, yes, I believe he will, but you are mistaken. I am not brave. I simply do not care. You have taught me that there are far worse things than death."

She watched dispassionately as he fought another round with his temper. He almost seemed to surge toward her, but after glancing around, he turned instead and strode away. She watched him until he had disappeared around the corner of the manor and finally rose from the bench. The sun had crested the horizon and she knew she should already have begun her day.

A muscle clenched low in her belly when she tried to straighten. The child was heavy and her body unaccustomed to the weight. She paused, massaging the cramp until it passed and finally straightened and turned toward the kitchen.

Lord Arnaud stood propped against the back wall of the kitchen and her heart fluttered painfully in her chest. She did not want to draw attention to her reluctance to pass near him, however, and after only a slight hesitation, she trained her gaze on her feet and headed toward the laundry shed instead.

He cut off her retreat, bracing an arm across the door frame, and she stopped, dropping a curtsey. "My lord?" she said questioningly, refusing to lift her gaze.

"You are not well?" he asked after a moment.

Surprised, she glanced upward. She saw his gaze was on her belly and looked away again when his gaze flickered to her face. "I am well enough. We Saxons are a hearty lot. You need not fear that I will cease to be useful."

He tensed, but instead of responding to the provocative remark, asked instead, "What did Renard speak to you about?"

She had a strong feeling that he'd heard much, if not all, of their conversation. They had not been standing nearly so close as she was to Lord Arnaud now, and voices carried quite well across the yard. She shrugged. "He asked if I would go with him when he left."

"And you said?"

She glanced at him again. "I am no longer a free woman. I can not choose."

He frowned, his displeasure obvious. "Would you choose to go with him if you were?"

She flushed. He was as thick skulled as his brother. She wondered if men ever thought with more than their cocks—it passed comprehension that they could be so enamored of them that they thought they only had to shove their 'wonder rod' into a woman to enslave her for life.

She had not thought Lord Arnaud such a fool as to believe she had been at all interested in having Renard rutting her. It infuriated her that he did, that he obviously considered her no better than a common whore. As tempted as she was to inform him that she rather thought having her fingernails pulled out one by one would be more pleasurable, however, she bit her tongue. "I am not free. I did not give it any thought," she said coolly.

He caught her chin, forcing her to look up at him. Her heart clutched painfully in her chest, but she regarded him steadily.

"Would you?" he ground out harshly.

She swallowed with an effort. "What answer do you seek?"

His eyes blazed. After a moment, however, he released her abruptly and strode away.

A sense of satisfaction filled her. She had routed

two Normans in one day and it was scarcely more than sunrise.

The sense of triumph did not last, of course. The moment he disappeared the satisfaction vanished with him.

Since she didn't want him to know that her trip to the laundry shed had been no more than a ruse, she went inside and sorted the laundry for washing.

She could not fathom the man. Had he believed Renard's lie that she was jealous that he had turned his attention elsewhere? Even if he did, why act as if it mattered? He had made it painfully clear that what she had believed was kindness and concern for her welfare was no more than caution and suspicion, and the cleverness to know that her treatment, for good or ill, strongly affected the servants who remained. They were not likely to attempt revolt in any case, but her assurances that they would be treated well if they accepted their new master had gone a long way toward keeping the peace—which had been his objective.

Was that it? He had believed Renard and thought she might try to flee with him? Was it … a warning? She had tried to kill Renard without considering the consequences of her actions, but she knew right well that she would have been executed if she had succeeded. Did he think that she might run away, forcing him to track her down and punish her—with all the repercussions that that would entail?

She shook her head in disgust with herself. She should have known that it must be something like that. If she were truthful with herself, she knew very well that she had responded to him as a man and that that was the only reason that she had been eager to look well upon all that he did. She had not truly questioned his motives at any point.

Perhaps she was as guilty of stupidity by conceit as Renard? Had she believed, somewhere in her mind, that he was attracted to her as she was to him? Or that he was being kind because he realized that she was the daughter of Odolf and deserved better treatment because of her birth? She had certainly not been spoiled as Lady Rosabel seemed to have been, but her father had been a wealthy man and she had, once upon a time, been considered a marriage prize.

She would have been settled by now if not for her father's dependence upon her to run his household, but she had not found a man to tempt her away from her home and so she had not pressed her father to settle her.

Perhaps, after all, it was just as well she had not. She would be a widow now, of a certainty, with children that she would need to worry about and protect. At least as it was she did not have that worry.

She found that she was glad her impulse had taken her to the laundry shed. Of all the tasks she performed, laundry was her least favorite, but it was a fine day to be working outside and the relative solitude of her task helped her to clear her mind a little. By the time she'd finished laundering Lady Rosabel's fine linens, her back had begun to feel as if it would break in two, however, and her hands were already red and raw from the lye. When Yvette and Pauline arrived to check her work suspiciously, as if Lady Rosabel, or they, thought that she might deliberately damage the clothing, she left the remainder of the laundry to them and went inside.

The servants were clearing away the noon meal as she passed through the kitchen once more. She managed to grab a piece of fowl and a crust of bread and gnawed at them as she made her way upstairs. She had

spent hours toiling over a pot of boiling laundry and
then hanging it to dry and she had not even combed her
hair upon rising. She would have to take a few moments to tidy herself before she went in to Lady
Rosabel's day room. Lady Rosabel required that her
maids be neat in appearance. Clearly she thought that
she and Griselda were the next thing to animals, but
Elspeth saw little point in giving the lady more to complain about.

To her relief, her belongings remained in the corner where she'd left them. Kneeling, she set the meat
and bread she hadn't finished on her rolled pallet, wiped
her hands on her apron and dug through the small bundle
of her belongings until she found her comb. Quickly
removing the leather thongs that she used to secure
her braids, she carefully parted her hair down the center once more, dragged one section across her shoulder and began working the snarls from it.

Her hair, she saw, had gotten far too long. It must
surely be nearly to her knees by now and it was a great
deal more work than she had time for. Pressing her
hand to her aching back, she shifted after a bit to sit on
the floor and paused long enough to finish her meal.

Hearing a heavy tread on the stairs, she glanced
around and saw to her surprise that Lord Arnaud had
come up. He rarely did so during the day unless it was
to visit his lady in her day room, or, occasionally, to
remove his mail and change into more comfortable
clothing if he had no plan to leave the manor.

Her heart skidded painfully, but she thought perhaps
he wouldn't notice her in the corner if she sat perfectly still. She waited breathlessly until the footsteps
stopped, listening for the sound of a door opening.
When she didn't hear one, she nerved herself to glance

around again.

He was standing at the door to the day room, but she could see that he was facing her, even though she looked no higher than his knees. Turning away again, she dropped the remains of her meal in her pocket and hastily brushed the crumbs from her clothing. When he still did not leave, she wiped her hands on her apron and began to hastily braid the hair she'd combed. She'd intended to form a single braid as she usually did, but she could scarcely think, knowing that he was watching her, wondering why he was watching her so intently.

Her fingers were trembling so badly, she made a mess of the braid before she'd sorted half its length. She stopped, studying the twisted hair and finally glanced toward him again, wondering if she'd been so preoccupied she simply hadn't heard him go into the room.

She saw that he was studying the hair she held clenched in her fist. The impulse to explain herself rose. She tamped it, waiting to see if he would accuse her of … anything, before she began to babble as if she truly was guilty of something, which she wasn't. Not really. She had begun work before the others and not taken the time to perform her daily grooming first—truthfully, she had dallied in the yard too long, and she knew it.

She should be in attendance on Lady Rosabel now, not huddled in the corner eating her mid day meal.

It was almost as if he had merely waited for her to acknowledge him, however, for after allowing his gaze to skate over her, he turned away and went into the room.

Breathing a little easier, Elspeth returned her attention to her hair, combing the tangles out of the other section of hair and then forming the single

70

braid down the back as she usually did. She left about a foot of hair free of the braid at the end, not only because her arms were aching with fatigue long before she had it all braided but because she meant to make certain that it didn't take her so long to arrange her hair again.

When she'd finished tying the leather thongs tightly around the braid to hold it in place, she gathered her belongings and took them into Lady Rosabel's bedchamber, depositing them next to Griselda's. Dragging her unfinished meal from her pocket, she flicked the lint off of it and quickly finished it, then opened a window and tossed the bone out.

Griselda had a small eating dagger that they shared. It was dull and she doubted very much that it would cut her hair, but she thought it worth a try and dug it out. She'd grasped the hair in a wad and was on the point of trying to saw through it when the door to the Lady Rosabel's chamber opened.

"Don't."

Chapter Seven

Elspeth jumped guiltily, dropping the knife. "My lord?"

He strode toward her, bending to scoop up the knife. "I would not like to see you butcher your hair ... nor injure yourself in the attempt with this dull blade."

She stared at him with a mixture of surprise and irritation. "I have nothing else to use and my hair is far too long. I will be stepping upon it ere I know it."

Without a word, he caught her hair, running his hand down the rope-like braid until he reached the unfettered end. "It gleams like gold," he said musingly, studying it where it lay against his palm. After a moment, he closed his fist around it, pulled his dagger from his belt and sliced the ends off cleanly.

"Lady Rosabel wants her needlework basket," he said as he looked down to slip his knife back into his belt.

Relieved that he had not come into the bedchamber in search of her, Elspeth nodded and went to fetch the basket, then escaped the room. Lady Rosabel did not seem pleased when Elspeth arrived with her basket instead of Lord Arnaud, whom she'd apparently sent to perform the task, but she smiled when he returned a few moments later and sprawled in the chair adjacent to hers. "I thought, perhaps, that you had become bored and left," she said chidingly.

Lord Arnaud smiled faintly. "I am not accustomed to being idle."

Lady Rosabel frowned, her lips tightening. Her response made it obvious that even Lord Arnaud could not escape her tendency to turn every word, gesture and comment over and over until she found an insult in it. "I am not accustomed to being idle either, but I have not been at all well with this child."

His gaze flickered over her speculatively. "That was not an accusation," he said coolly. "I merely meant to point out that I was not bored with your company."

She sniffed threateningly, but apparently decided after a glance at Lord Arnaud to try a different tact and sighed gustily. "I am bored. Why don't you play something for me, Guillume?" she said, brightening.

Lord Arnaud glanced toward the lute that had been hung on the wall by a peg and finally rose and retrieved it. Settling once more, he began to check the strings, tuning each in turn.

"Here girl. Make yourself useful and separate these threads for me," she said, extending the basket without glancing in Elspeth's direction. Elspeth rose at once and took the basket, returning to the bench beneath the window that she had been sharing with Griselda. Without a word, Griselda took a handful of the threads and began carefully sorting them.

"What would you like for me to play?"

Lady Rosabel smiled and clapped her hands in delight. "I have so missed court! Anything! A love ballad!"

Elspeth glanced toward the two of them curiously. Somehow, she would never have imagined that Lord Arnaud possessed any musical talent at all. It seemed at odds with his role as warrior, particularly since she knew from what she had heard his men say of him that he had distinguished himself so well on the field of battle that he had gained William the Bastard's attention, and admiration.

She saw that he had flushed uncomfortably at Lady Rosabel's request and amusement touched her as it occurred to her to wonder if he actually could play the lute. He seemed familiar with the instrument, though, so perhaps he was only uncomfortable with that particular request?

The moment he began to strum the instrument and lifted his voice in song, shivers raced all over her body. She had thought his deep voice pleasing to the ear when he spoke. When he sang, it seemed to reach deeply inside of her. His voice, the music, and the words of the ballad he sang played such havoc with her senses that she made a tangled mess of the threads she was trying to separate.

Griselda's hand closed over hers, stilling her movements, and she glanced at the older woman. The knowing look in her gaze was almost as disturbing as the warning she saw there. She looked down at her hands once more. Griselda took the threads from her, handed her those that she'd sorted and wound into skeins and set to work untangling the mess that Elspeth had made.

Nodding at the silent command, Elspeth rose and placed the sorted skeins within Lady Rosabel's reach. Before she could return to her seat, however, Lady Rosabel spoke quietly to her, sending her to fetch refreshment for her and her lord.

Elspeth had never thought to be grateful to the woman, but in that moment she was so happy to have an excuse to escape that she felt almost tearful with relief. Bobbing a curtsey, she fled the room. She only wished that she could flee from herself.

* * * *

Lord Arnaud seemed determined to better acquaint himself with the wife that he had spent more time apart from than with. Or perhaps it was only that he had tired of her constant complaints of neglect, boredom and home sickness, and thought to make peace—or because of his concern for her that she was seemed to be having a difficult pregnancy. Whatever the case, he spent far more time in her company than he had before.

Despite that, and the fact that she had no way to escape since she was constantly at Lady Rosabel's beck and call, Elspeth managed to either avoid him altogether or remain well out of sight much of the time.

She suspected that was at least in part because Lord Arnaud wished to keep his distance, as well. For, although he did not seem to actually avoid her, more often than not he joined his lady when she was working elsewhere.

Griselda, for reasons she did not discuss with Elspeth, aided her surprisingly ably.

It was her considered opinion, and Elspeth trusted Griselda implicitly in such matters, that Lady Rosabel was not nearly as ill as she liked to pretend, but that she had indulged herself far too much. Griselda had advised her to rest when she felt ill, particularly in the early months of her pregnancy. She had not meant that Lady Rosabel should spend her entire pregnancy ensconced in her bed or a chair in her sitting room.

Griselda had not mastered the Norman tongue, however, and Lady Rosabel simply pretended she couldn't understand her when Griselda tried to coax her into daily walks that would help to strengthen her for the ordeal she must soon face. Finally, Griselda demanded that Elspeth speak with Lord Arnaud about the situation.

Elspeth had spent weeks avoiding him. She was not only indignant that Griselda would ask, she refused point blank to seek him out. Griselda would give her no peace, however.

"You are that concerned about her?" Elspeth had finally demanded. "After all that you have said about our hated enemies, the Normans?"

Griselda glared at her. "I am not comfortable ignoring danger to her health when Lord Arnaud specifically charged me with seeing to it that she and the child were well taken care of."

Elspeth bit her lip at that. "You truly think that her child is at risk?"

"I truly think that both her and the child are at risk or I would have said nothing! She has done nothing but sat about and eat since she ceased to be ill and she will not have the strength in her body to expel the child when the time comes! Think you the lord will thank us if his wife and heir die in child bed? Or that he will blame us for not taking better care of her? And what is to become of us if she dies in child bed even if he does not blame us for it?"

Elspeth could not like Lady Rosabel, but she did not want the woman's death on her conscience. "Why can you not speak with him yourself?"

Griselda glared at her impatiently. "Because I can not understand the half of what he says, nor he what I say."

"We could speak with Jean," Elspeth said on sudden inspiration. She had seen almost nothing of him since she had been sent to serve Lady Rosabel—because Lady Rosabel had scarcely been down the stairs since she had arrived, but she knew there would be no problem making him understand.

Griselda wasn't particularly happy with that solution, but she agreed that they would try it. When another week passed, however, and they had not managed to catch Jean to speak to him, Griselda began to pester Elspeth again.

Elspeth finally agreed, but that, too, proved difficult. She didn't want to speak to him in front of Lady Rosabel, knowing full well that it would only send her mistress into a rage. Finally, she decided there was no hope for it. When next Lord Arnaud ordered a bath, instead of sending someone else to take her place as she had since the night he had sent her away, Elspeth joined Griselda. Her nerves were on edge, however.

She had not approached him before, which made it difficult enough in itself even if she could have dismissed the animosity that she had worked to shield herself with since he had told her he looked upon her only as his enemy. Even if there had not been so much tension between them, she feared he would react badly to discussing his wife with a servant, especially her.

It did not make things any easier that, when he entered the room, he checked at the sight of her standing before the hearth with Griselda. It was the barest of pauses. She might not have noticed at all except that she had glanced at him nervously at that precise moment.

The unwelcoming look upon his face was enough in itself to make her long to flee and she glanced at Griselda, wondering, once again, if she should even attempt to speak to him. Griselda only frowned at her and gave her a nudge forward as Lord Arnaud settled on the stool beside the tub.

Finally, Elspeth knelt before him. "My lord—may I speak?"

"Concerning what matter?" he said after a notable pause, and although his voice sounded carefully neutral, it was that in itself that increased her anxiety.

"Griseld—it is about your wife," Elspeth said quickly before she lost her nerve, and then dared a glance up at him.

If he had looked even vaguely receptive before, he lost even that much, his face hardening until it looked as if it might have been carved from stone. "Take care you do not forget your place," he said coldly.

The words washed over her in a frigid wave and Elspeth glanced at Griselda again.

"Speak," Griselda said in a harsh whisper, nudging her again. "He thinks you mean to complain ... or insult his lady."

"We are ... Griselda is concerned for her health, my lord," Elspeth said hurriedly. "She has spent too much time abed. She grows weak, and she will have difficulty when her time comes."

It could not be said that any of the tension left him, but the cold fury was replaced by anxiety. "She eats well now. She seems healthy enough to me," he said after a moment, suspicion rife in his voice. "Are you suggesting that there is something I can do about it, even if what you say is true?"

Elspeth bit her lip as Griselda nodded eagerly and dropped to her knees beside her, gesturing toward his legs and belly as she explained the need for strength in the lower body. Lord Arnaud merely stared at her in incomprehension, however.

"You must persuade her to walk so that she will grow stronger. She is weak and the child heavy. It pains her to walk, and she is convinced that it is bad for the child. She will not listen to Griselda."

78

He frowned. "If she believes it bad for the child, perhaps she knows better where it concerns herself."

Elspeth released a sigh of exasperation. "She has not borne a child before. She knows only that she is afraid."

His eyes narrowed at her tone. "You are younger than she. You are so much wiser?"

Elspeth felt color fill her cheeks. "Griselda attended my mother through the births of five babes. I trust her judgment."

"But can I?"

Elspeth sat back on her heels, staring up at him in dismay. She had known he would not like to discuss his wife with her. She understood it. But she had not thought his distrust ran so deep that he would question their motives, that he might think that they were trying to hurt her rather than help. He held her gaze for several moments before he turned away to study the fire on the hearth.

Almost absently, he fished a leather thong from beneath his surcoat and pulled it off over his head, holding the small pouch attached to it in his palm and studying it for several moments before he clenched his fist around it. "More than any other, I have entrusted her care to the two of you. Think not that I will not hold you responsible if ill comes of it."

Elspeth swallowed with an effort as he turned to look at her once more. "Then you might just as well kill us now," she said stiffly. "For she is as pig headed as you are and suspicious of every attempt to help her, no matter how well meaning."

His eyes narrowed on her face, but Elspeth met his gaze unflinchingly, refusing to back down. After a moment, some of the tension left him and he nodded.

It would have been a vast understatement to say that Lady Rosabel did not take the suggestion well. She had been enjoying her invalidism and the attention it gained her far too much to willingly give it up. Lord Arnaud spent the first week coaxing her to walk with him, even carrying her downstairs to walk along the paths of the tiny kitchen garden.

She complained endlessly, and swore each time that she walked for more than a few steps that she was having heart palpitations, or contractions, or both. By the second week, Lord Arnaud's patience began to rapidly unravel. He ceased trying to cajole her and commanded her instead, which only resulted in tearful hysterics and even less cooperation than before.

She accused him of trying to hasten her to her death. She accused Elspeth and Griselda of conspiring against her to murder her. Yvette and Pauline, who had never looked upon either of them with anything but thinly veiled hostility and suspicion, fed her doubts until what had begun as no more than thoughtless anger became a certainty in her mind. Soon, the rumor spread beyond the confines of Lady Rosabel's chambers into the general populace of the keep and the Normans began to look upon all of the Saxons with a great deal of suspicion, and vice versa.

There seemed no way to squelch the rumors once begun. The fact was that the truce between the two factions had never been more than a thin facade. Animosity lingered not far beneath the surface, waiting to erupt, and needing only a tiny catalyst. Elspeth found it difficult to accept that anyone actually believed such things, but whether they did or not, it was an excuse for disputes.

Lord Arnaud found more and more of his time was spent settling petty squabbles and trying to keep the peace. Lady Rosabel seemed content with the results. As much as she seemed to enjoy Lord Arnaud's attention, she preferred him dancing attendance upon her as invalid. His determination to deprive her of glorying in her delicate condition made him lose favor with her very quickly.

When she topped off weeks of giving him the cold shoulder and provoking a fight each time he demanded his rights as her husband by informing him that she was no longer in any condition to perform her duties as his wife, Elspeth expected an explosion the likes of which they had not seen heretofore. Instead, Lord Arnaud, furious, but looking far more relieved than disappointed, ceased to inflict himself upon her at all.

Neither Elspeth nor Griselda was relieved. The cold feud between Lord Arnaud and his wife only made their situation far more difficult. Neither of them thought for one moment that he would be any more inclined to take pity on them if Lady Rosabel's labor went badly, but without him to enforce the order for her daily walks, Rosabel balked, and Yvette and Pauline staunchly aided and abetted her.

Short of engaging in a daily battle that threatened to escalate from verbal to physical, the only time that they were able to drag her from her bed and force her to walk was when Yvette or Pauline, or both, were sent to attend other matters.

The only heartening aspect was that Rosabel did seem to be improving. She would still complain when she was walked from her chamber to the sitting room and back again, and swear that she was nigh fainting, or that she was going into labor, but she had ceased to tremble as if her legs would give way.

They switched from walking her to her sitting room and back to walking her to the head of the stairs. The distance was greater, and Elspeth, at least, thought her curiosity might overcome her reluctance if she saw that she might have the entertainment of company if only she went downstairs.

It was obvious she was tempted. She had seemed pleased, at first, that she had thoroughly routed Lord Arnaud, but that had not lasted once she discovered that he would not sit with her in her day room and entertain her with his lute either.

"Jean often plays his lute once they have finished supping," Elspeth suggested tentatively.

Lady Rosabel glanced at her sharply. "Jean?"

Elspeth nodded. "He is a troubadour from Vereins."

Lady Rosabel frowned. "I am too heavy and clumsy to try the stairs. I would have to be carried."

Elspeth held her temper with an effort. "It can not take much to walk down. Only hold on to the rail and I will help you."

Lady Rosabel's eyes narrowed suspiciously, but since Jean chose that moment to begin tuning his lute, she hesitated. "Go and tell my lord that I wish to be carried down."

Elspeth's lips tightened. "You can walk down the stairs if only you will try," she said, keeping her voice even with an effort. She knew she should simply concede defeat, but she also knew that Lady Rosabel would not budge an inch if she ceased trying to prod her.

Lady Rosabel's face was instantly suffused with rage. "How dare you speak back to me, you Saxon slut! Do as I say or I will have you whipped for defying me!"

Elspeth felt the blood drain from her face. "You are upset. I will help you to your room," she said, trying to placate the woman.

Lady Rosabel slapped her. It didn't hurt as badly as it sounded, for the sound seemed to echo down the stairwell like a clap of thunder. It was also unexpected and caught Elspeth off guard. She wavered and fell back against the wall. Her heart pounded painfully as she glanced down at the stairs, which had never seemed nearly as steep and frightening as they did at that moment.

Instead of being satisfied, however, the eruption of physical rage seemed to have unleashed a tidal wave of fury that Lady Rosabel had been nursing. Or, perhaps, it only enraged her further that Elspeth did not seem either cowed or particularly harmed by the blow. Whatever the case, the moment Elspeth righted herself, Lady Rosabel flew into a frenzy of rage, screaming and slapping her over and over again about the face and head.

Elspeth shielded her head with one hand, searching blindly with her other to find something to hold onto to keep her balance. The handrail was on the outside of the stairs, however. There was nothing along the inner wall where she stood, to grasp. Almost as if time had suddenly slowed, she felt her balance waver, shift, and then she saw the stairs flying up toward her face.

Strangely, she felt no pain when she landed, only the pressure of the blow, as if she were cushioned from any sensation of pain. Dimly, she knew that she would continue to fall and reached for something to catch herself, but again, it was as if time had slowed, or she had been caught in a nightmare that retarded her efforts to move. She tumbled over and over until she was dizzy and so disoriented that she could no longer tell up from down.

She landed on her back. When at last she ceased to fall she merely lay still, trying to catch her breath, trying to grasp what had happened, expecting momentarily to feel the pain she had not yet felt. Griselda leaned over her, her face contorted, tears streaming down her cheeks, but Elspeth couldn't seem to hear her at first, or understand her when she finally distinguished her voice. She realized finally that there were a sea of faces above her.

Jean's face swam into view. She saw that he was holding her hand, kneading it. "Lady! Lady Elspeth, are you hurt?"

Fear surged through her, but almost as if his voice had finally ripped away whatever it was that had protected her from the pain, it began to surge through her, building quickly until it took her breath away. Her hand tightened on his. She found her voice with an effort. "Take me to the cottage, Jean."

He was thrust roughly away and Lord Arnaud's face was above her instead. His face was chalky white and she knew only from looking at his expression that she was going to die. He glanced toward the people that had gathered around them, ordering them back before he turned to her once. "You will be more comfortable here, chere. Put your arms around my neck."

Her arms hardly seemed to belong to her. She had to command herself to lift them at all. He caught her hands, leaning low and wrapping her arms around his neck, then sliding one arm beneath her shoulders and the other beneath her knees. The pain only seemed to intensify as he lifted her. She dropped her head against his shoulder, unable to think for the pain that seemed to be growing stronger and stronger. It took an effort even to tilt her head back to speak to him and once she had done so, she found she couldn't lift it again. "Take me to the cottage," she whispered urgently. "I do not want to die among my enemies."

He stiffened, hesitating with one foot on the stairs. "Please."

At that, he looked upward, staring at Lady Rosabel, who stood frozen in horror at the top of the stairs. Abruptly, he turned away from the stairs and strode through the great hall.

Chapter Eight

The night was chill with the crispness of fall. Despite the heat emanating from Lord Arnaud's body, Elspeth's teeth were chattering by the time they reached the tiny cottage that she had shared with Griselda. There was neither light nor heat and Lord Arnaud cursed when he had pushed the door ajar and moved inside.

"You can not stay here," he said harshly. "I will take you inside where you can be more comfortable."

"Nay! Leave me. At least my last sight will not be of their gloating faces!"

"Cease!" Lord Arnaud growled hoarsely. "You will not die."

Elspeth barely heard him. Pain had become the focus of her world. She groaned. "The child is coming."

After a moment, he settled her on the packed earth and rose to search for the makings of a fire. Elspeth curled into a ball, panting as each wave of pain washed over her, groaning mindlessly as it reached its peak and slowly began to taper off.

By the time Griselda arrived, Lord Arnaud had built a small fire in the fire pit. Feeble warmth and light and smoke filled the tiny cottage that was little more than a daub and stick hut. Griselda had fetched her medicines and their bedding, however, and set to work at once spreading first her own and then Elspeth's bedding, one atop the other. When she had finished, she began trying to help Elspeth to sit up. Lord Arnaud pushed her aside, scooped Elspeth up and settled her on the bedding.

"She thinks the child is coming," he said without glancing at Griselda, his gaze pinned on Elspeth's face.

Griselda ran a hand over Elspeth's abdomen and hissed an epitaph beneath her breath. Pushing Elspeth's knees up, she flipped her gown back. "She is bleeding. The child is coming."

Lord Arnaud had been stroking Elspeth's cheek soothingly, but at that his hand stilled and his head snapped around. "It is too soon, surely?"

Griselda looked him in the eye. "Yes ... but it comes, nevertheless."

He swallowed audibly. "What do you need?"

Griselda's faced crumpled. "Time."

Lord Arnaud stared at her for a long moment and finally gripped her arms, shaking her. "Calm yourself," he ground out in a fierce whisper. "So help me God, if you let her die you will long for death ere I grant it!"

"She is like my own daughter to me," Griselda said angrily. "I would give my life for her, but I could not protect her from that pig! And I can not save her from the consequences. She is strong enough to save herself ... or she is not. I am not a witch, whatever that Norman female says. Nature will take its course, and there is little that I can do beyond making her comfortable."

Lord Arnaud's face hardened, twisted with pain. Finally, he released her. "Do what you can for her." Rising abruptly, he left the tiny cottage.

When he'd gone, Griselda mopped her face and moved to the pallet. Despite the chill that lingered in the cottage, Elspeth was sweating and thrashing about as if fevered. Climbing to her feet with an effort, she found a pail and left the cottage to fetch water.

Lord Arnaud was pacing just outside. He glanced from her face to the pail and took it from her, turning and striding toward the well.

Shrugging, Griselda went back inside and settled beside the pallet, stroking Elspeth's hand and murmuring any words of encouragement that came to mind. The contractions were hard. Either she would expel the child from her body soon, or she would be too weak to do so before very long. She had no idea whether the fall had simply brought on her labor early or if Elspeth had been hurt beyond mending. She could not find any bones that appeared to be broken. Her face was bruised and had begun to swell. There were other bruises, as well, but the bruises would heal and as badly as they looked Griselda wasn't particularly worried about them.

She began praying—to the old gods, to the Christian god, to any deity that might be inclined to look upon her with pity and grant her wish.

When Lord Arnaud returned with the water, she poured a portion in a kettle to heat and set the remainder near the pallet so that she could bathe Elspeth and try to make her more comfortable. Returning to her bundle of belongings, she extracted the things that she'd collected to help with the birthing. Lord Arnaud, she saw, had knelt beside the pallet once more. She handed him a thick strip of leather. He stared down at it with out comprehension. "Place it between her teeth. It will give her something to focus on besides the pain."

He caught her jaw, forcing her teeth apart and placed the strip of leather between them. She bit down on it as her belly tightened once more. He stared at the shifting of her muscles and finally turned to Griselda again. "What are you doing?"

"Brewing herbal tea. It will make her mind strange for a bit, but it will also ease the pain."

He rose abruptly. "I will be outside if you need anything."

She stared at the door when he'd closed it behind him. "And good riddance," she muttered.

Elspeth's eyes were disoriented and glazed with pain when Griselda lifted her shoulders and held the cup of tea to her lips. "I do not want to die," she said hoarsely.

Griselda smiled, stroking her cheek. "Good. Then don't."

Lord Arnaud returned twice to place more wood on the fire and keep it burning. By the time Elspeth's child made it into the world near dawn, the cottage felt like a hot house. He did not linger long enough for Griselda to complain, however. It was as if he could neither bear to remain outside in ignorance of what was happening inside, nor remain inside and watch.

Finally, when she had Elspeth comfortable and the squalling babe nestled at her breast, she left the cottage. Lord Arnaud was seated on a block of wood near the door, idly brushing something back and forth across his palm. When he sensed her presence, he took the lock of hair and thrust it back into the pouch that hung from the leather thong around his neck. "Is she…?"

Griselda sighed and settled on a log beside him. "The bleeding has slowed. If it does not begin again … and if she does not become fevered."

He said nothing, merely stared off into the distance, and she wondered if he had even heard her.

"I would like to stay with her and take care of her," she said hesitantly, determined that she would, with or without his permission.

"Do you believe that Rosabel intended to cause her harm?" he said after a moment.

Griselda was tempted to fling a furious 'yes' in his face, but in truth, she didn't believe the woman had had malice on her mind. She was simply too self-centered and temperamental to consider the consequences of her actions. There was no doubt in her mind that Lady Rosabel had been horrified when she saw what she had done.

Of course, that might have been because Lord Arnaud had looked up at her with murder evident in his eyes. She thought it unlikely that anyone who had seen his face could be in any doubt that it was only the shock of seeing Elspeth lying still and white on the floor that had kept him from climbing the stairs and slaying her on the spot.

His own men had looked at each other in dismay, obviously fearing they would have to try to restrain him.

If there could be said to be any good that had come of the incident, it was that there was no longer doubt in Saxon mind or Norman where Lord Arnaud's heart lay and she knew it had gone a long way toward bringing the peace once more.

She shrugged. "No. I do not," she said finally, believing it, though she thought she would have said as much regardless. The old lord was dead. The Saxon way of life had gone with those who'd fallen beneath the swords of the Normans. Elspeth had been willing to make peace with the Normans as soon as Lord

Arnaud had shown them that he was a fair minded man and they would not be mistreated so long as they co-operated. She would not approve of conflict on her behalf, not when it effected the lives of so many.

He glanced at her then, studying her. Abruptly, he nodded and rose. "Stay with her."

Lord Arnaud did not visit again. Three days later, a messenger arrived from King William, commanding Lord Arnaud's presence and he gathered his army together once more and left Rasgarth.

Elspeth's son, born nearly two months before he should have been, struggled to cling to life for nearly three torturous weeks before he died. Elspeth had not wanted him, and when she saw how tiny and weak he was, she had known he could not survive. She had wanted not to care, but in the end she had not been able to stop herself from loving him. She was devastated by his death.

Little more than a week after she buried him, Lady Rosabel went into labor and she and Griselda were summoned to attend her.

Elspeth was inclined to ignore the summons. She had not really blamed Lady Rosabel for her fall, but she hated her for the death of her son. "I can not wet nurse that ... woman's child! I will not!" she said angrily. Her chin wobbled. "Not when I would be nursing my own if not for her nasty temper!"

Griselda studied her in tight lipped silence for several moments, but she was more worried than angry. Lord Arnaud had left orders that they were to attend his wife, and the captain stood outside with two men at arms to see that they did. "You can not blame the child for the mother's sins."

Elspeth dragged in a ragged breath. "I do not—but I see no reason why she can not nurse him herself."

"It is Lord Arnaud's child, Elspeth," Griselda said quietly. "You would not leave the poor babe at her mercy, knowing how she is?"

Elspeth glared at her, but the fight had gone out of her. Rising, she found her shift and dragged it over her head while Griselda gathered her herbs. Wrapping their shawls tightly about them, they headed toward the manor.

They could hear Lady Rosabel's screams the moment they entered the great hall.

They exchanged a glance. "She will be worn herself out before she even comes to the difficult part," Griselda predicted.

The birthing was a nightmare for all concerned. Yvette and Pauline were as prone to hysteria as their mistress, and each fed off the other's until they managed to exhaust themselves and had to rest before pitching yet another temperamental fit. Lady Rosabel's contractions grew stronger and stronger, but Griselda could discern no real progress. When she finally demanded that Lady Rosabel get up and walk, in an attempt to get the weight of the child itself to help matters along, Lady Rosabel called them every foul name she could lay her tongue to and her maids shoved them aside and refused to allow them near her.

Griselda was torn between the desire to do battle and the certainty that it would be a waste of time and energy. Finally, she turned and stalked from the room. Elspeth followed her.

Lord Arnaud's captain met them at the foot of the stairs. "You were summoned to attend Lord Arnaud's wife," he said grimly, blocking their path and refusing to move out of the way.

"We were ordered to leave," Elspeth threw back at him.

"No order supersedes Lord Arnaud's save the

King's," the man ground out.

Elspeth and Griselda exchanged a look and turned, climbing the stairs once more. To their dismay, the captain and the two guards who had escorted them to the manor to begin with, followed them up the stairs once more.

The captain opened the door for them. "By Lord Arnaud's order, these Saxon women were sent to attend Lady Rosabel. I am ordered to remove anyone who interferes."

Yvette and Pauline gaped at the man, exchanged frightened glances and abandoned their station near Lady Rosabel's bed to huddle in the corner. Lady Rosabel immediately began cursing him and threatening retribution once Lord Arnaud returned, but he withdrew without a word, closing the door.

Griselda studied Lady Rosabel through narrowed eyes for several moments and finally moved to the hearth. Elspeth followed her, watching her in silence for several moments. "You're brewing the tea for her?"

Griselda shrugged. "It would be better to wait if she were more reasonable. She has not made near the progress she should. But she is already growing tired and I do not think we will be able to do anything at all with her until she has settled down. The tea will soothe her as well as dull the pain."

Elspeth frowned. "She will be sleepy, though," she said tentatively. "That is not a good thing, is it?"

Griselda sighed. "There is nothing that is good about this. We will be lucky if either she or the child survives, but I do not think the chances at all good that both will."

Elspeth glanced fearfully toward the door, wondering what the men had been told to do if she and Griselda failed, but there was little point in focusing on it when it would distract them from what they needed to do.

Lady Rosabel accused them of trying to poison her when they brought the tea. Griselda lost her temper and cursed her. Fortunately, her accent was such that Lady Rosabel could scarcely understand her under ordinary conditions. Elspeth's temper was little better. Grasping the woman's cheeks, she gritted her teeth at her. "I would as soon poison you if it would not mean my own death, but I do not think you are worth throwing my life away. Are you so stupid that the idea of dying and taking your child with you seems—romantic to you? What good do you think it will do you for everyone to weep and bemoan your passing? You will not be here to enjoy it!"

Rosabel's eyes nearly bulged out at that, but it was fear, not fury that gripped her. "I do not want to die," she gasped in a frightened whisper.

"Then drink the tea. It will make you calmer and dull the pain—and then walk with us, else the child will die inside of you before much longer and then you will die also."

She complained, but she drank the tea. When she had finished it, Elspeth and Griselda helped her from the bed. Drawing an arm over their shoulders, they supported her between them and walked slowly back and forth across the room until Rosabel began to weep for them to allow her to lie down again.

They helped her into the bed again and Griselda examined her. "There," she said, patting Rosabel's hand, "that is better. We make progress."

Rosabel looked at her vaguely. "It is coming now?"
"Soon."

Despite everything the woman had done to make her own life a misery to her, Elspeth felt a stirring of pity. She knew what pain the woman must be suffering. She also knew that Rosabel's fear was very real—and not misplaced. Enemy or not, man could not invent a means of punishment more torturous than bearing a child, and it was impossible not to pity anyone enduring it.

When they had allowed her to rest for a little while, they pulled her from the bed and walked her again.

Elspeth lost track of the time. It had not been daylight when they had been summoned, and yet when she thought to look outside, it was still dark. She was disoriented until she realized that Rosabel had been laboring a full day and into night again. The fear that thought inspired wiped her weariness from her. How long, she wondered, since Rosabel had been able even to help them when they walked her back and forth across the room instead of hanging limply between them?

"She's foundering," Griselda muttered under her breath as if her mind followed the same path. "I will give her no more tea. She's too tired now to have the energy to fight us anyway."

"How fares the babe?"

Griselda shook her head. "I can not tell. It has not moved in hours, but they rarely move much once the labor begins. Most likely the poor little mite is growing weaker as the mother does."

"What are we to do?" Elspeth asked fearfully.

Griselda rubbed her head wearily. "I know of nothing. I think, perhaps, her hips are too narrow for the child, but I can not be certain. Most likely it is only that her contractions are too weak to help him move. I warned the lazy she dog that she would not have the strength to bear the child," she finished angrily.

Elspeth drew a shuddering breath. "That is not likely to do us much good when we must explain why she and the child died."

Griselda's lips set in a tight line. "I will save Lord Arnaud's child if I have to tear it from her. I would as soon not, so long as there is a chance that she might expel it herself, for they are bound to believe I killed her on purpose."

Almost as one, they surged to their feet and moved to the bed once more. Dragging Rosabel upright, Elspeth slapped her cheeks lightly until she roused enough to open her eyes. Instead of taking a few turns about the room, this time they walked her until they were ready to collapse with her, then they merely rested against the edge of the bed a few moments and began to walk her again.

The weight of the child, or the movement, or both, brought the contractions on stronger, and still they continued to move her around the room, dragging her much of the time, until the pains became intense enough that she found the energy to begin screaming again.

Elspeth thought her back would break in half as she struggled to help Griselda get Rosabel on the bed once more. She could only imagine what it must be like for Griselda, who was thrice her age. When Griselda checked her progress, however, she saw that it had been worth the effort. The babe had finally crowned.

Energized by the realization that the ordeal was almost over, Elspeth grasped Rosabel's face and shook her to gain her attention. "Rosabel! The babe is coming. You must push now. Can you do that?"

Rosabel nodded vaguely, gritting her teeth. Elspeth could not see that it helped much, however. "When her belly tightens again, help her to push," Griselda said, a thread of excitement in her voice now despite her weariness.

The baby began to squall angrily the moment its head

95

was freed. Elspeth clapped a hand over her mouth, laughing and crying at the same time. "See, lady! He is as impatient as his father to take the world."

"Get it out!" Rosabel screamed in revulsion as Griselda tried to work the infant's shoulders gently free. "Get it out!"

Elspeth stared at the woman in dismay. A moment before she'd seemed nigh dead. She would not have believed Rosabel still had the strength for a bout of hysteria.

"Push!" Griselda demanded. "You must help him."

"Pull it out!"

Griselda boxed her ears. "Push!" she screamed at her.

She did as she was told, heaving even when they told her to stop. At last the infant slipped from her body and dropped heavily onto the bed. He screamed almost nonstop. Galvanized by the baby's distress, Elspeth rushed away to test the water they had heated to clean him, tipping the cold water into the heated water. By the time she'd made it back to the bed, Griselda had bound the cord and severed it and she scooped the baby up and moved to the other side of the bed to clean him up.

He looked to be almost twice the size of her own baby. She checked him carefully as she washed him off, but she could see nothing but perfection. Even his coloring was good. Mopping the tears from her cheeks, she looked up at Lady Rosabel. "He is perfect! Your son is perfect! And so beautiful! He is the image of his father! He will be so pleased that you have given him a son!"

Yvette and Pauline, who had huddled in one corner from the time the captain had threatened them, surged forward, pushing Elspeth out of the way and cooing over the baby. A spark of anger rose in her, but she was far too weary to stoke it and it died almost as quickly as it arose. Moving around the bed, she helped Griselda clean Lady Rosabel up once she'd expelled the afterbirth.

They were both bloody from head to foot but too weary to do more than splash halfheartedly at cleaning themselves up. Elspeth was so tired, she lost consciousness almost the moment her face touched the thin pallet.

She was awakened some time later by the persistent wails of the baby and the tightening of her breasts as the milk flowed into them in response. Groggily, she sat up and looked around.

Pauline, looking the next thing to panic, was walking the baby back and forth across the floor.

"Give him to me and I will feed him," Elspeth said.

Pauline sent her a resentful glare, but reluctantly handed the baby to her. Lying down once more, she settled the baby beside her, opened the neck of her shift and offered him her nipple. He snuffled around it a moment, like a little puppy searching for its dinner, and finally latched onto it, suckling greedily. She chuckled, stroking his black, spiky hair.

When she woke again, it was to screams and wails of a different sort entirely.

Lady Rosabel was dead and Yvette and Pauline were screaming murder.

Chapter Nine

The commotion woke the baby, frightening him, and he immediately began to wail. Shushing him, Elspeth scooped him into her arms and began rocking him as she looked around in confusion, trying to jog her exhausted mind into interpreting what was going on.

The captain of the guard, grim faced, was listening while Yvette and Pauline pelted him with their own interpretations of the events. Griselda, still looking so exhausted that her eyes were glazed and blank, merely stared at them.

"She threatened to poison her," Yvette snarled, pointing a shaking finger at Elspeth.

"She said she would cut the child from its mother. Look at the blood!" Pauline screamed, pointing at Griselda.

The captain glanced from one woman to the next, his hands on his hips. "Did you murder the lady?" he demanded, staring at Griselda.

Griselda only stared at him uncomprehendingly.

Elspeth got to her feet with an effort. "She did all that could be done!" she cried. "You can not accuse her of murder!"

The captain looked around in disgust. "Take them all and lock them up. Lord Arnaud can sort through this when he comes."

Elspeth gaped at him. "But … how will I feed the baby?"

He stared at her in dismay. "We will find another wet nurse."

Elspeth clutched the baby tightly. "Lord Arnaud said I was to be his wet nurse," she said angrily.

His eyes narrowed. "That was before he thought you would die," he said tightly.

"If he didn't tell you any differently before he left, then he meant that I was to nurse the child if I didn't die," Elspeth said hotly.

He scratched his head. "Lock the others up. We will place this one under house arrest."

"Griselda is old. Leave her with me and she can help to tend the child."

"She is accused of murder!"

"You accused me, too! Look at Lady Rosabel! You will see she died in child bed. We did all that could be done. Griselda is nigh dead from attending her."

He glanced toward the bed in revulsion, but he didn't move so much as a step closer. After casting a desperate glance around the room, he fixed Yvette and Pauline with a hard glare. "You two—prepare the mistress for burial." He turned to look at Griselda and Elspeth. "You and you, come with me."

He escorted them to a room down the hall, thrust them inside and bolted the door from the outside.

"Send for someone to look at her. You will see we did nothing to harm her!" she yelled at the door.

Lord Arnaud did not come. A messenger arrived with the news that he was in the midst of a campaign to contain unrest near the borders and could not take leave. To Elspeth's relief, however, the captain sent his men in search of anyone with any knowledge of medicine or child birthing and dragged them in to examine Lady Rosabel. When none found anything amiss, she and Griselda were released and they returned to their cottage.

The captain was doubtful about her taking the infant, but since he hadn't been given specific instructions about it and Lord Arnaud had taken Elspeth to the cottage himself, he allowed it.

Unlike her own child, Lord Arnaud's son was strong, and he flourished. He filled the hole left in her soul from the loss of her own son. She knew she was asking for pain to allow herself to grow attached, but she could no more prevent it than she had been able to prevent herself from loving her own child.

By the time he began to look up at her and study her quizzically while he suckled, he had completely stolen her heart. She chuckled as she looked down at him. "He is wondering why I am standing over his dinner," she murmured. "And not at all pleased with me from the frown on his face."

Griselda huddled close, stroking his soft cheek. "You were right. He has the look of his father."

Elspeth sighed. "He will be walking before he has a name. You are certain Lady Rosabel did not give him one?"

Griselda's lips tightened. "She did not even hold him in her arms. No, she did not."

"Lord Arnaud's name is Guillume," Elspeth said tentatively.

Griselda studied her for several moments and finally sighed. "He is not Lars, Elspeth," she said gently.

Elspeth glanced at her sharply, feeling tears fill her eyes at her son's name. She had named him for her eldest brother. She nodded. "I know."

"You should give him up to another to nurse. Lord knows, there are a plenty now who could nurse him. Lord Arnaud will have no shortage of serfs in a few year's time."

Elspeth bent her head to study the infant. "I want to keep him."

"That's just my point, Elspeth. He is not yours. In a year or so, he will be taken away and then you will be lucky to see him at all. You will … have to give him up. As much as it pains me, in the eyes of the Normans, you are lady no more. You are nothing to them but a common peasant."

Elspeth drew a difficult breath. "I will have him for a little while."

"You will come to love him and it will be all the more difficult to give him up."

"I love him now!" she said angrily.

"You only think you do because he has filled your empty arms. If you give him up, you will see that I am right. You will still mourn your own child, but you will not be trying to replace him with this child."

Elspeth's jaw set. "It is my choice for now. I will live with the pain later if I am given no choice. For now, he needs love as much as he needs nourishment and I can give it to him. There is no one else to give him that."

It was the dead of winter before Lord Arnaud returned at last, and everyone had ceased to expect him to return before spring. Elspeth was huddled under every scrap of fabric that she owned near the fire in the pit when she heard the sound of activity outside.

She exchanged a look of alarm with Griselda, but there was no sound of clashing steel, only the hoof beats of many horses on the packed snow, the jingle of harness on the crisp air—the sound of many male voices.

"Do you think it is Lord Arnaud?" Griselda whispered anxiously.

Elspeth bit her lip, listening. "It must be else the alarm would have been raised."

"We should take the child and go," Griselda said decisively.

"Now? It is nigh dark, and cold as a witch's tit! He is like to freeze before we get there." She looked down at the sleeping baby. "Besides, I have just gotten him to sleep."

Griselda's brows rose. "Lord Arnaud is like to be wroth with us. Especially if Yvette and Pauline are to tell their side of the story first."

Elspeth frowned. "First? Last? Will it make a difference, do you think? He will believe them … or he will believe us. In truth, I hope that the captain will convince him before we must face him. Perhaps his temper will have cooled by morning."

Despite the argument, neither of them were easy in their mind. They listened for a while until the sounds of arrival began to quiet down. Elspeth had just begun to relax when someone began pounding upon the door of the cottage hard enough it looked likely to cave in momentarily.

Griselda leapt to her feet and raced to open it. She fell back when she saw who stood there. Elspeth was still struggling to gain her feet when Lord Arnaud stepped inside. She stared up at him, her heart pounding in her chest so frantically she thought it would suffocate her.

His face was drawn with weariness, but his dark eyes blazed almost feverishly. "I have come for my son," he said harshly, though his eyes never left her face.

His voice startled the infant awake, drawing Elspeth's attention. "Shhh, sweeting. It is all right," she said soothingly, holding him tightly and rocking him.

Lord Arnaud squatted, so that he was near eye level with her. "Mayhap you will tell me why I return to find my son and heir in this … sty," he ground out furiously.

Elspeth blinked at him in surprise. "He has come to no harm."

He ground his teeth. "It is nigh as cold in here as it is outside."

"It wasn't until you burst through the door!" Elspeth snapped.

Grasping her arm, he hauled her to her feet unceremoniously and marched her toward the door. She glanced back at Griselda uneasily as he dragged her from the cottage.

Almost as an after thought, he turned back to Griselda. "You too!"

Her uneasiness deepened at that, but it took all of her concentration to hold onto her blankets and the baby and try to keep step with him. When she stumbled and almost fell, he scooped both her and the baby up and carried them the remainder of the way. Expecting him to set her on her feet once they were inside, he surprised her by striding across the great room and up the stairs. When they reached his room at last, he set her on her feet, opened the door, and pushed her inside.

Elspeth moved to the center of the room and turned to face him warily. The baby continued to wail, how

103

ever, and finally she focused on quieting him. Moving closer to the hearth, she discarded the blankets she had wrapped around them and finally opened her shift and offered him her breast. He latched onto instantly, balling his hands into fists. Elspeth smiled down at him, stroking his soft cheek and finally began rocking him when she saw that he had calmed enough to go back to sleep.

"What happened to your son?"

Elspeth's throat closed. She looked up to discover that he had moved to the hearth. "He died."

His gaze flickered to the child at her breast. "Yvette said you strangled him at birth."

Elspeth felt a wave of horror wash over her. Her chin quivered despite all she could do. "He was too weak to survive … too small, but he did not die at birth. He struggled to cling to life for nigh a month. I did not kill my child. I did all that I could to save him."

"As you did Lady Rosabel?"

Elspeth stared at him steadily. "Yes."

"And yet, you despised them both."

Elspeth drew a ragged breath. "If you wish to interrogate me, at least let me put the baby down to sleep. Loud voices frighten him."

He was silent for several moments. "He is nigh four months old and I have yet to see him."

As badly as Elspeth hated disturbing the baby, she could certainly see his point. Blowing on her fingers to make sure they weren't still cold, she unwrapped the baby carefully for his inspection. Lord Arnaud knelt beside her, studying the sleeping child for several moments before his gaze moved to her breast. A blush started on the upper slopes of her breasts and traveled upward. Tugging her nipple from the infant's mouth, she pushed her breast back inside her gown and held it closed with her hand.

104

He frowned. After a moment he rose and strode from the room. When he returned, he was carrying the cradle that had been fashioned for the infant. After glancing around briefly, he set the cradle near the side of the bed nearest the hearth. Elspeth watched him doubtfully, but when he had settled the cradle, she got up from the stool and carefully laid the baby down, rocking it slowly until the baby ceased moving about restlessly.

When she turned, she saw that Lord Arnaud had settled on the stool beside the hearth. It dawned upon her then why he had summoned both her and Griselda. He'd become accustomed to having a hot bath awaiting him when he returned from his travels, tired and filthy from the road.

The tub was in its place and buckets lined up along the hearth, heating.

Griselda, who had come quietly into the room when Lord Arnaud had brought the cradle, was already moving toward him. Elspeth hesitated, but when he turned from his contemplation of the fire to look at her, she moved forward to help.

The ritual should have long since been something that she had become accustomed to, and yet she found that she had not. Each time that she helped him to removed his armor, and the clothing beneath, she marveled at the sight of his body, felt her heart thundering in her ears. Breathlessness seized her.

He had new wounds, mostly healed now. The sight of them made her heart seize in her chest as the realization sank into her that any one of them might have cost him his life. The thought chilled her.

Lifting her gaze, she saw he still wore the thong around his neck that held the small leather pouch. She studied it curiously, but when she reached for it, he removed it himself, dropping it to the hearth beside his stool.

"You have ... seen much fighting?" she asked hesitantly as she glanced up at him.

His expression hardened as his gaze moved over her face. "Some. Do you want to know how many Saxons I killed?"

Elspeth swallowed with an effort, realizing she did not care so long as none managed to slay him. The realization rocked her and she glanced at Griselda guiltily.

"Shall I get my herbs, my lord?"

"If they have not killed me in this time, they are not like to," he said tiredly, rising and removing his chausses. Stepping into the tub, he gripped the edges as he settled himself, as if his sore, tired muscles resisted the movement.

His hair had grown long, brushing his shoulders, far longer than the Normans were want to wear their hair, though by no means nearing the length that her kinsmen had worn their hair.

He had several day's growth of beard, as well. It was odd that she had grown so accustomed to a clean shaven face when it had seemed so naked to her at first, so—bleak when she was accustomed to bearded men.

When she had finished scrubbing his hair, she cupped his chin, tilting his head back and ran her other hand over his hair as Griselda lifted one of the buckets and poured it slowly over his head. Her gaze flickered to his face when she had rinsed the dark mass clear of suds and she saw that he was watching her.

Her heart seemed to trip over itself and race to catch its balance.

She jumped when she heard the clatter of the bucket as Griselda set it down once more.

Apparently, the noise carried to the infant, for he began to fuss. Elspeth turned immediately, but Lord Arnaud caught her arm.

"I will take the baby where it is quieter and bring him back when you have finished your bath," Griselda said hurriedly, rushing over to the cradle and scooping the baby into her arms.

"Bring him back when he needs to be fed," Lord Arnaud said as she reached the door, his gaze never moving from Elspeth's face.

Griselda hesitated, then nodded and left.

Elspeth swallowed with an effort, her heart thundering in her ears. When he released her, she moved behind him, staring at the soap and washcloth for many moments before she picked them up and began to scrub his shoulders and back. His muscles, she saw, were knotted with tension, but as she massaged the soapy cloth over him, they became more pliant, less painfully tight with tension.

When she had finished washing his back, she handed him the soap and wash cloth and moved to the hearth to add heated water to the tub as he finished bathing. He did not linger. Scrubbing the cloth over his chest and arms, he stood up, rubbing the cloth over his genitals. Mesmerized, Elspeth stared at his engorged cock for several moments before she remembered herself and bent to lift a bucket to rinse the soap. He took it from her, pouring it over his chest. She watched the gleaming cascade until he handed the bucket back to her and asked for the linen to dry himself.

Setting the bucket down as he climbed from the tub, she reached for the linen and moved around the tub, shaking it out and handing it to him, then turned to scoop the soap and wash cloth from the water while he dried off. Placing the soap on the hearth to dry, she wrung the cloth out and set it aside, then bent to collect the buckets.

"Leave them."

Nodding nervously, she set them down once more and turned to look at him. "If that's all, my lord ....?"

"Nay. It is not." He caught her braid as she turned to go, tugging her to a halt. Her eyes widened, as he pulled the leather thong from her hair and began to unravel the braid with his fingers. Her mouth had gone dry. She moistened her lips as he tugged her closer, releasing her hair and pulling the lacing from the front of her gown. "My lord?"

He lifted his gaze to hers as he pushed the gown from her shoulders and down her arms until it fell to her ankles. "I have honored my vows, in deed if not in mind," he said hoarsely as he caught her arms and pulled her against him, "though they chafed me mercilessly. In my mind and my heart I have forsaken my vows a thousand times. Before God, I could do nothing else, Elspeth." He caught her face between his palms, his eyes blazing with hunger as he stared down at her. "Waking or sleeping, I could see no face but yours, hear no voice, feel no flesh. I have tasted you on my tongue a thousand times, sank my flesh into your body. I am sick for want of you ... and I will wait no more if I am damned for it."

Elspeth stared up at him speechlessly, torn between fear and the need she had tried so hard to ignore—fearing the need that raced through her veins like poison, leaving her weak and trembling, without the will to protest or resist. "My lord, you can not do this," she whispered finally. "There will be more talk."

"Let them," he said harshly. He bent his head, brushing his lips so lightly across hers that the contact made her lips tingle with sensation as her flesh awoke to his touch. His breath rushed from his chest at the light contact of his flesh to hers, as if he had been holding it. Elspeth's head swam dizzily as she tasted him on her tongue, breathed his scent into her lungs. She went perfectly still, waiting breathlessly for his touch to come again. When it did, his lips melded with hers, clung briefly, parted reluctantly.

Without conscious thought, she swayed toward him, lifting up onto her toes as she sought the heat of his mouth. He sucked her upper lip between his own, as if plucking a sweet into his mouth, running his tongue along the sensitive surface, savoring the taste and texture before he released it and plucked at her lower lip.

A hot tide washed through her, leaving weakness in its wake and Elspeth lifted her hands to his chest. Faint tremors ran through his flesh, as if he were holding himself so tensely that his muscles quivered with the effort.

After a moment, he lifted his head and gazed down at her. Elspeth opened her eyes with an effort and looked back at him. He swallowed convulsively, glanced over her head toward the bed. Bending, he scooped her into his arms and strode across the room with her. Leaning down, he lay her atop the coverlet and covered her body with his own, covered her mouth with his mouth, swallowed her gasp of surprise as he thrust his tongue past the barrier of her lips and possessed her mouth with the ravenous need he no longer stemmed, or no longer had the strength to deny.

Even as his tongue possessed her mouth, he pushed her thighs apart, wedging his hips between hers. The head of his cock nudged the dampness of her cleft, skated along it as he curled his hips upward.

Elspeth gasped into his mouth, stiffened in sudden doubt. He lifted his head, staring down at her as moved his hips until his cock head found her opening and delved it. "Open your eyes, Elspeth. Look at me," he whispered harshly. When she opened her eyes slowly, he pressed against her once more, sank deeper inside her damp, clinging passage. She gasped in discomfort as he stretched her, as she felt her muscles resisting his intrusion. He withdrew slightly, pressed forward again, sinking a little deeper than before as her body lubricated the way for him. She swallowed, wanting to close her eyes, unable to break the hold his gaze held on her, feeling her heart thundering against her ear drums as she stared up at his taut face and felt his flesh slowly possessing hers. She gasped again, reaching up to close her fingers around his taut upper arms as he withdrew and then plunged deeper still. "My lord."

"Guillume," he said, his teeth clenched, sweat beading his brow, his body trembling with the effort to hold himself in check as he slowly claimed her, allowed her body to adjust to him.

"Guillume," she said, her voice threaded with need.

He groaned, thrusting sharply and sinking into her to the root of his cock. She gasped, more that half fearing pain when she felt her body stretching to accept him. Instead, a wave of pleasure moved along her senses. Her passage clenched around him, clutching his engorged flesh.

Shaking, he withdrew until only the head of his cock remained inside of her, levering his upper body upwards and bending to mold his mouth to hers. He kissed her deeply, hungry to taste and possess her all at once, thrusting his tongue in and out of her mouth as he had thrust his cock into her nether mouth. She moaned as heated pleasure jolted through her system in a dizzying wave, moving restlessly beneath him, sliding a caressing hand along he straining muscles of his back and finally digging her fingers into his buttock.

He tore his mouth from hers as she arched upward toward him, dropping his head forward on his shoulders, gasping harshly. Abruptly, he lowered himself, burying his head against the crook of her neck and shoulder as he slipped a hand beneath her hips and drove deeply, withdrew and swiftly drove into her again, his movements jerky and awkward with blinding need as he lost the battle to hold himself in check.

Elspeth's gasps of pleasure became sharper, skated the edge of hoarse cries as the pleasure burgeoned, built, grew stronger and stronger inside of her with each stroke of his cock along the trembling walls of her sex, until finally it reached the point where it could expand no more. It shattered then, blinding her with its glory. Light and blackness seemed to explode inside her mind. Liquid heat and intense rapture flooded her body. The walls of her sex convulsed around his shaft.

His cock jerked against the kneading walls of her sex, convulsed, spilling fiery warmth inside of her. He shuddered, groaned, and finally went limp atop her, gasping hoarsely as he fought to catch his breath.

When Elspeth stirred beneath him, he rolled off of her with obvious effort, dragged the coverlet down and then pulled her against him, covering them.

Chapter Ten

Elspeth was too stunned by what she had felt, and too drained of all energy even to think to protest when he dragged her beneath the covers with him and pulled her so that she lay draped half across him. Almost idly, he stroked her hair, smoothing it, working the braid free all the way to her scalp until her hair cascaded over her nakedness.

Lifting a lock from her shoulder, he held it to his face and breathed deeply. "I have imagined you clothed in nothing but this golden veil," he murmured, "since the day I saw you combing it."

He pushed her to her back and rolled over, holding himself away from her as he smoothed the hair over her breasts and flat belly. Carefully arranging the fall of hair so that only her distended nipple poked through, he leaned down and flicked the sensitive tip with his tongue, plucked at it with his lips.

Elspeth swallowed. "I should go."

He lifted his head. His expression grew taut. "You

will not."

Brushing her hair from her body, he leaned close, breathing deeply as he nuzzled the turn of her neck. "The only thing in this world more heady than your fragrance in my nostrils is the scent of me on you and the essence of our coupling."

Pushing her thighs apart with his knee, he moved over her, settling the weight of his lower body against the bed. He caught her hands in his then, lacing his fingers through hers and pressing her hands against the mattress on either side of her head. For several moments, he did nothing more than gaze down at her, his eyelids heavy with desire, his eyes gleaming with the heat of it. And yet the possessiveness of his gaze, the look upon his face was enough itself to resurrect the passion that had burned itself to embers only minutes before.

His gaze moved down her face to her lips, still swollen from his kisses, making her mouth go dry with the craving to feel his lips once more, to taste him on her tongue. It lingered until her lips slowly parted with the increasing labor of her breath, then wandered downward to her breasts that trembled and shuddered with each panting breath and the tips that had puckered and grown engorged with need. Slowly, he lowered his head, sucking one taut peak into his mouth as if it were a ripe berry, swirling his tongue around it, catching it between his tongue and the roof of his mouth and sucking it as if to savor the taste of her flesh. She gasped, digging her head into the mattress and arching upward as his mouth stimulated a surge of fiery ardor that stabbed through her to her groin, making her passage quake with need for his possession.

Her reaction to his caress spurred him to lavish his devotion upon her body, and he titillated her senses with his mouth and tongue, teasing first one nipple and then other, caressing the heaving flesh between with his lips, his tongue and the gentle adhesion of his mouth. Her breath caught in her throat on a gasp as he shifted downward, stroking her trembling belly with the damp heat of his tongue, sucking tiny bits of flesh in to his mouth.

He lifted his head at her gasp, surged slowly upward so that his engorged cock nudged her cleft, parting the flesh that sheltered her genitals, gathering moisture as it sought her passage and claimed it. Holding himself above her, he curled his hips slowly upward, impaling her body with exquisite, torturous, languor that tore his name from her throat on a needful groan. With the same tortuous leisure, he withdrew and then slowly pressed deeply inside of her again, and then again. With each unhurried stroke, he stoked the embers to heat, the heat to flame, and the flame to a raging inferno of need so that she was moving feverishly beneath him, panting for the release he would not give her, moaning his name like a mantra.

When she opened her eyes at last to look up at him, she saw his expression was as tortured as her own. He let out a harsh breath, lowering himself slowly until her breasts were pressed tightly against his chest. Opening his mouth over hers, he stroked her mouth with his tongue, inhaling her whimpers of need as he began to thrust into her with swifter, more powerful strokes that quickly brought her body to a crescendo so potent, and so prolonged her heart seemed almost to stop in her chest and the blackness of nothingness consumed her senses for many moments.

Slowly, awareness filtered into her mind once more. More slowly still, the tremors of absolute absence of strength subsided and the tiny jolts of pleasure mellowed into the warmth of sated flesh. She drifted on the sea of wondrous release for a time, enjoying the stroke of his palms over her body and finally knew nothing at all.

When the first thin wails of hunger penetrated her stupor, Elspeth sat up with a fearful start, looking around for the infant.

"Come!" Lord Arnaud growled, his voice husky from sleep.

The door opened and Griselda glanced around. Seeing Elspeth in the great bed, she moved quickly toward her, handed her the baby and left once more. Still too disoriented to think beyond the need to sleep, Elspeth cradled the baby in her arms and offered him her breast, drowsing as he suckled hungrily.

Lord Arnaud shifted, propping his head on his arm and leaning against her back as he watched the infant. Elspeth's eyes widened as she felt his cock grow hard against her ass, nudging the cleft. Reaching between them, he guided his erection between her legs, thrusting along her cleft lazily as he reached around her and stroked her breast. The infant's eyes opened. He frowned, his waving fist connecting with Lord Arnaud's hand.

A smile curled Elspeth's lips. "He doesn't like being interrupted."

"Neither do I," Lord Arnaud growled, smiling against her shoulder as he nipped the flesh there.

She glanced toward him sleepily. "Surely your hunger was appeased?"

His gaze moved to her face and he lifted his hand, stroking her cheek. "I fear there is no cure for this hunger, only temporary respite, for the more I feed, the more I want."

Pressing his lips briefly to her shoulder, he rolled away and climbed from the bed.

She watched him through half closed eyes as he

strode to the hearth, admiring the lean lines of his body, and the bunching and flexing of his muscles as he squatted on the hearth to stoke the fire, feeding the flames from the pile of wood beside the fireplace as the fire began to leap higher.

Checking the pails on the hearth, he moved one closer to the heat and rose, striding to the chest at the foot of the bed and opening it. She waited, curious. When he closed it at last, he'd donned chausses. In his hands were two shiny bright pieces of metal, one squared, the other more knife like. Setting the two objects on the mantel above the hearth, he knelt beside the bucket, splashed water over his face and then soaped it. When he straightened once more, he grasped the blade and, staring at his reflection in the shiny square of metal, began to scrape the blade across his face.

She watched in fascination as the dark stubble slowly vanished, revealing the pale skin beneath. When he'd finished, he wiped the blade and began sawing off the hair that brushed his shoulders a lock at the time, shortening it to the base of his skull and tossing the hair he'd cut toward the fire. The pungent smell of burning hair stung her nose.

She rolled over with the baby, giving him her other breast to suckle while she allowed her thoughts to drift with the uncertainties that assailed her as the dregs of sleep dissipated. If she were light of wit, or knew Lord Arnaud to be, she might be inclined to view what had passed between them as no more than it appeared to be—the slaking of his needs upon the handiest female.

She did not think she could trust the pretty words that he had given her. She had not forgotten that he had told her long ago that he would claim her save for the vows he had already spoken. She had seen hunger in his eyes since, but she was not fool enough to believe that was only for her, whatever he said now. He had slaked his lust upon his wife right well, and he had felt no tenderness for her, only the respect her position as his wife guaranteed her. Theirs had been an arranged marriage, and unlike the marriage that would have been arranged for her had her father lived, it had been strictly an exchange of power and property, a business arrangement. She had seen with her own eyes that neither of them had much liking for the other, let alone so much as a spark of love.

Regardless, he had taken his vows seriously, upheld them even when Lady Rosabel had not truly honored her own vows. Strictly speaking, those vows were terminated by death, but it was customary to honor a period of mourning, even when the surviving spouse felt none, even among Normans, and she knew Lord Arnaud well enough, she believed, to know that only something powerfully compelling would make him break with accepted custom.

If he had used discretion, perhaps she could have accepted that he had been without a woman so many months that his needs overrode his good sense, but she knew well enough that there would not be a soul within the boundaries of the keep who did not know he had taken her into his bed.

She had been accused of murdering his wife. The captain had dismissed the accusation once he had been assured her death was natural, but to chose the woman who'd been accused was bound to produce a rumor of conspiracy—that they had hatched the plot together.

He would realize that as surely as she did, so why? Why had he not simply chosen another woman for his needs?

Realizing the baby had drifted to sleep, she scooped him up and sat up, climbing from the bed to settle him in his cradle. He stirred when she lay him down and she stroked him soothingly, laying her cheek against the side of the cradle and studying his small face lovingly.

When she rose, she saw that Lord Arnaud, now fully dressed, had seated himself in his chair near the hearth, his long legs sprawled before him, his gaze upon her speculative. Shivering, she retrieved her clothing from the floor where he'd dropped it the night before and pulled it on.

"I was told another tale last eve when I came that ... disturbed me."

Elspeth looked up at him, feeling something unpleasant knot in her stomach.

He seemed to be waiting for her to comment. When she didn't, he continued. "The tale is that you switched the infants. That mine was slain and yours substituted as my heir."

Elspeth felt the color leave her face. It was not fear, however, so much as it was a wounding of her soul, that he could believe her capable of such a thing. "And you believe this?" she managed to ask, although her lips felt as numb and unresponsive as the remainder of her body.

His gaze slid to the fire. "It would be a clever revenge upon your enemies—to place your own son in a position to inherit what would have been his grandfather's had your enemies not come."

She looked down at her hands. "I am not capable of killing a child," she whispered.

"You are capable of killing your enemies."

Her head jerked up. For a moment, she thought he was accusing her of having killed Rosabel—perhaps he was, but she thought it more likely that he referred to her attempt to skewer Renard with his own blade. Or perhaps he was saying that she had attempted it twice and succeeded at least once? "Even if you could believe me capable of such a ... cold and calculating thing as you accuse me of, you must know it was not possible. Lars ... my son died more than a week before Lady Rosabel's time came upon her. And Griselda and I were brought here under guard. They stood outside throughout the birthing. How could I have brought mine to make the exchange? How could I have disposed of Lady Rosabel's child?"

He sat up. "By hiding your own beneath your shawl...and by allowing mine to die within his mother's womb and be buried with her."

Elspeth stared at him in horror, realizing that someone had thought of an answer to counter every truth she uttered and make it into a lie—Lord Arnaud? Or had Yvette and Pauline spent these many months figuring every angle and realized that she could not prove anything that she claimed? "The captain summoned two different mid-wives to look at her to assure himself that we had not caused her death."

"They looked to see signs of poisoning—or the use of a weapon. They were not asked if she had given birth. And they would not have been able to tell if you had simply done nothing at all for her and allowed her to die laboring for naught."

Elspeth rubbed her aching head. She had been accused of so many foul things, many of them conflicting, that she could not seem even to think how to defend herself.

"I love your son. You must see that I do."

"That is the part that disturbs me."

Elspeth blinked at him in confusion. "I do not understand."

"You claimed you hated Renard, and yet you also claim you loved his son. And if you did, then you must have hated Rosabel for her part in his death, but you claim to love the son of the woman who killed your child."

She glanced at the sleeping infant and then back at Lord Arnaud. "I still hate Renard. I will always hate Renard with every fiber of my being for what he did to me. But the baby was mine. I carried him inside of me. I nurtured him with my body. I felt him grow and when he was born, it was I who struggled to bring him into this world, suffered pain you can not even begin to imagine only to give him breath. I wanted to hate him because of Renard, but when I held him to my breast and saw that only my nearness gave him peace and comfort…." She pressed her hand over her mouth as a sob tore its way up her throat, fighting to regain her calm. "I could not help but love him. Even knowing he was too small and weak to live, I could not stop it."

He scrubbed his hand over his face and stood up abruptly. Turning away from her, he stared down at the fire. "Which only means that you might have loved him enough to allow my son to die so that you could secure the future of your own."

"My son died. It is true I blamed her for it and hated her for it, but I did not hate the baby for what she had done. When you have opened your heart to love, you can not close it again. I could not help loving him even if I had tried, and I did not try."

"Even though he was Rosabel's?"

"Because he is yours."

His head snapped around. He stared at her hard, his gaze penetrating. Abruptly, he pushed away from the fireplace and strode toward the door. When it had closed, the sobs she had been trying so hard to hold inside escaped her. She needed to release the pain. She felt that she couldn't hold it inside, but the infant woke almost at once, his lip primping at the sounds of her sorrow. Taking him from the cradle, she sat on the edge of the bed to rock him, trying to calm herself so that she could calm him.

She'd just managed to regain control when the door opened once more. Glancing toward it, she saw that Griselda had come in and she began to cry all over again. The baby burst into tears the moment she did.

Griselda frowned. "What ails you, child? You are distressing the baby!"

Elspeth sniffed, mopped the tears from her cheeks with her hand and lifted the baby to her shoulder. "I am accused of the most foul things imaginable … and … and he believes them!"

Griselda sat beside her and patted her back consolingly. "That is why there is a guard at the door, I suppose."

Elspeth stared at her wide eyed and burst into tears again. Griselda took the baby from her and began walking him. "I can not calm the baby if you persist in squalling like an infant yourself," she said testily after several moments. "You have not wept and carried on like this since we learned of your father's and brothers' deaths! That, at least was understandable."

Elspeth calmed herself with an effort and finally got up and tore a piece from the bath linen to use as a handkerchief. "I do not understand these Normans," she said finally, sniffing.

Griselda gave her a hard look. "You mean you do not understand Lord Arnaud."

Elspeth swallowed convulsively, fighting the urge to burst into fresh tears. "No. I do not understand him at all. How can … how could a man feel lust for a woman when they believe that they have done something truly horrible?"

Griselda frowned, obviously having difficulty following her. "I think you just have no understanding of men at all, child. From what I have seen myself, as

121

often as not, they simply lust and must take their ease. It has nothing to do with any woman in particular. They could ease themselves upon a goat. What does he believe you have done?"

"I am not entirely sure," Elspeth said, sniffing again. "I do not think that he is. Yvette and Pauline have designed so many lies—but I am evil whatever tale they invent. I have strangled my child at birth—or killed Lord Arnaud's child and put mine in his place. I have poisoned Lady Rosabel or simply stood by and watched her die in agony without lifting a finger to help. I am cold and calculating and a murderess besides."

Griselda snorted. "The evil twins. I can not conceive how they could fool anyone at all. They are a plague to peace … and of the same fabric as their mistress. That one was most certainly cold and calculating—truth to tell, the Normans are a cold lot."

Elspeth bit her lip. "They say the same of us."

She snorted. "They have the cold, emotionless eyes of serpents."

"And they say ours are like ice."

Griselda studied her a moment. "If he will only open his eyes, he will see that there is no darkness in you. In time, perhaps he will."

Elspeth sighed wearily. "I can not believe that time will make a difference. Of a certainty, so long as Yvette and Pauline are here, something will be stirring. Disharmony is the air that they breathe."

Chapter Eleven

Elspeth was surprised when she was told that she was expected to take her meals in the great hall. She had thought that she would not be allowed to leave the room, just as she and Griselda had been confined before when Yvette and Pauline had accused them. She would almost have preferred to remain in her room, however, than to be escorted under guard. She did not particularly care what the Normans thought of her, but it shamed her to be treated as a common criminal in front of people who had known her her whole life.

She supposed it was no more shameful than being treated as a whore, but it was certainly on a par with it when she had been looked upon before as someone of worth.

She was escorted to the head table, which confused her almost as much as everything else that had happened. It was a place of honor. It was the place that Lady Rosabel should have occupied except that she never had.

It confused everyone else as much as it did her.

The man who served her called her Lady Elspeth. She glanced up at him in surprise since no one had spoken of her position since the Normans had first come. She saw, however, that, despite his subservient manner he had not 'slipped'. He had used it very deliberately. To show his loyalty to her and her family?

When she looked around, she saw that he had spoken loud enough that it had drawn the attention of everyone at the table. Ignoring them, she did her best to focus on her meal, trying to get the food into her mouth without dropping it on the infant in her lap. She had fashioned a sling to carry him around, but the unaccustomed noise of the great hall had woken him. To her surprise and relief, he had not immediately begun to wail. Instead, he opened his eyes wide and stared at everything that passed within his vision. He was a strong child, but young still, and although he could hold his head up well, when he tired, he had the tendency to simply drop it forward on his chest. She had to watch him to keep him from slamming his head against the table.

When Lord Arnaud reached down to take him from her lap, she almost choked on her food. It took every ounce of restraint to keep from leaping to her feet and snatching him back, but she saw after a few nervous moments that Lord Arnaud seemed to be handling him well enough and returned at least half her attention to her food.

He was dully—dutifully—admired by everyone at the table, who made all the appropriate compliments as Lord Arnaud held him up for inspection. When he'd finished showing the baby around, he cleared the space in front of him and sat the child on the table. He frowned thoughtfully at the child for several moments, while the baby stared back at him as if mesmerized, his eyes wide, his mouth gaping. Finally, holding the baby with one hand, he lifted the other and rubbed at a dark spot beside the baby's mouth.

"It will not come off. It is a mark that he was born with," she said quietly.

Lord Arnaud glanced at her and then picked the baby up and studied him more closely. The baby lifted his arms and reached for his face, pulling at his nose. Lord Arnaud's lips curled in a smile. "I will call him Etienne—for my grandfather."

When she'd finished her meal, she rose. Lord Arnaud studied her for a moment and finally gave her the baby. Relief surged through her. Cradling him to her chest, she made her way back upstairs to the master's chamber. She found Griselda there, busily tidying up. The tub had been emptied and removed and the floor cleaned.

"We are to stay here, then?"

Griselda turned to look at her in surprise. "I know no more than you. Not as much, I suppose. Did Lord Arnaud say nothing?"

Elspeth bit her lip and shook her head. "Beyond accusing me, no."

"What of the guard?"

Elspeth frowned. "Except for telling me that I was to go down to the great hall, he only follows me about like a shadow. He has not said that I can not go where ever I please." She thought it over. "But then, I have only been downstairs to the hall and back again. Perhaps we are allowed to move about the manor?"

Griselda shrugged and went back to her task. After a few moments, Elspeth settled the baby in his cradle and looked around for something to entertain him. The reflecting shield was shiny, but she was not at all certain that Lord Arnaud would appreciate her touching it and, in any case, it had sharp corners if the baby should happen to get hold of it. Finally, she merely propped him up so that he could watch her and Griselda and helped Griselda finish setting the room to rights. It did not take long with the two of them working together.

When they'd finished, Elspeth fed the baby and put him down in his cradle to nap and she and Griselda went to sit on the pallets they had arranged in the far corner of Lord Arnaud's chamber.

Neither of them were inclined to talk. Elspeth thought that Griselda was very likely as worried as she was about what would come of the latest accusation, but she tried her best not to think about it, particularly since there was nothing that she could do. She had to suppose that Yvette and Pauline—she knew it had to have been them who had accused her—had considered the possibility more carefully after the last time. They had made certain that this time Elspeth had no defense but her word—which did not account for much since she was Saxon.

After a little bit, Griselda sighed impatiently. "I had never thought that I would complain that I had nothing to do, but time on your hands allows far too much time to think. I think that I will see if I can fetch Lady Rosabel's basket of needlework. I have not done any needlework in nigh a year—not since—"

"You should not do that. It belongs to Lady Rosabel."

Griselda gave her a look. "She is not likely to come back and finish the work herself. In any case, no one asked us before they took all that was ours. I can not see harm in working on these pieces, but if you would rather, I will find something that needs mending."

Elspeth felt more comfortable about the mending. There was plenty in the household in need of it. Plenty more that was beyond mending. They started by sort ing the linens, separating everything out that was no longer good for anything but cleaning rags and stacking the linens they might rescue in another pile.

Mid-afternoon, a servant from below stairs was shown into the room and asked Elspeth if she would tell them what they should prepare for the evening meal. The Normans had begun to complain about the monotony of the meals the cook came up with. Elspeth was not at all certain that Lord Arnaud would appreciate her interference in the running of his household, but she set her mending aside and went down to see what she could do to help.

She ended up spending much of the remainder of the afternoon overseeing the preparations. By the time Griselda arrived with Etienne demanding his dinner at the top of his lungs, she thought she had things fairly well organized, however, and went upstairs with him to feed him and settle him for the night.

She'd scarcely settled him when the guard informed her that she was expected to join the company downstairs. She looked down at herself in dismay, for she had been working in the gown she had on all day and had collected much of her work on herself. It would not have been so bad if she were not expected to sit at the high table. She would have looked no worse than any of the other servants, but she would still have hated to sit down to dinner in her filth.

Unfortunately, the only other gown she possessed was the one that Renard had torn from her and it looked worse, if possible, than the one she was wearing. Shrugging, she finally decided that it was at least clean and asked the guard if he would wait and let her tidy herself. He did not look inclined to do so, but finally he went out again and Elspeth quickly bathed off and changed, tidying her hair as best she could.

Lord Arnaud looked at her disapprovingly for arriving late, but said nothing as she took her seat and a servant came to set a trencher in front of her. Elspeth looked down at the food with approval, saw that it looked far more appetizing than the noon meal, and turned to smile at the servant.

"The food is better," Lord Arnaud commented.

Elspeth glanced at him. It wasn't exactly high praise, but at least he seemed to have noticed. "Our ... the old cook was ... died. His apprentice is not as good, but then he is not accustomed to cooking for so many. I am sure he will do better."

Lord Arnaud merely looked at her. She wasn't certain if it was because she had stumbled over the explanation about the loss of the old cook, and he thought she was pointing out that it was the Normans' fault if there was a problem—which it was—Or if he meant to emphasize that the new cook had had more than ample time to grow accustomed to cooking for so many. His next comment seemed to support the last.

"Lord Odolf's household was not this large?"

She flushed. He must know very well that it could not have been, for the place was bursting at the seams with the overflow and scarcely half of the people who had once occupied Rasgarth had survived the invasion. "No."

He gave her a look, as if waiting for her to continue. She was reluctant, but then she could see no real reason not to tell him whatever he wished to know. It could certainly make no difference to them now. "Besides my father and brothers, perhaps twice the serfs you see now—perhaps half or three quarters the number of men you have."

"You had no sisters?"

"Thankfully, no."

His brows rose at that.

"I was the last born. I would not have wanted for my sister …."

He was silent for some time. "Your mother?"

"I did not know her. She died when I was born. Griselda raised me."

"Your father did not wed again? He must have still been a young man."

Elspeth studied the food on her trencher, toying with it idly. "My father loved my mother with all his heart. He had nothing left when she died … could not bear the thought of seeing another woman in her place. He had his laymen. He seemed content enough with that.

"Truthfully, I am surprised that he did not hate me for the loss of my mother—perhaps he did at first, but he seemed to look upon me as his consolation for losing her. He always said that I was just like my mother."

He frowned. "Is that why he did not settle you in marriage? Because he could not bear to part with you?"

It seemed a judgment of her father and she frowned. "Perhaps, but I do not believe he would have stood in my way if I had been willing to accept any of the suitors who came."

"He allowed you to chose?" He sounded both surprised and disapproving, which irritated her, particularly since she could not see that his own arranged marriage had brought him either contentment or happiness. Wealth and power possibly, although she did not know the particulars of the arrangement—but of what good were either if one could not find contentment at least? Her father had always said that, no matter what people said their goal in life was, the end goal was to find happiness if possible, and contentment if that could not be had. It did not matter what it was that they thought would bring them happiness—for everyone the object differed—in the end it still boiled down to the search for happiness. She had always considered that that was why he had sought nothing more. Her mother had given him happiness, and he knew he could not find that again. When she died, he had settled for the contentment of rearing his children and making certain that all who depended upon him were comfortable.

She sent him a look. "From among those he considered suitable, yes. He was not an ambitious man. He was content with what he had and felt no need to profit from my marriage—beyond my happiness."

His eyes narrowed. He knew very well that she had intended to insult him in return. She didn't care. He had no right to sit in judgment on her father. He might have been rough, and loud, and unrefined to the Norman way of thinking, but he had been a good hearted man, loving, generous and just … and honorable. If he had ignored the summons to war, he might well have lived to see his grandchildren.

She felt like weeping at the thought that conjured of her own son, but resolutely pushed it far back in her mind.

The truth was, he had died defending their homeland. If he had not gone, the only difference would have been that he would have died defending his home, for the Normans would have come regardless.

"May I leave, my lord?"

He nodded without glancing at her and she rose and quit the great room. The baby had not stirred, she saw when she sent Griselda to find her own meal and checked on him, and she sat for a time mending until her eyes grew too tired in the dim light. Finally, she set the work aside and curled up on her pallet.

Sleep was slow to come.

She was tired, but tense also, wondering what was to become of them. She was surprised, after his accusations, that Lord Arnaud had not removed Etienne from her care. Perhaps because he truly believed the baby was hers? But if that was true, why had he not sent both of them away? Or had her placed in a cell until he could decide her fate?

She was still awake when Lord Arnaud came up to retire. He stood over her for a time, studying her and she fought to regulate her breathing, feigning sleep. Finally, he moved away and she heard him undressing for bed.

She relaxed. She had just begun to drift into the edges of sleep, when she realized that he had moved toward her once more instead of dousing the lights and climbing into bed.

"Get up."

She opened her eyes to look up at him, but she did not argue. She could tell nothing from his tone of voice, except that he did not sound at all pleased. When she had stood up, he reached for the ties of her gown and removed it and she thought her heart would beat its way from her chest—partly from dread—partly, she was ashamed to admit even to herself, from anticipation.

"Get in bed—my bed."

Nodding jerkily, Elspeth climbed into his bed and lay down, watching him nervously as he banked the fire and doused the candle that he had brought with him to light his way.

She stiffened as he settled beside her in the bed and dragged her toward him, but he only settled her back against his belly, dropped an arm around her waist and composed himself for sleep. Disconcerted, she lay stiffly for a while, listening to his breathing and finally drifted off herself, still wondering why he would insist that she lay with him if he was not of a mind to use her body.

When a week passed in much the same way, she ceased to be relieved that he made no attempt to couple with her, becoming more deeply confused instead.

After the things he had accused her of, she had not felt that she would be able to enjoy his attentions, or even to pretend that she did. When he made no attempt to couple with her, she decided he must feel the same, and she had been relieved.

It made no sense that she could see, however, that he insisted upon sleeping with her in his bed. He scarcely needed to do so to keep watch upon her. He generally sent the guard away at night, but he could as easily have ordered him to stay.

There were other changes that confused her even more. Little by little, she found herself managing the household as she had done before. At first, it was only a question by a servant here and there, but when she took care of the situation and Lord Arnaud did not seem to object, the servants fell into their old habits and looked to her to for guidance and instructions.

Yvette and Pauline were packed up and sent back to Normandy.

She could not say that she was sorry to see them go. She was vastly relieved, for they had created unrest within the household from the moment they had arrived. She was not completely easy in her mind, however. As impossible as it seemed that they could continue to create problems from across the sea, she could not completely convince herself that they could not—particularly when the accusations they had launched against her had never actually been addressed.

Lord Arnaud began to examine the manor from top to bottom, studying it. It was winter and there was little that could be done outside. He took men and hunted regularly for fresh game, but aside from that everyone was pretty much confined within the manor and, naturally enough, tempers shortened.

He set men to work cleaning up the space beneath the rafters and laying down more solid flooring. When they had finished, the servants were told that they would thereafter be sleeping in the attic space.

After studying the second floor for some time, he set the men to work creating a series of rooms linking with his own. A door was knocked from the wall between the master chamber and the next and that room transformed into a sitting room. That room was connected by way of another door to a second bed chamber.

The dust and sawing and hammering went on from daylight to dark for nearly two weeks, making life difficult for her since Etienne did not rest well with all the noise. Eventually, however, the hammering stopped and she was informed that the sitting room was hers. The bed chamber opposite the master chamber was now the nursery, and that would be occupied by Griselda and the baby.

She was expected to share his room and his bed.

She did not argue. She had never seen the sense of arguing only for the sake of doing so when she knew very well that it would change nothing. She was in no position to argue in any case.

If she had been Lord Arnaud's wife, she might have thought the effort would be worth the risk of angering him. If she had even been his layman, she might have thought her wishes would hold some sway.

He had not touched her since he had accused her and she had withdrawn from him, however. She wasn't altogether certain why he had not. It would not have occurred to her to refuse him, however hurt and angry she was. If he wanted to take her, he did not need her approval or her cooperation. He could simply beat her into submission and take what he wanted as Renard had.

When he did neither, she began to feel ill used. She could tell herself that she was glad, and that she did not want him to couple with her until she ran out of breath and she still would not be able to convince herself when she lay awake half the night listening to his breathing—feeling it against her neck—and trying to ignore the stirrings of arousal that went through her every time he tucked her against him—and then promptly fell asleep.

When the hurt and anger had finally dulled, she had been content for a little while to wait until he initiated sex with her to spurn him so that he would know she had not forgiven him. When he did not give her the opportunity to, she was angry all over again. That, too, had passed, however, when the cravings of her own body had begun to campaign against her. She began then to consider if there was some way that she might entice him and still save face.

Nothing came to mind. She ceased to leave her hair braided at night, because he had said he liked to see it loose about her shoulders. She had tried undressing for him, but instead of watching her, he always seemed preoccupied with his own thoughts, staring into the fire as if he would find wisdom there. When she helped him to bathe, she made it a point to 'accidentally' stroke him with her hands instead of just the wash cloth, but she could not see that that had any more effect upon him.

Finally, after nigh two weeks of uncertainty, she found that she simply could not endure it any longer. When he had tucked her against his belly and settled to sleep, she lay stiffly for a time, battling her pride and then throwing it to the wind. "If you do not want me, I do not know why you will not send me away," she murmured.

He stiffened. After a moment, he rose slightly, caught her shoulder and turned her onto her back so that he could look down at her face.

Chapter Twelve

Elspeth met his penetrating gaze with a mixture of hope and doubt. Sighing gustily, as if he had been holding his breath, he lowered his head and opened his mouth over hers, forcing her lips to part with the pressure of his mouth and the insistence of his tongue, and then plundering the sensitive inner surfaces with fervent, rapacious heat. His ardor scorched her. Liquid fire engulfed her. Pleasure shivered along every nerve ending like the vibrations along the strings of a lute. She lifted her hands, skated them along his chest and then locked them around his shoulders, threading her fingers through his hair and cupping his base of his skull as she kissed him back with her own voracious need.

A grunt that was part surprise, part appreciation erupted from his chest and his longing escalated from hunger to frantic need. His lack of restraint unleashed a tidal wave of urgency inside of her. Running a hand along her body to her hips, he skated it over her thigh, settled in against her belly, parting the lips of her nether mouth with his fingers and delving the damp cleft. She gasped as his fingers rubbed along her clit, arching up to meet his touch, rubbing herself against him.

A quaking moved through him at her reaction. When he felt how wet she was for him he lost the little restraint that he had placed upon himself. Thrusting her thighs apart with a shaking hand, he shifted to cover her with his body, probing her cleft with the head of his cock, curling his hips and pressing against her.

She tore her lips from his to cry out as the head of his cock bumped along her cleft and found purchase, sinking into her wet passage. Gritting his teeth, he scooped an arm beneath her shoulders, and one beneath her hips, pumping his hips in short, hard thrusts until he had claimed her fully. With scarcely a pause to catch his breath, he withdrew and thrust again and again, almost savagely, groaning as if he was in agony, setting a cadence that tore little cries of ecstasy from Elspeth as her body abruptly convulsed around his cock and seemed to explode with pleasure.

He jerked, tensed all over and ground his pubic bone against hers as his own body convulsed, ejecting his hot seed deeply inside of her.

When his body had ceased to spasm with release, he simply lay limply on top of her, as if he could not even summon the strength to hold his weight from her, let alone roll off. Elspeth found it welcome, despite the discomfort. It offered her the illusion, at least, of belonging, of being more than merely a vessel for his lust.

When he had caught his breath, he pushed himself off of her with an effort and dragged her across him, stroking her hair along her back.

As completely sated as she was, she was a little miffed, as well, realizing the moment that her brain had begun to function once more that he had out waited her, forcing her into the position of supplicant. "It was not very chivalrous of you to make me ask," she muttered.

His hand stilled. "If I had asked would you have said yes?"

"I would have said nay, and then I would have felt better."

"I feared as much," he said after a moment. There was a hint of suppressed laughter in his voice.

She lifted her head to look at him and saw that his eyes were gleaming with amusement. She narrowed her eyes at him, but she could not resist the teasing gleam in his eyes. Lifting her hand, she stroked his cheek. "You must know very well that I would never tell you nay."

He swallowed with an effort, the amusement fading from his eyes as a gleam of another kind lit them. His lips twisted wryly. Rising, he pushed her back onto the pillows and lowered his lips to her throat. "I dared not chance it. I could not have borne it," he murmured, walking kisses across her throat and along the side of her neck to her ear. "My manhood would have shriveled."

Elspeth uttered a choked laugh, pressing her palms against his chest to push him away. After a moment, he lifted slightly to look down at her. Uttering a sigh of pained acceptance, he rolled away, staring up at the ceiling. Elspeth followed him, catching his face between her palms and brushing her lips lightly across his. His lips parted, a deep sigh of satisfaction hissing from his lips. She plucked at them with her own lips as they parted, sucked gently on his lower lip and finally stroked her tongue across the smooth surface, feeling heat rise inside of her as she delved her tongue between his parted lips and tasted him, explored the heat of his mouth and the texture of his tongue with hers.

He held himself perfectly still, as if savoring her caresses, or perhaps curious as to how far she was willing to go. A heady excitement burgeoned inside of her, the thought making her feel reckless with abandon. Shifting closer, she moved her lips down his throat to his chest, sculpting her palms over the hard musculature of his male breasts; enjoying the texture of his skin and the roughness of the dark hair that covered his chest; the heat that wafted his scent to her; the racing of his heart; the little catch in his breath each time her lips found another sweet patch of flesh to taste.

He jerked all over when her hand caressed his cock and then her fingers closed around it tightly. Lifting her head, she watched his face as she stroked him, saw moisture bead on his brows as he strained to hold himself still. He dug his head into the pillow beneath his head, his face contorted as if he was in agony, his breath ragged.

She moved over him. Placing a knee on either side of his hips, she pushed the head of his cock into her cleft and slowly traced it from her clit to the mouth of her passage. He surged upwards on a harsh breath, catching her hips in his hands, his fingers clenching, digging into her as she lowered herself slightly, pushing his distended flesh inside of her. He settled again, his head tipped up as he watched her slowly working his cock into her passage.

She closed her eyes when she had impaled herself fully, pausing to savor the feel of him stretching her, filling her. When she opened her eyes again, she saw that his gaze was on her face. Slowly she lifted up onto her knees again, and then pressed downward. He watched the melding of their bodies, his eyes glazed, fevered.

Finally, when she could not bear the delight of slow torture any longer, she leaned forward, bracing her palms on either side of his head as she sought a tempo of movement that began building the delightful tremors to harder, more forceful shocks of bliss. He slid his hands upward to her waist, rocking his hips and thrusting upward to match each downward stroke of her passage over his flesh. Lifting his head, he captured the peak of one swaying breast, suckling her in a way that sent darts of pleasure into her belly to join the delight the stroke of his cock created. She cried out, feeling her body leap toward the precipice she sought. When he released the nipple he held and sucked the other into his mouth, it forced her over the edge.

Wrapping his arms tightly around her, he sat up, tipped her onto her back and thrust into her until his own culmination erupted through him, tearing an agonized groan from his throat. He went still as it died away, shuddering from the force of his release, his face buried against her throat as he gasped hoarsely, trying to catch his breath and calm the pounding of his heart.

When he had recovered somewhat, he lifted his head and stroked her hair from her cheeks, kissing her with such tenderness Elspeth's heart tightened painfully. She opened her eyes to look up at him as he pulled away, surprising a look on his face that she found difficult to fathom.

It disappeared in the next moment as he sat up, pulling her with him and then shifting until they were comfortably situated beneath the covers. She fell asleep, still curled across his chest, the comforting sound of his heart in he ear.

He had dressed and gone by the time Griselda woke her to feed the baby, and she was vaguely disappointed, but she felt too gloriously alive to allow it to mar her happiness for long.

She found herself singing as she moved about the manor performing her tasks, smiling at nothing in particular. It was too much to hope it would go unnoticed, but she found tentative smiles met hers, and everyone seemed to go a little more briskly about their work, their steps lighter.

It was nearing dusk when Lord Arnaud returned with the hunting party he had taken out. He was cold, fatigued, and irritated that they had only succeeded in bringing down a couple of bucks. She refused to allow his mood to darken hers, however, drawing him to the room where she had a hot bath and mulled wine waiting for him.

He seemed wary, almost distrustful of her light mood, but his own humor brightened considerably as she bathed the cold and fatigue from him. The almost festive mood in the great hall when they went down for the evening meal seemed to perplex him, but by the time he'd eaten he seemed to have accepted that the change was something to be welcomed.

Despite the stores he had brought with him, it was late winter and supplies had begun to run low, and as they did, everyone's spirits had sunk in direct proportion to the diminishing stores. Both Saxon and Norman temperaments had grown short. Whatever had lifted their spirits, however short lived it might be, it was sorely needed.

He did not linger in the hall long when they had finished eating, instead following Elspeth upstairs within only a few minutes. He found her waiting in his bed, wearing nothing but her golden hair, a faint smile of welcome on her lips.

It was all the encouragement he needed to join her and make love to her until they both fell into sated slumber.

The dwindling supplies made it imperative to hunt daily, but Guillume found the lure of spending at least part of his days with Elspeth and Etienne in the sitting room irresistible. If they managed to bring down enough meat to last for several days, he would spend at least one sprawled in his chair before the hearth, watching Etienne's efforts to hold himself upright, or inch along the floor, with amusement.

Occasionally, he would take his lute from the wall and play for Elspeth. She never asked. She didn't want to make him feel as if he was welcome only if he came to entertain her, but she loved to listen to him.

Mostly, he would merely watch her, sometimes with amusement when she was trying to put Etienne through his paces to show him what he'd learned, sometimes with the gleam of desire in his eyes, but more often with an expression of doubt, or wariness, or even anxiety.

Elspeth wasn't certain what brought on that expression, but she was afraid it was because he had never completely reconciled in his mind the accusations Pauline and Yvette had made.

She hoped that Griselda was right and that, in time, he would come to realize that she could never have done what she was accused of.

It was the only dark cloud on her horizon—the ever present fear that his desire for her would burn itself out and he would turn away from her because he had never learned to trust her enough to truly care for her.

When she returned to the chamber they shared one day to discover that her trunk had joined his at the foot of the massive bed, and that most all of the things that had once been hers before the Normans came had been restored to her, she had been speechless with joy. She had believed then that he must care for her if he could realize how important it was to her to have her own belongings—the gowns that her father had had made for her, the combs that had been her mother's, and the fine lawn sleeping gowns that had been made for her—not that he allowed her to wear them, for he far preferred that she sleep naked beside him.

Even the weather seemed to favor her, for the snow ceased to fall and the earth began to thaw with an early spring, bringing relief to everyone that the ground would soon be thawed enough to begin to till the soil. Her people, still strongly tied to the old superstitions, saw it as a good omen, a sign that they were favored because the Norman lord had restored their mistress to her rightful place.

Her happiness lasted until the arrival of a messenger from Normandy.

Pauline and Yvette had fled directly back to the home of their former mistress and had convinced Rosabel's father that she had met with foul play. He had used it as an excuse to gather an army and had lain siege to Guillume's holdings in Normandy.

Leaving orders for his army to begin making immediate preparations to move, he left to request permission from King William to take his army to Normandy and to make arrangements for the crossing.

Guillume was so enraged, his temper so volatile from the moment he learned of it, that it brought all of Elspeth's fears to the forefront.

She could not help but think his withdrawal meant that he blamed her as the root of all of his troubles.

Chapter Thirteen

When the news came that riders approached, Elspeth was in her sitting room. Lord Arnaud had left to speak with King William more than a fortnight before and she moved anxiously to a window and pulled the covering back to peer out into the approaching evening. She saw them as they crested the rise, moving quickly. Her heart skipped a beat when she recognized Guillume's standard.

She turned to look at Griselda. "It is Lord Arnaud!"

"Go. I will tend the babe."

Checking her gown and her hair quickly, she flew from the room and down the stairs, catching a serf as she reached the great room and ordering a bath prepared for him and then dashing to the kitchen to make certain food was made ready for him and the men who had traveled with him.

She was breathless by the time she reached the stoop at the front of the manor. Lord Arnaud and his men were just coming through the gate and it took an effort

144

of will to stop herself from rushing across the keep to greet him. As if he sensed her presence, he glanced toward the manor at that moment and some of the weariness seemed to leave his face.

She knew it was indecorous, and that he might not welcome such a display from his layman, but the moment he dismounted and handed his horse over to a stable hand, she rushed from the stoop to meet him. He staggered back a step as he caught her full against his chest, his arms going around her instinctively. Briefly, his arms tightened and then he set her away from him.

His expression was grim when she looked up at him, but she did not sense that he was displeased with her.

"You are leaving?"

He laced her arm through his and turned toward the manor. "At dawn."

Elspeth swallowed against the knot of fear and misery in her throat. "I know you are weary unto death from your travel. I have told them to ready a bath for you, but you must eat first. And then it will be ready and you can take your ease and rest."

When she had made all ready, she sent Griselda away so that she could have Guillume all to herself. He lifted his brows when he came in and saw that only Elspeth would attend him, but said nothing, moving wearily to the stool and removing his footwear.

He sighed in relief when he had settled into the tub of heated water and Elspeth massaged his head and back, removing the tension and fatigue as she removed the dirt from the road.

When she had handed him the soap and cloth to finish his bath, she moved to the side of the tub so that he could watch as she removed her own clothing. He went still, the bath forgotten, his eyes glazing over with desire.

She had intended only to await him in the bed, but he grasped her before she could move away, pulling her into the tub with him. She gasped as the water washed over her and then chuckled huskily at his impatience.

Squeezing the water from her braid, she coiled it atop her head, using the ends of the leather thong that bound it to tie it in place.

Lord Arnaud watched her with interest, but when she reached for the cloth to help him finish his bath, he held it away. Dropping the soap, he ran the lathered cloth over her breasts, massaging them. Elspeth closed her eyes, feeling the drugging warmth passion flooding through her as his hands kneaded her breasts and then moved over her body, exploring every inch of her flesh slowly, as if he were determined to savor every moment.

When he had left no part of her in wanting for his touch, arousing heated currents with each caress of his hand, he dragged her toward him, nibbling almost teasingly at her lips before he opened his mouth over hers and slipped his tongue along the exquisitely sensitive inner surfaces of her mouth. Surprise jolted through her and a tide of liquid heat fast behind that as she tasted him, felt the faintly rough texture of his tongue along her own.

When he withdrew, disappointment filled her. She studied him chidingly through half closed eyes, but finally took the cloth from him and began to bathe him as he had bathed her, swiping the sudsy cloth over the hard muscles of his chest and working downward until she felt the brush of his cock along her arm. Holding his gaze, and wrapped her hand around it. He flinched, gritted his teeth on a hiss of a breath. She tightened her fingers and slowly moved her hand downward along his shaft. His eyelids slid closed as she continued

146

massaging the throbbing, distended flesh.

After a moment, he caught her wrist, studying her for several pounding heartbeats. Abruptly, he surged upward, taking her with him, and stepped from the tub. The chill air of the room instantly wrapped cool fingers around them. Elspeth shivered, reaching for the drying cloths as Lord Arnaud grabbed them up and wrapped it around them, cocoon like, pulling her tightly against him and leaning down to kiss her as he rubbed the moisture from her back.

She uttered a faint protest as he dropped the linen and caught her up in his arms, carrying her to the bed, but the heat of his body and the desire he created within her quickly chased the chill from her damp skin. With his mouth and tongue, he bathed her in heat, teasing the sensitive tips of her breasts until she was writhing in fevered need beneath him, then moving downward over her belly, drawing sharp gasps. She lifted her head to look at him when he pushed her thighs apart and stared down at her genitals, his gaze intense as he reached down to brush the golden thatch of hair aside and parted the petals of flesh.

She inhaled sharply at his touch, closing her eyes, jerked as she felt his mouth nibbling a trail of heat along her inner thigh. She was gasping for air by the time he'd woven a similar trail along her other thigh, clutching at him, urging him to enter her.

Instead, he lowered his head to the nest of curls, stroking her cleft with his tongue. Her hips came up off the bed at the excruciating sensation. She grasped his hair frantically, certain she could not endure much of that particular torment. Ignoring her, he opened his mouth over her mound and explored her cleft with his tongue in a leisurely way that had her near to weeping with unbearable pleasure.

147

She fought to escape that torturous heat, but he grasped her wrists, pinning her to the bed, and continued to stroke her with his tongue, massaging her clit, and sucking it into his mouth to taunt her until release burst upon her shatteringly. She screamed at the force of it, bucking against him mindlessly as he held her down and continued to tease her, drawing her culmination out until blackness began to envelope her and she went limp beneath him.

She was only vaguely aware of him as he moved up beside her, studying her as she struggled with her frantically pounding heart. She'd scarcely caught her breath when he began to move over her languidly, kissing and stroking her until the explosive release she'd only just experienced gathered in upon itself once more, binding her in a blinding haze of desire once more. "Guillume," she whispered hoarsely. "Do not torture me so. I do not think I can bear it."

She found she could, for he would not give her peace, carrying her to the point where she thought she would shatter with release and then withholding it, over and over until she thought she would loose her mind.

She was sobbing for surcease before he moved between her thighs and thrust into her. Her body, so long denied of the need for release, clenched around his cock convulsively, impeding his possession. She grasped his buttocks, arching her hips to meet his frustrating sorties of conquest, too desperate to feel him deeply inside of her for patience.

He gritted his teeth, resisting the urge to yield to her demand as he allowed her body to accept him, pushing, withdrawing slightly and pressing forward again until the natural lubricants of their bodies allowed full possession, grinding his pubic bone against hers when at last he'd sunk into her to the root of his cock. He

148

held himself still for several moments when he'd claimed her completely, striving to hold to his control, to hold his release at bay.

Elspeth fought him, striving to grasp the release so long denied her, moving against him until, with a harsh cry, he withdrew and set a savage cadence that brought them both to explosive release within moments.

The release sapped the strength from her so completely it shattered her thoughts. She was barely conscious as he dragged her against him, cuddling her close and stroking her soothingly. One fear emerged even from the darkness that was sucking her down into oblivion. "Come back to me, my love," she whispered even as the darkness swept her away.

He was gone when she woke. She stared around the room, empty of his belongings, and felt only a terrible loss that he had gone without even saying goodbye. Slipping from the bed, she dragged a gown and robe from her trunk and rushed to the door. The guard blocked her path. She stared up at him in dismay. "I only want to wish him a safe journey."

"Lord Arnaud is gone—this past hour and more."

Devastated, she closed the door once more and climbed back into the bed, struggling to hold her tears at bay. Finally, gathering the pillow to her that still retained his scent, she wept until exhaustion claimed her once more.

She was awakened by Etienne's familiar wail for sustenance. Sitting up groggily, she ignored Griselda's disapproving look and took the baby, giving him her breast to quiet him.

"I hope you do not mean to mimic the ways of the lazy Norman she-dog and begin to lie abed half the day," she said testily.

Elspeth regarded her dully. "He left while I slept.

He did not even say good bye. He did not give me the chance to wish him a safe journey."

Griselda snorted. "Mayhap he had no wish to carry the image with him of you blubbering and wailing like an infant."

Elspeth flushed at the rebuke, knowing it was warranted. She could not fathom why she possessed so little self-control where Guillume was concerned. "Do you think I have given him a distaste for me with my lack of control?" she asked fearfully.

Griselda studied Elspeth a moment. "He seemed pleased enough with that lack last eve."

Elspeth felt the color suffuse her cheeks so hotly it seemed to pulse for several moments. "You heard?" she asked, horrified.

"If there was anyone within the manor who did not, he must be sadly deaf!" Griselda retorted. "I was nigh convinced he was killing you."

Elspeth covered her face with her hand. "I will die of mortification."

"Unfortunately, that has killed no one yet—perhaps fortunately, for many would have fallen long ago. You will recover. The thing is, I can not see how you could feel that he did not bid you farewell most fondly—and more than half the night, I might add. If he does not fall from his horse from exhaustion of having bid you farewell, he is a mighty man indeed!"

Elspeth bit her lip, but the amusement quickly died as her anxiety rose one more. "You think that was his way of saying farewell?"

Griselda rolled her eyes. "I do not think pretty speech comes easily to that one—he has been bred a man of action."

Elspeth swallowed against the urge to weep all over again. "I fear he will not come back to me. Lady Rosabel was wont to say this is a crude, dirty place.

Perhaps the lure of their more refined way of life will tempt him to stay once he has finished what he set out to do. Beyond his son, there is nothing to hold him here, and he could send for Etienne."

"I am not going to pander to your determination to grieve. He will come to no harm, and he will return to you. He will not be able to stop himself. You are a blind fool if you can not see that he worships you and that he always has. Battered as you were, I saw the moment he first looked at you that our white rose of Saxony had made a conquest of our dread Norman invader. From that moment onward, he has scarcely taken his eyes from you when you were near. Did it not seem odd to you that he has always known precisely where you were at any moment of any day?"

Hope reared itself, but Elspeth found it difficult to trust it. "He desires me. He told me that long ago."

Griselda pursed her lips in disgust. "He loves you. Why else would he carry a lock of your hair close to his heart these many months?"

Elspeth looked at her sharply. "How do you know that?"

She shrugged. "I thought it curious when he began to wear it, but I had not guessed why until the night when you fell and we thought you would die. The look on his face then was such that no one who saw it could doubt how he felt. Later, when the babe had finally come and I went outside the cottage to catch my breath, I found him waiting to know if you would live. I do not think he realizes that I saw that it was a lock of your hair, for he put it away at once."

Elspeth said nothing, torn between doubt, hope and the fear that she would lose what she had so desperately wanted. "I did not tell him. He left and I did not get the chance to tell him," she said anxiously.

"Be still!" Griselda said sharply. "You will tell him when he returns. Mind the child and mind your chores and you will see he will return before you have had much time to miss him."

Griselda was wrong, however. Elspeth found she had more than enough time to miss him. He had left little more than a skeleton army to guard Rasgarth, taking the bulk of his men with him. Lord Arnaud's absence was enough to make the place seem empty, but the few who remained emphasized it with every gathering.

Weeks passed in a sluggish flow of time. The man he had left in charge emptied the manor of able souls and set them to work tilling the fields to prepare them for planting. The work on the walls, which had stopped when winter set in, was resumed, though little progress was made with so few to work on it.

Elspeth spent the latter half of the month watching hopefully for Lord Arnaud's return, and the second month in despair that Griselda had been wrong and he would not return at all—and fear, that something had happened to him, though she dared not even allow those thoughts to take form in her mind for fear it would bring him bad luck.

He did not send word, and even though Elspeth knew that she was no more than his layman and could not expect to be kept informed of her lord's movements, it hurt and angered her.

By the beginning of the third month after his departure, the child she carried made its presence known as her belly swelled beyond concealing it. Griselda, as Elspeth had guessed, was not pleased. "T'would have been better if you had healed longer from the last time," she muttered irritably, "but I suppose as determined as Lord Arnaud was to plow your fields and as anxious as you were to allow it that it is only to be expected."

Elspeth blushed, but glared at her nurse. "It has been nigh a year. I am strong again."   "T'would have been better if those fields had lain fallow a year before reseeding," Griselda said tartly. "That was no normal birthing. If it had been, I would have no anxiety at all. But there is little point in bemoaning it now. You must take care. That is all." She thought it over. "Small wonder you have been so weak and weepy when you are breeding again. It is enough to make any woman so."

Elspeth supposed that was say Griselda had leavened her disapproval over her wayward emotions, but it made her feel no better that Griselda was concerned about her condition.

She did not have a great deal of time to worry herself over it, however, for by mid month, riders were seen approaching from the East. Certain it must be Lord Arnaud at long last, Elspeth strained to peer into the distance until the standard they carried could be seen. The colors, she thought, were not just the same, but she found she could not dismiss the hope that had swelled inside of her and dashed down to greet the riders when they reached the gates.

Her heart seemed to stop in her chest when the lead rider stopped before the stoop and removed his helm.

Renard leered at her. "You have missed me, I see."

Feeling weak and sick, it took Elspeth several moments even to command herself to move. Finally, without a word, she whirled and fled inside. She did not stop until she had reached the sitting room.

Griselda took one look at her face and turned chalk white herself. "What is it?" she gasped fearfully.

"Renard—Renard has come," Elspeth gasped, dropping into a chair before she fainted.

* * * *

"They have not let him in!" Griselda gasped in alarm.

"He is Lord Arnaud's brother! They would not think to turn him away."

"Why is he here!" Griselda demanded, obviously as fearful as Elspeth was.

Elspeth dropped her face into her hands. "You think they would tell me, even if I had asked? I am only Lord Arnaud's layman! They tell me nothing of his business! He has been gone nigh three months already and I have not been told anything—not when he is expected to return, not if he is ill or wounded—nothing!"

"Hush! There have been no messengers. There is nothing more that anyone else knows." She frowned. "You are guarded. I am certain they will not allow Renard to harm you," she said a little doubtfully.

Elspeth was no more certain, but when the first of her fear had passed, she found her backbone and refused to allow the man to so terrorize her as to make her hide herself away in the lord's chambers. She found, in any case, that it was not a feat that was possible, for he lingered, showing no interest in moving on, watching her like a stalking cat each time she crossed within his sight.

As nervous as she was, it was impossible to maintain her guard at its peak for very long. When nigh a week passed and Renard made no attempt to approach her, she ceased jumping at shadows.

She'd been out to check the progress of the laundry. When she left the shed to go back into the manor, Renard was leaning against the wall next to the door. She stopped abruptly, her head whipping around toward the guard who always followed her. To her relief, he was only a few steps behind her.

She glanced toward Renard again, still reluctant to pass him, but finally decided that it would be better to have it over with than to continue trying to avoid him. Bracing herself, she continued toward the house, uncomfortably aware that he had surveyed her thoroughly as she approached him.

"I see my brother wasted no time in claiming you as his layman once his wife had been planted."

His gaze was on the telltale swell of her belly, but she saw no reason to respond to the statement.

"I am curious about my son."

Elspeth's eyes narrowed. She stopped. "You have no son."

"So I was told—but then I was also told my son resides in the master's suite. You are more clever and devious than I had credited."

Elspeth felt anger color her cheeks. As strongly as the desire was to insult him, however, she would not insult the memory of her son only to cut his father. "My son died. Etienne is Lord Arnaud's son."

A smile curled his lips. "So everyone seems to accept—now. But then you are still under guard, are you not? I detect a lack of trust on my brother's part."

He had placed that arrow well. Elspeth had done her best not to think about the implications, had, in truth, become so accustomed to her 'shadow' that she did not give him much thought, but she knew the order would have been rescinded if Lord Arnaud truly believed her. Her eyes narrowed. "I detect far too much interest in business that does not concern you," she said through clenched teeth.

He shrugged, grinning at her. "I was merely pointing out that you rejected a far better offer. But perhaps you regret it now?"

Elspeth's lips tightened. "If you believe that for one moment, then you most certainly can not believe that I am at all clever."

With that, she moved to brush past him. He caught her arm, detaining her, and Elspeth glanced once more toward the guard. His face had hardened and he had surged forward, but she could see that there was doubt there, also. "Release her. None are allowed to touch Lord Arnaud's woman."

Renard reddened, but he released her and stepped

back.

Shaken, Elspeth decided flight was the better part of valor. She had thought, after the last time that Lord Arnaud had threatened him, Renard would not dare to actually accost her. That he had done so in front of her guard was proof that he considered nothing but Lord Arnaud's presence a hindrance. She decided that she would not risk another encounter. She would stay in Lord Arnaud's apartments until he returned, or Renard left again.

* * * *

Elspeth was not certain what awakened her except that it was some noise that she was not accustomed tohearing. She lay still for several moments, listening.

The scrape of a tread on the floor near the bed sent a wave of cold over her, freezing her to the spot. Even as she struggled to form logical thought, to sit up and confront who ever it was to see if the threat was real, a rough hand covered her face.

"If you make a sound I will slit your throat and any who come to your summons."

Elspeth swallowed, her mind still too chaotic with fear to do much more than supply the face that went with the voice—Renard. He would almost certainly have entered through the chamber door—which meant the guard was dead, or in league with him.

Griselda was the only other person near enough to come quickly.

She nodded and was dragged upright. "Where is the boy?"

"Why?"

He slapped her. "In the next room?"

"You can not take him. Lord Arnaud would have every man seeking you."

"He is mine. I will not leave him," he growled.

Elspeth swallowed her terror, trying to jog her mind into productive thought. "Do .. do you not want your son to inherit what you can not?" she asked shakily. "If you leave him, he will be lord here one day—and of the property in Normandy, as well," she added when he seemed to be considering what she'd said.

"So it is true?"

Elspeth nodded shakily. "I could not bear to think he would have nothing. Rosabel's—Lord Arnaud's child died. I thought it could not hurt—and he is entitled to this, at least. It was my father's. Leave him."

"It is tempting, but Guillume suspects already. He is likely to dispose of the boy when he realizes he is mine."

"He will think Etienne must be his if I would abandon him here. And ... and you will have Lord Arnaud's child to hold against him."

He snorted. "His bastard is not likely to hold much interest for him."

Elspeth said nothing. She could think of nothing else that might persuade him to leave Etienne. Perhaps, though, if he took her she could call out a warning to Griselda? Perhaps she could buy her the time to flee to safety with the baby?

"Perhaps it is best this way, after all. We will have to ride hard tonight to elude Guillume's men. It would be more difficult if we have a squalling infant along."

Elspeth nodded shakily. "Yes! That is true."

For a moment, she thought her anxiety to leave the baby had had the opposite effect. Finally, he seemed to come to a decision and dragged her from the bed. Pulling a length of cloth from his belt, he stuffed the rag into her mouth and bound it around her head. "In case you get last minute doubts and decide to warn the guard yourself," he said, chuckling as Elspeth tried to break his hold. He bound her wrists before her, then dragged her toward the door.

The guard lay on the floor just outside. She peered at him as Renard dragged her past, but she couldn't tell if he was still breathing.

Despair filled her as they reached the great hall. All was quiet and she knew Renard and his men had disposed of those on watch. Her only chance now was to try to awaken someone as they passed through the hall.

Apparently, he had thought of that, as well, for they'd no sooner stepped from the stairs than he struck her along the jaw and she descended into a blackness more profound that she had ever known.

* * * *

"Lord Arnaud! We are pleased to see that you have returned from settling your little domestic problem hale and hearty!"

Lord Arnaud bowed. "Aye, sire. In truth, there was more boredom than action involved."

"You settled the problem to your satisfaction, however?"

"Aye."

King William studied him for several moments. "As it happens, I am glad that you came straight away to report your success to me. I have had you much on my mind."

Lord Arnaud studied him uneasily. "I am flattered, sire."

King William's eyes narrowed, but after a moment he smiled thinly. "Your countenance is like stone, Arnaud. You do not seem flattered to me."

Lord Arnaud flushed. "I was only surprised, sire, that you would give me any thought at all when such weighty matters besiege you."

King William nodded. "Tis truth." He sighed gustily. "But we are well in hand, now. What put me in mind of you, however, was that I have an heiress that I would like to see settled. Matilda reminded me that your wife had died some time ago in child bed, and that we had settled only a rather insignificant estate upon you for your services. She is no filly, but still of good child bearing age and she is a proven breeder."

A cold sweat broke on Lord Arnaud's brow as he stared at his king, trying to sort through his chaotic thoughts and find the words that would save him. "I am deeply honored, sire."

William's eyes narrowed. "But?"

Despite his best efforts, Guillume found himself reddening once more. "I had come to petition you for permission to wed Lady Elspeth, daughter of Odolf."

William frowned, but it was more thoughtful now than angry. "I am not familiar with this young lady or her sire."

"Lord Odolf was the Saxon who held Rasgarth before me."

William's brows rose almost to his hair line. He studied Lord Arnaud in silence for some moments. "A clever political move, certainly, but you have nothing to gain beyond settling the strain of our new relations. I have already given you Rasgarth."

He studied Lord Arnaud's reception to that remark for several moments, and finally smiled. "Ah. I see. I must suppose that the Lady Elspeth, herself, is the jewel you mean to acquire. You must bring her to court once you have wed. I am anxious to see this rose of old Saxony."

Profound relief swept through Guillume. He bowed once more and rose. "Thank you, sire."

Leaving the bulk of his army behind to follow more slowly, Guillume set out with a dozen knights to reach Rasgarth by the most direct route, far more anxious to reach Rasgarth, and Elspeth, than he would ever have admitted, or thought possible.

He knew, even before he reached the gates that something was not as it should be. There was far more activity in the keep than there should have been.

He gaze went immediately toward the manor, but Elspeth did not meet him as he and his men rode through the gates. Instead, Griselda stumbled through the doors, Etienne in her arms, wailing almost as loudly as she was.

Stark terror stabbed at him as he scrambled from his horse and strode toward her.

"She is gone! She is gone! Stolen while we slept!"

"Who?" Guillume asked sharply, dreading the an-

159

swer.

"Elspeth!"

Feeling coldness sweep over him, Lord Arnaud thrust her aside, crossed the great room, and strode quickly up the stairs. Griselda followed him, still sobbing. "She is not there, I tell you!"

Slamming the door to his chamber back, he looked around the room for signs of a struggle and saw none. He turned to Griselda, grabbing her arm. "Cease that racket and tell me what has happened!"

Griselda sniffed, bouncing the baby and trying to quiet him. "I brought Etienne in for his feeding this morn and she was gone, the guard at the door slain, the men at watch, also. It was Renard. I knew the moment he came that he had come for mischief."

"Renard was here?" he asked grimly.

Griselda nodded. "He came nigh two weeks ago and would not leave. Elspeth was afraid even to leave the chamber."

Guillume strode into the middle of the room. "And you heard nothing? She did not call out for help?"

Griselda gaped at him. "The guard was dead. She would not have called out for me to defend her from Renard. She would have been afraid for me."

The rage that suffused his face frightened her.

"I see the turn of your mind, my lord, but she did not go willingly."

He looked at her, his eyes cold now. "Did she not? When there is no sign of a struggle? When she did not even cry out? The faithless—"

Griselda glared at him when he stopped. He had no need to finish for her to know what was going through his mind. "Your jealousy will spell her death."

He flushed. "Take care, woman. I have tolerated much from you for Elspeth's sake, but do not think that you can speak to me in that manner with impunity."

Her face crumpled. "Slay me then if it will make you feel one whit better! I will die of a broken heart anyway if you harm Elspeth in your jealous rage. She hated Renard. She has always hated him and feared him and yet you could think that she would run away with him when she carries your child!"

He paled. "She is with child?"

"Aye. Four months gone."

His lips tightened. "For all I know it is his child."

"The jealousy has turned your mind! You know it is yours! She loves you. I had thought that I understood why. Now I am not so sure that I do. It will break her spirit if she sees that you still have no faith in her, no trust, when she has given her heart to you, withheld nothing.

"She needs you. Renard will kill her—whether intentional or not. You saw how he beat her. She is not recovered enough from the last time to survive if he treats her as he did before!"

The madness left his eyes abruptly, replaced by stark fear. "How long has she been gone?"

Griselda thought about it. "She was gone when I came with the babe just before dawn. The bed was still warm. I thought, until I saw the guard, that she had only gone to relieve herself."

Lord Arnaud nodded and strode toward the door. "That means he has nigh a six hour lead."

"Lord Arnaud!"

He stopped and turned to look at her.

"You will see that you are wrong about her, but know this. If you break her heart, you will never have it back again as it was. Nothing that has been mended is ever the same again. I beg you, do not do anything that you will both regret."

His face hardened. "Find someone to feed the child. I will bring her back."

Chapter Fourteen

They had fled as if the hounds of hell pursued them. Renard had said it was only to throw off the possibility that they were being hunted, but she did not think that he believed it. Whatever had possessed him to steal her away, whatever lies he had told himself, they had not sustained him long. He fled like a man who knew he was being chased and knew just as certainly that he would die if he were caught.

He had not removed her gag even when she had come to and they had stopped long enough to tie her to her own horse—yet another indication that someone followed, for he obviously did not want his horse burdened by two riders.

That hope sustained her throughout much of the day. Obviously, he and his men had slain the men on watch if they were so certain they would be pursued. It seemed doubtful that a hunting party would be sent only for her.

She didn't particularly care why, however, only that

they would come.

As darkness began to move in upon them, and the aches and pains of having ridden all day swarmed over her, refusing to be ignored, her spirits began to sink with the sun.

Since she'd come to, they had been heading north, leaving a trail that would be easy enough to follow. Once the sun set, he could turn and strike off in another direction entirely and lose whoever was tracking them. By the time it was light enough for them to see again, Renard could be well beyond their reach.

The one bright spot, so far, was that Renard was too intent upon escaping to enjoy his prize for the moment. They had only stopped briefly a couple of times since they had left.

Which, she wondered, would be worse? If Renard decided to continue riding through the night to throw off pursuit? Or if he was unwise enough to decide to stop for the night, in which case he would almost certainly rape her?

In her heart, she knew that Guillume would suspect that she had gone willingly. She had not fought for fear that Griselda would be hurt, or that he would change his mind about the baby, but the fact that she'd left no sign of her unwillingness would be damning. Especially since Lord Arnaud had never really trusted her. Particularly since she had not even tried to convince him that she would prefer death to Renard.

It was all very well—then—to allow her pride to overrule her head, to convince herself that he was being unreasonable and unjust and should know better than to think such things of her, but look where that pride had gotten her!

She was his enemy by birth, and by combat. She had no right to expect to be trusted. It had been stupid and childish to think otherwise. Trust was not a thing easily earned in such circumstances—but it had to be earned. If Lord Arnaud had been the sort to blindly yield trust, he would not have gotten far in life.

She spent part of her time praying to any deity that might be willing to listen that Guillume would return and come after her, and the other part praying that she would be rescued by his men and he need never know.

When it grew too dark to see, they stopped to wait for the rising moon. Elspeth dropped wearily to the ground, too tired even to be afraid. Her ass was numb from the pounding saddle. Her hands were numb from the binding. Her wrists were raw and bleeding.

She stiffened when Renard made his way over to her and sat down beside her. When he pulled the gag away and offered her a skin of water, however, she grabbed for it eagerly, gulping as much as she could before he tore it from her grasp. "I think we have lost them."

Elspeth said nothing for several moments. "You said they would not follow. That I was only Lord Arnaud's whore and they would not stir themselves to come after me."

He snorted. "They would not. On the other hand, we did kill three of Guillume's men. They were bound to be righteously indignant over that. But not so angry, I think, that they would continue the hunt when it has grown too dark to track us. Most likely they will have returned by now."

"My lord!" one of his men called out in a harsh whisper.

Renard's head snapped up. "What is it?"

"Come! See what you make of this!"

Renard got up and moved away from her. "Merde!" he exclaimed after several moments.

"Torches. I count twelve—no sixteen. Do you think it is men from Rasgarth?"

"I think we will not stay and see. They are twice our number," Renard said grimly.

Elspeth struggled to her feet as he turned toward her, straining to see the torches, hope spreading through her and bringing renewed strength to her aching limbs. She caught no more than a glimpse as Renard shoved her toward the horse and helped her to mount, but her heart did a nose dive. The torches seemed far away and she feared that, once they were on the move again, that distance would grow.

As they set out once more, she began trying to think what, if anything, she could do to help her rescuers find her. She began trying to tear a strip of cloth from her gown. It was white. With the torches, they would almost certainly see it if they were following the tracks. She found, however, that the fabric resisted her efforts. She could not find a weak point to start, and had nothing to use but her fingers.

Finally, she pushed herself back along the saddle far enough to rub her gag against the pommel. The racing horse made it more difficult than she'd expected. In the first attempt, she banged her mouth so hard she felt her lip split. It brought tears to her eyes. Blinking them away, she turned her head slightly and tried raking her cheek along the bouncing pommel. She bruised her cheek, but she felt the gag slip slightly and renewed her efforts. After some time of struggling with it, she managed to free her mouth and sat up once more to look behind her.

The torches seemed closer, but she wasn't certain if it was pure hopefulness on her part or not. She decided to chance it before any of the men noticed she had managed to remove the gag. Drawing in a deep breath, she screamed as loudly as she could. "Here! I'm here! Help—"

She didn't get the last out. One of Renard's men jerked his horse closer and struck her on the side of her head with his fist. Her terror shielded her from the pain, but not the impact of his fist. Even as she felt blackness engulfing her, she felt herself flying side

165

ways off the horse. She hit the ground so hard it knocked the air from her lungs. She was aware of rolling, tumbling over and over and then nothing else.

"Hold!"

The voice penetrated the fog that seemed to surround her and Elspeth felt fear force everything else from her mind. They were coming back for her. Focusing only on the need to escape, she dug her fingers into the ground, dragging herself forward several inches.

"Elspeth!"

She tried to crawl faster, but someone caught her, rolling her onto her back. She threw up her arm to ward him off. "No!"

She felt a trembling seize her.

"Elspeth! How badly are you hurt, chere?"

Elspeth swallowed with an effort, lowering her arm. "Guillume?" she asked disbelievingly.

He gathered her into his arms, holding her closely against his chest for several moments. Finally, he scooped her up and stood. Striding to where the other riders waited, he lifted her up to one of his men. Once he had mounted, he moved his horse closer and pulled her across his lap, tucking her securely against him. "Six men with me. The rest—track them. Do not return until you have them or can assure me they have been dealt with," he said grimly.

They rode only a little while before they stopped and made camp. The shock had long since worn off, however, and Elspeth felt every jolt of the horse in every aching joint and bruise. She was relieved when she was taken from the horse and lain carefully on a bedroll that had been spread on the ground, only vaguely aware of Guillume's hands moving over her as he carefully probed her for broken bones.

"I can not find anything broken, Elspeth, but your mouth is bleeding. Did you hurt your mouth?" His voice was urgent, threaded with some emotion she could not grasp.

166

She nodded. "I was trying to use the pommel to remove the gag so I could call out."

He frowned, examining her face in the flickering light from the fire. "Your face is bruised. From the pommel?"

She nodded. "He hit me."

"Who?"

Elspeth frowned, trying to gather her scattered wits. "Renard—when he took me from the house. He knocked me unconscious. One of his men when I started screaming." She caught his arm when he sat back on his heels. "He said he would kill Griselda if I tried to call for help. He wanted to take Etienne. I only went with him to get him away from Etienne. I swear it, my lord, on my father's soul!"

"Be still. We will talk of this later."

"Please, Guillume—Lord Arnaud. I did not run away. I swear it."

He swallowed audibly and caressed her cheek gently. "I know, chere. I should never have doubted you." He left her for several moments. When he returned, he held something to her lips. Expecting water, she took a large gulp. It burned a trail of fire down her throat—burned her lip. Tears filled her eyes. She choked, holding her ribs while she coughed.

Setting the wine skin aside, Lord Arnaud settled beside her, pulling her against him. "Rest. Tomorrow, I will take you home."

The word 'home' comforted her as much as his heat and strength. Relieved that he seemed to believe her, she relaxed and slept.

It was full dark by the time they drew the horses up before the gates of Rasgarth once more. Elspeth had never seen a more welcome sight. Lord Arnaud had ridden slowly and had stopped frequently to allow her to rest, but the ride had been an agonizing one nonetheless. Regardless, Elspeth had not wanted to stop at all. She hurt, whether she was on the horse or not, and could think of nothing but reaching home where she could lie still without worrying about having to get on a horse once more.

She felt like weeping with relief when they rode through the gates and she heard Griselda's voice.

A groan escaped her when Lord Arnaud had carried her upstairs and settled her finally in his bed. Griselda, who'd followed them upstairs, immediately began pushing and pulling at her, however, tugging her filthy gown off. She complained, for all the good it did.

The bath was better. She would have far preferred if she had been allowed to soak in the tub, in hot water, but it was still a relief to feel the dirt bathed carefully from her skin. She was more than half asleep by the time Griselda had finished. "How is the babe?"

Elspeth searched her mind. "I do not think he took any hurt."

Griselda checked her anyway, but seemed satisfied. "Your poor face is so battered I would not have known you."

Elspeth opened her eyes with an effort. "I am hideous?"

"You are bruised and swollen from the top of your head to your toes, but the bruises will fade and so, too, will the swelling. I must get my salves for your wrists. But first, you must drink the tea, sweeting."

Elspeth drank obediently, smiling faintly as she lay back once more. "I must look terrible if you are calling me sweeting."

Griselda snorted and stalked away.

When she had gone, Elspeth realized that Lord Arnaud was standing in front of the fireplace, watching her. Covering her face, she rolled over with an effort. She heard him cross the room. In a moment, the bed dipped as he sat down beside her. He stroked her arm soothingly.

"I have carried your image in my mind many months, Elspeth. It … pains me to see you so hurt, but you are still beautiful to me."

She sighed, but she didn't turn over. Instead, she

caught his hand and carried it to her lips. "I have missed you so terribly. I had begun to fear that you would not come back.

"I know that you have never trusted me—I understand, but I had thought if I showed you how desperately I loved you that you would come to see that I could never do anything that would hurt you."

"I have not doubted you in a very long time."

She tilted her head to look at him. "But … you thought that I had gone willingly with Renard."

He sighed, scrubbing his hand over his jaw. "I had hoped that you would not realize that—Jealousy knows no reason. I did not truly believe it of you, but I could not completely ignore the fear and doubt. You were his before you were mine."

"I was never his. He took my body, but that did not make me his. Only I can decide who I belong to. I think, from the moment you rescued me from him, that I was yours. I know you did not do it for that reason, but it didn't matter."

He rubbed his forehead, as if his head ached. "I feared as much, but I did not want your gratitude, Elspeth."

"That why you had me guarded, because you believed it was only gratitude and that I would turn against you? How can you say you do not doubt me when you still can not accept that I love you with all my heart?"

"The guard was to protect you," he said harshly. "I did not trust that Renard would not try something."

He was silent for several moments. Finally, he swallowed audibly and clasped her hand tightly. "I … am not much for pretty words, Elspeth. Mayhap I had not truly accepted it myself when I left, but I knew when I got to Normandy that I had left my heart here … with you, and that I could not live without it."

Elspeth squeezed her eyes tightly, hardly daring to accept the joy that flooded through her, making her heart pound crazily. "Truly?"

He cleared his throat. "I have petitioned King William for permission to wed with you."

Elspeth forgot all about her embarrassment over the condition of her face. She whirled to look at him with startled eyes. "You have ....?"

He reddened faintly. "If you will consider my suit?"

Ignoring the stabs of pain the effort cost her, Elspeth sat up and threw her arms around him, hugging him tightly. "Guillume! I love you so! Nothing would make me happier."

He cupped a hand around the back of her head. "Griselda does not think I deserve you."

Elspeth drew back in surprise. "She did not say that!"

A wry smile twisted his lips. "Words to that effect."

She shook her head. "She is such a schemer! She has been assuring me for months that you loved me— and that you would come to trust me in time."

His dark brows rose. A faint flush suffused his cheeks. "I had thought I hid it better than that."

"Then you did love me? You do?"

"Have I not said so?"

Elspeth thought it over. "No."

"I told you that you held my heart," he said pensively.

In truth, that was even better. She snuggled closer. "When will we be wed?"

"As soon as the bride is ready—as soon as may be— when you are well enough."

* * * *

The Saxon bride wore a gown the pale green of spring. On her head was a coronet woven of spring flowers as she faced her Norman groom before the priest and vowed to love, honor and cherish him ... forever. And when her Norman had vowed the same, he pulled her into his arms and gave her the kiss of peace.

The End

Vulgar

GOLDIE MCBRIDE

Chapter One

Alinor had never traveled beyond her father's holdings in all her short life. Under other circumstances, she would have been enthralled, would have studied everything they passed with keen interest. She was so sick with trepidation, however, that she could not find it in herself to have any interest in her surroundings.

She was not a child. She had matured into womanhood nigh two years past, reached the age when her menses began and she was ripe to bear children for the man chosen for her. She should have left all childish things far behind. And yet, she found that she had nursed the childish hope that her own wishes would outweigh the arrangement that had been made for her, despite the fact that her mother had done her utmost to drum it into her head that, for people of their class, marriage was not an estate to be entered into blinded by emotional attachment. It was a binding together of wealth and power, and most ideally, of superior bloodlines.

Jean-Pierre was by far the most illustrious of those

who had offered for her hand. In truth—as they had pointed out to her—she should have been grateful that her parents had chosen a man in the prime of his life when it could easily have been otherwise, particularly since Jean-Pierre was considered by most to be an exceptionally handsome man.

Unfortunately, the beauty of his exterior hid a black soul—one she alone, apparently, could see, but then he had almost seemed to glory in revealing to her his darkness, which he kept carefully concealed from all others.

She had been cold to her parents when she departed. She regretted it now, for it seemed unlikely she would see them again in this lifetime.

Jean-Pierre, no doubt drunk on his newest conquest, had arranged their marriage and sent an escort for her to transport her across the channel to England. Whether it was their usual manner, or Jean-Pierre had given them orders to that effect, they had traveled at a grueling pace, reaching the coast in little more than a day and half. They rested there only a matter of hours and then took ship.

The crossing had been like nothing Alinor could have imagined in her worst nightmares. It was nearing winter, and the channel was treacherous with storms. She had been too terrified by the crashing waves even to fight them when her escort had whisked her aboard, and too sick and fearful afterwards to do more than cling frantically to the nearness support and pray for a quick death, expecting momentarily to meet it.

She had been so weak when they reached the coast of England at last and she was carried ashore that she could not even hold herself upright. The moment the man had set her down, she had collapsed in an ignoble heap on the wet sand. Not so much of a stitch of her clothing had been dry, but neither had she had a more thorough soaking than the one she received when she sank to the sand within reach of the crashing waves, which immediately reached for her and tried to drag her out to sea once more.

Their leader had waded into the water cursing, dragged her out and tossed her onto the back of the horse that had been brought for her. More miserable than she had ever been in her life, Alinor, her jaw locked to fight the chattering of her teeth, had looked around dully at the strange land that would be her new home.

On the cliffs above them, she had seen a solitary rider. His hair, long, falling well past his shoulders, and as dark as a raven's wing, fluttered around a face that was featureless at this distance, but she had the impression that he was relatively young—no youth from his build, but certainly not old. His bare chest and shoulders seemed broad, deep—massive. Around his shoulders a cape was flung almost carelessly. Of a color somewhere between a deep red and brown, the color alone seemed almost a challenge to those below to notice his presence.

Something about him caused her heart to leap in her chest. His stillness, the tension in every line of his body had convinced her that it was not mere curiosity that held him in thrall, watching as the small party that had met them brought forth fresh horses for the men who'd accompanied her thus far.

She didn't know why she hadn't called attention to him. She had told herself that she was simply too surprised; that she was too ill and miserable to think of it; that the others would probably have noticed him, as well—that he might even be a part of the party who'd come to escort her to Jean-Pierre.

She knew better.

She had glanced around, instinctively, after she'd

174

spotted him, to see if any of the others had noticed him. When she'd looked again, he'd disappeared.

She'd told herself there was little point in saying anything then, but she had caught a glimpse of him again, late in the day, had known that he must be following them—and still she'd said nothing.

Alinor found that, despite her exhaustion from traveling, she could only sleep fitfully. Tomorrow, or no later than the following day, she was to be presented to her groom, Jean-Pierre. He'd assured her parents that the wedding had already been arranged and that the wedding festivities were poised to proceed the moment she arrived.

That thought alone made sleep impossible. With the best will in the world, she had not been able to convince herself that he was not as she remembered, that she had only imagined the cruelty she sensed in him. She could not, despite her mother's efforts, and indeed certainty, that it was no more than natural maidenly fears of the marriage bed.

She would almost have preferred to face her wedding night in ignorance. She knew her mother had been well intentioned, but her careful instructions had been far worse than the ignorance that had frightened her before. It was impossible, in any case, that she could have grown up with no knowledge at all of the act of mating. The dogs that roamed the keep mated with a complete disregard for the size, or discomfort, of their audience. For that matter, she had stumbled upon the men-at-arms and maids on more than one occasion and though she'd fled immediately, she had seen enough to have a fair notion of what it was all about.

Her mother's helpful instructions had left nothing at all to the imagination, however, no room to convince herself that it couldn't possibly be nearly as degrading and revolting as it looked.

A whisper of sound distracted her from her mental ramblings and Alinor stiffened, listening. She sat up abruptly when it came again, her heart hammering in her chest.

She was seized abruptly, one hand gripping her chest in a bruising hold that flattened her breasts, the other large hand clamped tightly to her mouth to muffle any cries she might have the presence of mind to make. That hand covered near the whole of her face and seemed likely to smother her if the man did not relent in short order.

As he shifted his hand to allow her to draw a decent breath, she closed her eyes, willing the fear to abate, willing her mind to calmer reflection. Panic would gain her nothing but a swifter death.

Her first, instinctual, fear had been that one of the men sent to escort her had crept into the tent and meant to violate her, but no man of Jean-Pierre's, she knew, would dare to touch her. Jean-Pierre would make him beg for death before he granted it. The man who held her so tightly could not be a member of her party.

Had he come to rob? To rape? To kill?

Despite the fear those thoughts evoked, there was almost a sense of hope, as well, the sense that it might be over for her quickly and she would never have to endure marriage to Jean-Pierre. After her first, instinctual effort to free herself from the bruising grip, she subsided.

A blade was pressed threateningly to her throat. She closed her eyes, waited, hoping the pain would not be unbearable. After a moment, to her surprise and something curiously akin to alarm, the blade was removed. The hand covering her mouth eased its pressure and then was cautiously removed.

Despite her fear, it leapt instantly to mind that si

lence was all that ensured life for either her or the man. She would die if she so much as gasped for breath, she knew. He had not had to speak the command to assure her that he was deadly serious. His actions were clear enough.

In a moment, the hand was withdrawn completely and a rag took its place, was bound tightly around her mouth to muffle any sound she might think to make that would alert the soldiers outside her tent. It smelled strongly of animal and she realized that it was not a rag of cloth, but a thin piece of scraped hide. The odor was almost overwhelming given that she had not really recovered from the crossing, and she had to fight the bile that rose in her throat to choke her.

A rustle of sound came again as the man moved around her. Despite the darkness, she could make out a darker form among the shadows, could see well enough to tell that he wore no armor—and was still massive. He was not a knight then—nor merely a peasant either. Peasants, half starved for the most part, rarely grew into such giants.

She realized abruptly that it must be the rider she had seen trailing them since they'd left the coast, though she'd caught no more than a glimpse of him either time. This, then, was his purpose—to steal her away. The question was, why?

Ransom almost certainly had to be the motive. Would Jean-Pierre pay? And, assuming he did, what would he do to her once he got her back? Her captor would almost certainly dishonor her. If she survived it, Jean-Pierre would blame her no matter how hard she fought—if she fought.

That thought stunned her for several moments until she realized that she would almost welcome being deflowered by anyone but Jean-Pierre—it was almost inconceivable that it could be worse—and still shame filled her for such wicked thoughts.

She wondered, if Jean-Pierre paid, if man would return her. Or would he merely use her to rob Jean-Pierre, to taunt him, and then slay her?

Such speculation was useless at this point. It seemed unlikely that he would win free of the camp with her. Jean-Pierre's men surrounded them. Big as he was, and no matter how competent a fighter, he could not hope to best them all.

Pulling her to her feet, he produced a length of rope and bound her wrists so tightly she couldn't contain a moan of pain. He stopped abruptly, studying her, she knew, in the darkness. Her heart skipped several beats while she waited see what he would do and he, apparently, waited to see if she would try to sound the alarm. To her surprise, he loosened the bonds slightly. Gratitude filled her, and hope. He could not, surely, use her cruelly if he could show concern over so slight an injury?

When he'd finished binding her wrists, he picked her up and tossed her over his shoulder. The impact of connecting with his hard shoulder knocked the wind from her. She stiffened as she fought for breath, but he did not appear to notice her distress. Turning, he tossed something onto the pallet he had pulled her from and then made his way toward the back of the tent. Emerging through the slit he'd cut in it, he paused, almost seeming to sniff the wind for the scent of the men who lay sleeping on their pallets.

After that brief hesitation, he struck off toward the tree line, moving as silently past the sleeping men as a wraith.

* * * *

"Je suis Alinor d'Arrus," Alinor told him who she

was in little more than a whisper when at last her captor removed her gag. They had traveled miles it seemed through the woods before they had come at last upon a small clearing where a horse had awaited. Without a word, he had tossed her up onto the front of the saddle, climbing up behind her while she struggled frantically to maintain her balance. Settling, he caught her as she lost the battle and righted her, holding her snugly against his hard belly with one hand and gathering the reins in the other. Almost as an after thought, he had tugged the gag down so that she could breathe more freely.

He did not respond to her tentative effort of communication, except by a grunt, which allowed a good deal of room for interpretation. Alinor wondered whether he hadn't really heard her—since she had been afraid to speak too loud for fear of angering him—if he did not understand her language, or if he was simply not of the frame of mind to allow her to draw him into any sort of conversation.

She frowned. Her mother had thought it imperative that she learn to speak at least enough words of the peasantry of England to direct the servants, but there had been little time to learn once she had located someone who claimed knowledge of the Saxon tongue.

The moon had risen above the tops of the trees before she reached a point in her mental search that she was fairly certain she had recalled the correct words to ask the questions she desperately needed answers for. With an effort, she swiveled around to look up at her captor.

Her heart seemed to jerk to a halt as she looked up at him. His face, concealed by the night as much as revealed by moonlight, was a terrifying mask of harsh planes and angles. His eyes, deep set beneath his straight, black brows, were nothing more than black pits. The first thing that leapt into her mind was 'devil'. "Oo are you?" she gasped in a frightened whisper.

Instead of answering immediately, he pulled the horse to a halt, grasped the gag that he'd pulled down around her throat earlier, and tugged it up once more until it rubbed the underside of her nostrils.

"Wulfgar," he growled as he kicked the horse into motion once more.

Chapter Two

Alinor was too weak with fear even to feel a great deal of shock when the man pulled her gag up once more. Anger finally supplanted it, that he'd gagged her again when she had made every effort to speak quietly, but she was hardly in a position to argue the matter even if he had not made it impossible to complain.

She faced forward again, sitting stiffly erect. He allowed it all of two seconds before pulling her tightly against his chest once more. Briefly, she struggled to pull away, but her anger had not routed fear altogether and, in any case, she soon saw the gesture was useless. In a physical battle of wills, there was no contest.

Slowly, the tension she'd tried very hard to retain slipped away as weariness set in. She relaxed and, to her surprise, slept. It was still dark when she woke, but the black had given way to a deep gray and she thought it must me nearing dawn.

She sensed that the man who called himself Wulfgar was gathering himself to dismount and braced herself, but the moment he withdrew his support she began to slip sideways, lost her balance and fell off the horse.

He made a grab for her and managed to break her fall, but the jolt sent pain flooding through her just the same. This time he didn't bother to toss her over his shoulder, he merely encircled her waist with one arm and carried her by his side as he might a bundle. Draped across one forearm, Alinor could see little in the dimness beyond the dead leaves of the forest floor.

He knelt finally and half pushed, half dragged her into a shelter of some sort. Alinor could tell nothing about his expression and thus nothing about his mood or intentions. She was not left long to worry the matter, however. As soon as he'd settled her, he bound her feet, turned and left.

Alinor stared indignantly at the opening for some moments, wondering if he would return. With surprise and a good deal of dismay, she heard him mount his horse and ride off again.

That puzzled her far more than anything else that he'd done.

She'd been given an opportunity to escape, she realized … but how much of an opportunity was it, really?

She was bound hand and foot now, weak, numb from both the cold and from being bound so long, and she was in a strange land that she knew nothing of.

It occurred to her after a little bit that he might have abandoned her for good. Perhaps he didn't have the stomach to slay a helpless female outright and had simply decided to leave her and allow nature to take its course?

Well, she was of no mind to simply lie still and allow herself to grow weaker until she hadn't the strength to free herself. She began working at her bindings, twisting her wrists and hands until the stickiness of blood convinced her that she'd loosened the thongs. If she had, it was still not enough, however, for, try though she might, she could not pull her hands free.

It occurred to her finally that he had not tied the gag tightly as it had been before, but had merely pulled it up to cover her mouth, and she began trying to nudge the gag down her face. She was sweating with effort by the time she'd managed it and dizzy from exhaustion. She gnawed at the thong that bound her wrist for a time but weariness finally got the best of her and she dozed.

She woke to bright day. Though she had no notion of how much time had passed, her body screamed for attention. In desperation, she managed to struggle upright and began to work on the bindings around her ankles. She was nearly weeping before she managed to untie the knots with her numb fingers and struggle to her knees. With an effort, she grasped the hem of her gown and crawled on her knees through the opening.

She found that she was not in a clearing as she'd thought. The shelter was little more than a box made of branches and covered with leaves and moss, blending in so completely with its surroundings that it was almost invisible before she'd taken a half dozen steps from it. She was of no mind to go far, however, only far enough to ensure a little privacy to relieve herself.

It was not an easy task to accomplish with her hands still bound before her, but finally she managed to situate her shirts.

When she'd finished, she looked around the forest, trying to remember which way she'd come so that she could retrace her steps.

To her dismay, she realized that she'd been so filled with need that she'd paid little heed. No matter which direction she turned, she could see nothing that stood apart from anything else. Finally, deciding upon a direction, she gripped her skirts in her fist and carefully picked her way through the woods. After traveling perhaps twenty paces, she looked around again.

There was no sign of the shelter.

* * * *

A sense of triumph and anticipation sustained Wulfgar throughout the arduous pace he set himself as he crossed and re-crossed his tracks, led the men on his trail in a wide circle that doubled back upon itself, then zigzagged into nowhere. They tracked him doggedly throughout much of the day, but, as he'd expected, they reached a point of frustration at last when they realized they would not be able to retrieve the woman without help. At last, they abandoned the hunt and rode off to inform their master that they had lost his bride.

He grinned wolfishly, envisioning his enemy's face when the news was brought to him.

When the men-at-arms had disappeared, he turned his weary mount around and wove another round-about trail to the place where he'd concealed the woman. The moment he thought of her, however, an image of her rose into his mind's eye and he frowned.

When he'd heard his enemy had sent for a bride, he had not seen beyond the chance the gods had given him to avenge his loss—a bride for a bride. He'd imagined taking the nameless, faceless woman and violating her as that pretty-faced French spawn of Satan had taken and defiled his own bride. He'd envisioned the tragedy playing itself out in reverse, where he had crushed the heart from Jean-Pierre, duc de l'Cran as his own heart had been crushed when he had discovered the lifeless body of his beloved Freda.

An outlaw now in his own land, he had returned from the great battle, nigh as dead as those he'd left behind on the fields, only to discover that the Norman devils had taken all that had once been his and crushed those who stood in their path.

And his gentle Freda, whom he had taken to wife little more than a week before he'd been called to fight, had been so cruelly used by Jean-Pierre and his men that she had taken her own life.

The burning need for revenge was all that had kept him alive in the time since.

He would let no one deprive him of tasting it at long last.

Yet, he could not banish the sense of uneasiness that had begun to creep insidiously through his mind. The woman was nameless and faceless no longer. She had told him she was Alinor of Arrus. She had gazed up at him in terror through the eyes of a frightened doe— huge in her small, pointed face, soft and full of inno- cence—and painfully young.

His gut clenched. Determinedly, he summoned the feel of her womanly form. Slight as she was, she was soft and rounded enough to please any man. To his relief, his body responded instantly to the memory of her soft bottom pressing against his groin, to the feel of her plump, pliant breasts resting against the arm he had held her with.

The anxiety, hardly acknowledged, that he would not be able to follow through with his plan receded. In its place, a new urgency grew. He had not lain with a woman since he had lost Freda. He would take the Norman bitch and use her to slake his lust and appease his need for revenge. She was no more to him that any other possession of the duc, an object only, and, as his possession, an extension of the duc himself.

Frustration, fear and rage filled him when he arrived back at the place where he had left the girl and discov- ered her gone; fear because it had leapt immediately to mind that she had fallen victim to some wild creature, or some two legged animal had stumbled upon her; frustration because he had intended to see the deed through before she could further corrupt his resolve; and rage because he had been thwarted by a mere slip of a girl.

There was no sign, however, that she had been savaged—no blood, only the discarded binding, and signs indicating that she had crawled from the lean to. Kneeling, he searched the ground carefully and finally discerned the direction she had taken.

She had not gone far and she looked so relieved to see him that he felt his rage abandon him in a sickening rush.

"Monsieur!" Alinor gasped when Wulfgar appeared, so relieved to discover that she hadn't been abandoned in what appeared to be an unending woodland that she had to fight the urge to burst into tears of relief. "I became lost," she added a little uneasily when she saw that he was flushed with anger.

He strode toward her, bent at the waist and pressed his face so closely to hers that they were practically nose to nose. Alinor looked back at him wide-eyed, but unflinching. "I will bind you better next time," he said through gritted teeth.

Alinor blinked, looked at him blankly, but he'd spoken far too quickly for her to grasp what he'd said. In any case, she was captivated by his eyes. They were the color of emeralds. "Monsieur!" she gasped. "You 'ave beautiful eyes!"

He looked disconcerted for several moments. A dark flush stole up his neck to his hairline and he straightened abruptly, studying her face carefully. He could see no sign that she was being deliberately provocative—either to test his temper or in a flirtatious manner. Nor did she appear to be short on wit. Her

186

eyes did not have that blank look of the slow-witted. They gleamed with intelligence.

After a moment, he grasped her upper arm without another word and began marching her back toward the temporary encampment.

Alinor did her best to keep up, but his stride was far longer than her own and she found she had to run to keep from being snatched off her feet. Belatedly, embarrassment set in. Her mother had beaten her many times for her thoughtless tongue—much use it had done her for she had never mastered 'thought before speech' and feared she never would.

It might well be the death of her.

He was angry, she realized abruptly, because he had been kind enough not to leave her bound too tightly and she had taken them off and wandered away. She'd known he would be angry if he discovered she had removed them. In point of fact, it had been her intention only to relieve herself and return and replace the bindings so that he would never know that she'd left.

She would have except that she had not been able to find her way back. She had a bad feeling, however, that even if she could explain something that complicated in his own tongue he would be no happier with it. "I did not run," she said a little breathlessly.

He didn't so much as glance in her direction.

"I had need," she added a little desperately.

He halted abruptly, looked her over frowningly.

She gestured a little helplessly toward the woods.

Something flickered in his eyes, understanding, she thought, but in the next moment he was moving again.

They reached the tiny clearing surrounding the encampment within moments, a disconcerting indication that she had wandered all around it for hours when she had practically been upon it the entire time. She had no time to feel embarrassment for her incompetence, however.

He pushed her none too gently onto a pile of furs and followed her down, shoving a hand under her skirts. Alinor gasped, a shock running through her as his hand moved up her thigh and cupped her femininity. Something hard and long, like the root of a tree, was pressed bruisingly against her thigh.

She had known this would come. She had battled all day between the certainty that she must prepare herself for this and the certainty that she would be far better off if she could simply not think of it at all.

Fear seized her, but she closed her eyes and her mind to it, bracing herself. Abruptly, her stomach, which had demanded sustenance off and on throughout the day, once again voiced complaint.

When the man stilled, she opened her eyes to look up at him.

He was frowning. The hard root that had been pressing into her seemed to have vanished. He rolled off of her and lay staring up at the trees for some time.

Finally, he got up and moved away. Hesitantly, Alinor sat up as well, pushing her skirts down, studying him warily as he moved to the pack on his horse and withdrew something from it.

When he returned, he squatted down beside her and opened a leather pouch. Withdrawing something dark and withered looking from it, he tore it in half and handed a piece to her. She took it, looked it over and finally sniffed it. It appeared to be meat of some kind, dried to the consistency of leather. She wasn't sure what she was supposed to do with it until he put the piece he still held to his mouth, tore off a piece with his teeth and began chewing.

"Merci!" she said gratefully, and cautiously bit down on the piece she held. She discovered it didn't just have the appearance of leather. It also had the consistency. Struggling for several moments, she finally managed to pull off a small piece and began chewing. At first, it was about as flavorful as chewing on leather, but it was not an unpleasant taste and the longer she chewed the softer it became. Her stomach, stimulated by the possibility of appeasement at long last, began clamoring once more in delighted anticipation. Finally, she decided she'd chewed it sufficiently and tried to swallow. It took several, convulsive efforts, but she finally managed to get it down.

When she looked up at him, her eyes were watering with the effort. Wulfgar, she saw, had returned to the horse for a wine skin while she was working on the piece of dried meat. Without a word, he handed the skin to her. She thought she saw his lips twitch, but when she glanced at him, he was frowning and she decided she'd imagined it.

She had been almost as thirsty as she was hungry, and she took the skin eagerly, but she was not accustomed to drinking from a wine skin and discovered very quickly that there was a trick to it. Her first attempt resulted in a squirt of wine in her eye. Squeezing her stinging eye shut, she tried again. About half of the second squirt went up her nose, but she managed to get some of it in her mouth.

Wulfgar snorted, rose abruptly and strode toward his horse once more. She peered at him suspiciously for several moments after she'd wiped the wine from her nose, eye, chin and neck, but although his shoulders shook slightly, he didn't appear to be laughing at her. Dismissing it, she returned her attention to her feast.

It was easier to get the wine than to chew the dried meat. Moreover, she'd been very thirsty before she'd tried to chew up the meat and that had only made her more so. She focused primarily upon the wine, therefore, although, in truth, she had never had wine that tasted any worse. Her head began to swim before it occurred to her that she should pace herself more carefully.

Apparently, Wulfgar noticed she'd been imbibing rather too freely at about the same time that she realized it, for he took the skin from her. Shrugging, she returned her attention to her meat and took another bite. A sense of well being settled over her and she smiled at Wulfgar in a friendly way. He returned her smile with a suspicious glare. "Do you not speak French at all, Monsieur?" she asked him in her own language.

He merely stared at her.

After a moment, she sighed. It was going to make things very difficult if he couldn't speak her language, because she didn't know much of his at all. "You are like a grumpy bear," she muttered. His eyes narrowed at the comment, but she had turned her attention to her surroundings and didn't notice. "I wonder if we will stay here until Jean-Pierre pays the ransom?" she speculated out loud.

"No ransom!" Wulfgar said sharply, drawing her attention back to him.

Alinor looked at him in surprise. "If you have not taken me for ransom, then why?"

He said nothing and she decided he had not really understood as she'd hoped, but had merely recognized the word ransom. She searched her mind for some time, but discovered that she simply could not come up with any idea of how to frame the question in his own tongue. "Ransom, no?" she prodded.

He refused to be drawn into a discussion on the matter, however, and Alinor wasn't certain what to think of it. She wasn't particularly perturbed either. She thought about it several moments, wondering if it was the wine, and finally decided that there was some possibility that the wine had dulled her anxieties.

She wondered if the wine was responsible for the fact that Wulfgar didn't look nearly as threatening to her as she'd originally thought. In fact, quite the opposite. Now that she'd had a chance to look him over at close range, she saw that he was quite well favored. The sharp features that had seemed so unnerving when his face was shrouded by night, seemed, in truth, rather predatory, but they also made for a face that was quite fascinating. She thought he was probably not much, if any, older than Jean-Pierre. Certainly, he could be no more than thirty.

She sighed, wiped her hands on her gown and looked up at him expectantly. "I am ready, Monsieur. You may ravish me now."

Chapter Three

Wulfgar scowled at her. "You are drunk," he growled.

Alinor giggled, but sobered immediately at the look he gave her. "No, Monsieur!"

Bending, he grasped her by both her arms and pulled her to her feet. She stood a little uncertainly, swaying slightly, watching him curiously as he snatched the furs from the ground, rolled them up and moved to tie them to the rump of the horse.

His movements as he gathered the few personal objects strewn about were jerky with irritation.

"You do not want to ravish me?" she asked a little uncertainly after she'd watched him stalk angrily about the campsite for several moments.

He didn't so much as glance at her and she frowned, wondering if she'd used the right words. "I say thees wrong, yes?"

Having finished packing the horse, he strode toward her. Alinor watched him advance with a mixture of unease and anticipation. She was disconcerted when he merely grasped her arm and dragged her toward the beast. Placing his hands around her waist, he lifted her, settling her on the front of the saddle. The moment he released her, Alinor fell backwards. Fortunately, the ground broke her fall. It also knocked the breath out of her and she was still lying stunned on the ground when Wulfgar circled the horse and dragged her to her feet once more. Hiking her skirts to her waist, he sat her on the horse once more, straddling it this time, then placed her hands on the pommel. "Hold on," he said slowly, as if to a half wit, his teeth gritted in annoyance.

Alinor nodded, gripping the pommel tightly while he mounted. She glanced back at him when he'd settled himself. "There ees no time for ravishment now?"

He glared at her in tightlipped annoyance for several moments, then reached for the gag she still wore around her neck and pulled it up.

Alinor looked at him blankly for several moments before her own irritation surfaced. She pulled the gag down. "If you do not want me to speak, Monsieur, you need only say so. I do not like that nasty thing. It stinks."

Wulfgar tugged the gag over her mouth once more.

After glaring at him for several moments while he pointedly ignored her, she faced forward once more, sniffing to allow him to know that she thought he was very rude. Grasping her around the waist, he hauled her back against him and kicked the horse into motion.

Grateful for the support, Alinor didn't even put up a token resistance. She settled herself comfortably and looked around at the forest for a while, but there was nothing of any real interest to see and she found herself drowsing. It was nearing dusk, she saw when he shook her awake. Groggily, she sat up as he thrust her

193

away and dismounted. She reached for him as he turned to help her down and fell into his arms. It was when he set her feet on the ground and released her that she discovered her legs had lost much of their sensation. She managed to take a few uncertain steps, but when Wulfgar tossed the bundle of furs at her, it was all that was needed to finish her off. She staggered back several steps and sat, hard enough it brought tears to her eyes. When the pain subsided, she realized that she was expected to help set up camp. She crawled to her knees and then finally stood and looked around. Wulfgar stopped what he was doing long enough to point out a spot.

Alinor nodded, but the moment she took a step it was born in upon her that her legs were not merely numb from having ridden so many hours. Her inner thighs protested screamingly over the fact that she'd spent so many hours riding the animal astride. Unconsciously, she rubbed the protesting muscles as she lugged the furs over to the spot Wulfgar had pointed to and began spreading them out. When she'd finished, she studied the pallet for some moments and finally decided it would be more comfortable if she gathered enough leaves to put under it to give it a little padding. She'd gathered her second arm load when Wulfgar strode angrily toward her and knocked them from her arms. She stared at him openmouthed, wondering what she'd done to so thoroughly anger him, feeling her own anger surge forth as he began to scatter the leaves once more.

It occurred to her after watching him for some moments, however, that the other encampment had been so carefully concealed, the area around it left as undisturbed as possible, that he was expecting they would be tracked by Jean-Pierre. If Jean-Pierre had good trackers, no doubt they would still discover the encampments, but he was determined not to make their task easy.

She was still angry. If he had only told her that she was not allowed to do anything that might disturb the ground, she wouldn't have touched the leaves. After a moment, she stalked over to the furs and sat down, folding her arms over her chest and glaring at him while he attended the horse.

They'd stopped, she realized, near a tiny brook. She'd been too preoccupied to notice the trickle of water before—for it was little more than that and choked with leaves. Her interest caught as Wulfgar led the horse to the water and she got up and followed, squatting along the edge and pushing the floating leaves out of the way to scoop water into her hand. It was cold, numbing her fingers, but it tasted quite good and quenched her thirst.

When he'd allowed the horse to drink his fill, he led the animal from the stream and tethered it. He returned after a moment and stood staring down at her until, noticing, Alinor looked up at him questioningly. He pointed to the water. Alinor followed the direction of his pointing finger and then looked at him again. He couldn't, surely, mean what she thought he meant.

Glaring at her, he gave her a nudge toward the water with the toe of his boot.

Alinor scurried out of reach, certain now that the man was insane. It was cold and the water was colder still. She was well aware she was probably in need of a bath. Save for being thoroughly drenched when she'd come ashore she hadn't had an opportunity to do more than dab at herself with a handkerchief—but there was no way she was going to get into that freezing brook. "Non!" she said, shaking her head vigorously.

"Oui!"

She might have appreciated his usage of her language at any other time. She wasn't presently in the mood to, however. She held up her half frozen fingers. "Cold!"

His face hardened. He reached for her. Alinor shrieked, leapt to her feet and fled.

It was inevitable that he would catch her. Alinor had had no clear destination in mind and she was hampered by her stature, the gown tangling around her ankles, and the residual stiffness from days in the saddle. She had not gone far before he swooped down upon her, grasped her around the waist and hauled her back to the water. Wading in with her until he was in the middle, he released her. The brook was just deep enough to completely submerge her. It snatched her breath right out of her chest. She came up, struggling for air, swinging wildly. Stepping back to avoid her swing, Wulfgar lost his footing and hit the water so hard it covered Alinor in a fresh avalanche. Enraged, she dove for him. Straddling his middle, she grasped his hair and shoved his head under. He pried her fingers loose and bucked her off. When she came up again, he'd already gained his feet. Reaching down, he grasped her wrists and hauled her from the water.

Dropping her onto the mossy bank, he caught his breath and began to struggle out of his wet clothes. Wrapping her arms around her knees and hugging them to herself, Alinor watched him in teeth chattering resentment for several moments.

He ignored her, wringing the water from his tunic and spreading it over branches to dry. Removing his boots after a great struggle, he upended them. A small fish hit the ground. Alinor stared at it a long moment and snickered. In the next moment, however, he began to loosen the lacing on his breeches. Gasping, Alinor covered her face with her hands, listening to the rustle of soggy clothing as he calmly removed them, rung the water from them and moved across the small clearing to toss his breeches over the bushes beside his tunic. He was gone for some moments. When he returned, something soft plopped into her lap.

Alinor peeked through her fingers. It was a length of linen, damp already from his body but far dryer than the clothing she was wearing. Stiffly, she got to her feet, intent on heading for the brush to remove her own wet clothing. He caught her, held her until she ceased to resist and began to loosen the lacings down the back of her gown, his hands as impersonal as a maid's. She remained still, watching as he wrung the gown out and hung it up, wondering what his ultimate intentions were. He stripped her, layer by layer, hung each article to dry with care and then returned, took the linen from her and buffed her skin dry. When he was done, he scooped her into his arms and strode to the furs with her and, kneeling, crawled among them, covering the two of them from neck to foot, tucking her bare back against his chest.

Slowly, Alinor's shivering subsided and warmth began to seep into her. He shifted, pushing her to her back. When she would have covered her breasts with her hands, he grasped them, bearing down until her arms were manacled against the ground on either side of her head. Her heart leapt, and began to gallop away. Her breath caught in her throat. Slowly, he relaxed his grip on one wrist and slid his hand along her arm until he reached her breast, cupping the mound than trembled with her pounding heartbeat, massaging it.

Alinor stared down at his large, dark hand on her pale breast, torn between fear and fascination. Her mother had explained that it would be painful her first time, but less so if her husband took the time to help her to relax and ease his joining with her. She wasn't terribly clear on what it was that he must do to help ease the joining, but knew that she must relax and accept whatever he did or cause herself more pain.

It took an effort to remain perfectly still when it felt so very strange to have someone touch her in such a way. Her breath caught in her throat as he grazed the nipple with the pad of his thumb, rubbing it back and forth while her nipple tightened and reached out to him, almost like a sunflower following the path of the sun. When she looked up at him, she saw that he was studying her face, his eyes dark, heated.

Slowly, he lowered his head, closing his lips around her nipple. Startled, Alinor stiffened, but strangely exciting sensations began to move through her as he tugged gently at her nipple and then suckled it. She gasped as the warm heat of his mouth covered her. Fire seemed to flow outward, trickling along tiny pathways through her breast, spreading even to the breast he had not so much as touched until it throbbed and ached.

Alinor squeezed her eyes shut, following that trail in her mind with a mixture of curiosity and pleased surprise as it ebbed and flowed, washing along her ribs to her belly until it finally reached the core of her femininity, pooling there with growing warmth as if it had found a tidal basin to collect the molten fire.

She had not thought that anything could feel so good and yet so disturbing at once. She felt oddly, as if she'd drank too much wine—warm, lightheaded, breathless.

He was breathing heavily when he lifted his head, his face flushed, his eyes dark and gleaming. Holding her gaze, he released her breast and slipped his hand downward, over her belly, the rough pads of his finger tips causing her flesh to twitch reflexively. When his fingers tangled in the thatch of hair just above her nether lips, Alinor gasped, feeling her body tighten in anticipation.

He lowered his head once more, took the peak of her other breast into his mouth, sucking hard as his slipped his hand between her thighs, urging her to part them. Distracted, enthralled by the sensations rushing at her from both points, Alinor was barely aware of moving her legs to accommodate his hand. His finger explored the moist crevice of her femininity and discovered a tiny nub of flesh that seemed to focus all that she'd been feeling into one point.

She gripped his upper arms, digging her fingers into them, panting, wanting to pull away from that intrusive finger and move closer at the same time. Something was building inside of her, excitement, the certain knowledge of something else just beyond her reach. She felt, as in a dream, that she was struggling hard to reach it but could not race toward it. She could only fight to move forward inch by agonizing inch.

Releasing her breast, Wulfgar pushed her thighs wider, insinuating his knee between them.

When she opened her eyes, she saw that he was watching her once more. He moved over her, spreading her legs wider still, settling his hips between them. Something hard nudged the place where his fingers still teased her. She gasped, felt it pressing harder against her flesh. Abruptly, her flesh parted, and that hard, heated part of him breached the opening.

She panted, willing her body to adjust to the intrusion, fighting the tension of fear than began to creep through her, chasing the thrill of excitement further from her reach, but he continued to press into her, filling her, stretching her until she began to feel as if he would rip her apart, felt a welling of panic that he simply would not fit.

He paused, breathing raggedly, beads of sweat break

ing from his pores. Brushing the drying hair from her cheek, he lowered his head and began to tease her lips as he'd teased her nipples. Surprised, captivated by the gentle brush of his lips, by the warmth of his breath, she held still, allowed her mind to focus on the taste of him, the exquisitely pleasurable merging of their mouths. The flick of his tongue startled her, but it sent something hot and sweet rushing through her. She felt the muscles in her femininity tighten around his flesh, embracing his intrusion.

He groaned as if in agony, thrusting his tongue fully into her mouth, and the heat and taste of him were like wine, dizzying, disorienting.

She felt him gathering himself to thrust past her maiden head. With an effort, she parted her thighs wider, breathed deeply and suckled his tongue as he had suckled her breast.

He shuddered, thrust hard, breaching her maidenhead and burying himself so deeply inside of her she felt as if she had been mortally wounded. She could not contain the groan of pain when he possessed her fully, but she sensed that he was oblivious to it now, oblivious to anything but the drive to complete what he'd begun. He had lost all semblance of control and with it the gentleness that had gone before. Groaning, he began thrusting inside of her hard and fast, burying himself deeply, withdrawing only a little and thrusting forward once more in a mindless sort of frenzy that was both thrilling and frightening at once. Within minutes she sensed a gathering inside of him such as she'd felt before the pain, his body tensing all over in anticipation.

He threw his head back, releasing a long, low growl of agony or pleasure, or both, his body shuddering, pumping into her convulsively. Something hot spilled inside of her womb, and then he went perfectly still, collapsing on top of her as bonelessly as if he had passed out.

Alinor lay perfectly still, wondering if it was over, feeling chaotic emotions rush at her from no where. She felt the urge both to cuddle him tightly and to thrust him away.

She had missed something, and she felt that it was something momentous. Many minutes passed and she was beginning to think he truly had lost consciousness—might have thought him dead except for the harsh rasp of his breath and the thundering of his heart against her squashed breasts. Finally, he shoved himself upwards and rolled off of her.

Something uncomfortably sticky trickled between her thighs. She wiggled uncomfortably, wishing she could cleanse herself.

As if he read her mind, he thrust the furs aside, rose and moved away. When he returned, he held something white in his hands—the linen, she thought. Pushing the furs aside, and her efforts to thrust him away, he nudged her thighs apart and wiped the stickiness from her. Humiliated, she could do nothing but endure until he'd finished. When he sat back on his heels, he held the cloth up, examining it.

It was her pantaloons, covered now in her blood and his seed. He turned to look at her, his face an expression of triumph. Tossing the pantaloons onto the ground, he climbed into the furs once more and pulled her tightly against him despite her efforts to pull away. Finally, she desisted, knowing it to be a useless effort.

His arm tightened around her waist. "Sleep," he said gruffly. "We must leave in a few hours."

Alinor glanced at him in surprise, for he'd spoken French with no apparent effort at all.

Chapter Four

"Lord Wulfgar?" From the man's voice he sounded as if he suspected a wraith had appeared at his door.

"Aye. I have come for news."

The rough plank door was opened wider. Wulfgar's hand tightened on Alinor's arm and he tugged her into the faint light spilling through the doorway of the tiny cottage, pushing her before him as he ducked his head and entered.

Alinor blinked, dazzled momentarily by the light, though there was little enough of it. Her eyes felt as if they had been coated with sand, and the smoke that filled the room did not help a whit. Her eyes watered, and she blinked rapidly, trying to focus her eyes as she glanced briefly around the single room. When Wulfgar released his hold on her, she moved closer to the fire and sat on the floor near it, ignoring the stares of perhaps a dozen pairs of eyes.

In one corner was a cot. A woman lay in the middle of it, surrounded by small children. More slept on a pallet on the floor near the cot, squirming sleepily like a litter of pups, all staring with a mixture of fear, awe, and curiosity at the two strangers.

She heard the scrape of chairs against the hard packed earthen floor as Wulfgar and the man took a seat at a rickety wooden table near the only door the cottage boasted.

"The soldiers pass through every few days searching for the Norman's whore. He has torn the land apart searching for her. It is not safe for you here, my lord."

Wulfgar's face tightened with anger. "The Lady Alinor is not the Norman's whore. He will not live long enough to make her his whore," he said coldly.

The man paled. "Beg pardon, my lord."

Wulfgar studied him a moment longer and finally nodded. "Tell me what you have heard."

"Word came that the party sent to fetch the Norman's … lady had been set upon by a band of men and the woman taken. But when Lord John questioned them, the man who had been set to watch—the one you left tied to a tree—confessed that you were alone and that you had challenged Lord John to meet you in single combat. He put the man to the sword afterwards and placed a bounty upon your head. When they found the woman's clothes in the woods, torn and bloodied, we were told that you had slain the woman and fed her to the beasts of the wood.

They gave him the wolf pelt you left in the woman's tent. He knows it is you, my lord."

Wulfgar nodded in satisfaction, but then frowned. "I had thought he would answer my challenge before now."

The man looked at Wulfgar fearfully. "He calls you a low born outlaw, my lord, and says you are not worthy of his sword."

Wulfgar came up from the table with a roar that shook the walls of the mud and daub hut.

"Mercy, my lord! I have only told you the slander he has put about!"

Wulfgar turned and studied Alinor for a long moment through narrowed eyes and her heart clutched in her chest fearfully. "He will meet me," Wulfgar said through gritted teeth, "or I will slit his throat while he sleeps. One way or another, I will have my revenge."

Alinor rose nervously as he strode toward her, flinching involuntarily at the look on his face. He merely grasped her wrist and hauled her behind him as he quitted the cottage, however.

Grasping her skirts, Alinor lifted them out of her way as she struggled to keep up with the furious pace he set. Despite her best efforts, she stumbled several times, but he scarcely seemed to notice.

When they reached the place where he had tethered the horse, he grasped her around the waist and lifted her wordlessly onto the saddle, mounted behind her and kicked the horse into a gallop. He did not touch her, did not hold her closely as he always had before, and Alinor clutched the pommel in a death grip, expecting to hit the ground and be trampled by the great horse's hooves at any moment. She had no idea how long he pressed the horse, but finally, when she thought that she could not hold on another moment, he slowed the foam flecked horse to a less breakneck pace. They halted at last when they emerged from the forest on a rise. In the distance, Alinor could see a huge manor house behind the partially constructed stone wall of a fortress.

Dragging her from the horse, Wulfgar led her to a tree at the edge of the woods and tethered the horse.

Pulling a length of leather rope from the saddle bag, he pushed her against a tree nearby and began to bind her tightly to it.

Alinor found that she was more terrified than she had been at any time since Wulfgar had stolen her from her tent a sen'night earlier, so frightened she couldn't think of anything to say. She didn't know which frightened her the most, the fact that it appeared that he was leaving her for Jean-Pierre, or the certainty that he was going to meet his death.

"Why?" she finally managed to ask him when he had finished tying her and it appeared that he would leave without saying a word to her.

He paused and turned to look at her. "If I do not return before dawn, they will find you."

She supposed it was meant as a reassurance, but it was hardly that. She'd heard what the man had said and although she had not been able to understand all of it, she had understood enough to know that Jean-Pierre had said that she was dead. Somehow, she felt that he would not be happy to find that she lived still—dishonored by his enemy, perhaps even now carrying the child of his hated enemy. "Jean-Pierre will kill you if you go there," she said quickly.

His eyes narrowed. "Mayhap ... and mayhap I will kill him."

"But ... why, monsieur? I don't understand why you must do this."

He stepped toward her, leaning close, he teeth clenched in fury. "Because your precious Jean-Pierre has crushed all that I held dear. I will avenge their deaths—or die."

Alinor swallowed with an effort. "Your wife?" she said faintly as understanding dawned at last.

Something flickered in his eyes. "For my beloved Freda," he gritted out and, turning, strode away. Pull ing his sword and pack from the horse, he moved swiftly into the darkness, disappearing from sight within moments.

The urge to weep swelled in Alinor's chest as she strained to catch a glimpse of movement, feeling, somehow, that as long as she could see him he would come to no harm. She had no idea whether the urge to cry was for herself, for those who had perished in the battle for England, or for Wulfgar.

What he had told her and what she had overheard in the cottage explained much, and yet it left almost as many questions unanswered.

She had told herself from the first that she could not allow herself to believe that she was anything more than a pawn in some struggle between Wulfgar and his enemy, the man she had been sent to wed. Wulfgar had been so gentle in taking her, though, that she had nursed a secret hope that whatever his intentions had been originally, he had come to see her as more than that.

He had not touched her since. She had been relieved at first, for she had been so tender that she had dreaded coupling with him again, but many days had passed since that time and he had shown no interest in her at all. It had worried at the back of her mind.

She should have known his lack of any interest in coupling with her was indication enough that she was less than nothing to him. If she had, in truth, been no more than a common whore, he would have used her for his needs. It was painfully obvious that he could not even stomach her.

She should be relieved that her ordeal was nearing an end. She was weary to the point of dropping where she stood. She had scarcely been off the back of a horse for more than a few hours in weeks now, even sleeping in the saddle when she reached a point of exhaustion where she could no longer stay awake.

Wulfgar had kept them on the move and had not once built a campfire—knowing they were being hunted—and thus she had had nothing to eat since she was captured but dried meat, moldy cheese, sour wine and bread so hardened that it crumbled to dust in her mouth. The dunking in the brook had been her only bath until they had come upon another some three days later. She was dirty, ragged, her hair hanging in rat tails, and, even to her, she looked almost skeletal.

Her gown scarcely touched her now. It was small wonder he could not stomach bedding her.

A tiny spark of anger surged through her, supplanting the self-pity she had been enjoying wallowing in. It was a woman's lot in life, she knew, always to be pawns in the games that men played, but it was grossly unfair. She had done nothing! She didn't deserve to be punished for something someone else had done!

She could not escape it, however. Just as Wulfgar had used her to punish Jean-Pierre for the death of his beloved wife, Jean-Pierre was bound to punish her for living after Wulfgar had soiled her, for not having fought to the death to defend her honor.

In truth, she had not fought at all. She could be grateful that Jean-Pierre could not know that. She was amazed now at the naiveté that had led her into thinking that yielding to Wulfgar would be her secret revenge upon Jean-Pierre for taking her to wife when she wanted none of him—that it might even persuade him to denounce her and send her home. He would take her anyway, for it was her dowry that was of interest to him and her dowry could only be had if he wed her. Most likely, she would meet a tragic end once her dowry was his—might have in any event, but most certainly he would not want to keep her now.

The worst of it was that she very much feared hell

would be hers before he granted her release.

* * * *

Despite what he had told the cotter, Wilhem, Wulfgar was of no mind to allow Jean-Pierre to die quickly. He had challenged the worm to mortal combat, and he would have it before he was done.

A prickle of uneasiness scratched at the back of his mind, however, as he swiftly and silently made his way to the keep, moving like a shadow among shadows as he crept closer and closer to his goal. He had still been caught in the grips of fury when he had left Alinor tied to the tree, unable to think much beyond the need to strike out at Jean-Pierre and to allow him to know that he could not sleep easily so long as Wulfgar lived.

He should not have left her so vulnerable. No doubt, if he were slain tonight, Jean-Pierre would find her come daylight as he had intended—but she was exposed, easy prey for any beast brazen enough to hunt so near the keep.

He almost turned back when that thought occurred to him, but he had already slipped past the guard. It could take little more time to see his deed through and return than to simply turn back and leave it undone.

Dismissing her from his mind, he focused on his objective. There were two guards stationed near the rear entrance of the manor. Wulfgar studied them for some moments, formulating a plan. Finally, he moved behind the small shed at the rear of the manor, where the cooking was done, looked around until he found a small stone, and scraped it against the side of the building.

"What was that?" one of the guards said in a harsh whisper.

"Nothing—some stray animal most likely."

"We should check it out."

"You check it out. Jean-Pierre will have both our heads if we leave this door unguarded."

For several moments Wulfgar wondered if his ruse had worked at all. He was on the point of trying again when he heard one of the men stride purposefully across the yard. He moved down the wall and rounded the corner, placing his back against the wall as he waited, listening intently as the guard crept along the wall, pausing every few steps to listen. As the man rounded the back corner, Wulfgar slipped a meaty arm around the man's shoulders, covering his mouth, and sliced his throat. Blood gushed in a fountain of deep black. The man went limp. Easing him to the ground, Wulfgar left the dead man sitting propped against the shed wall and slipped around the other side.

The other guard had left his post by the time Wulfgar rounded the end of the shed. Uttering a mental curse, Wulfgar moved quickly down the building, hesitated at the corner and listened to the sound of gravel crunching under the man's feet as he walked half the length of the building and stopped. After a moment, he whirled and headed back toward his post. Wulfgar caught him as he had the first guard, dispatching him, as well, leaving him propped in a sitting position as he had the first.

He had already turned away when a thought occurred to him. He turned to look at the body speculatively a moment and then, with a wolfish grin, lobbed the man's head off.

He moved swiftly then, through the door, up the stairs and into the master's chambers. Laying the wolf pelt he'd brought with him at the foot of the bed, he sat the guard's head upon it, turning it so that the guard's vacant stare could greet Jean-Pierre when he woke.

He had covered less than half the distance from the keep to the forest when the alarm sounded. He abandoned stealth then and sprinted for the woods. He was winded by the time he reached the concealment. He hadn't been spotted, despite the fact that he'd made no attempt to keep to the shadows. He had headed straight for his goal, but he knew that would matter little. They would be rushing to saddle horses even now to give chase.

When he reached the rise, his gaze went at once to Alinor. Gritting his teeth, he turned away and ran to his horse, sheathing his sword, snatching the reins free and leaping into the saddle.

She had served her purpose. She would be better off if he left her. She would slow him. If he left her, the men searching for him even now were bound to find her and take her to safety.

Against all logic he found he couldn't abandon her. Whirling the horse, he returned for her, drawing his sword even as he leapt from his saddle, hitting the ground at a run. She cringed as he swung the blade, falling to her knees as he sliced the bindings cleanly. Grasping her around the waist, he half carried, half dragged her back to the dancing horse, shoved his sword into its sheath once more and tossed her up onto the saddle. She grabbed frantically for purchase as he mounted. Slipping an arm around her waist, he held her tightly against him as he turned the horse into the woods.

He had no hope of outrunning the party that would be coming for him. Light as she was, Alinor was nevertheless an added burden and would slow him dangerously if he headed for the open road.

He knew the woods as few others could claim, however, for he'd hunted them from the time he had learned to use his first bow. He would lose them and then he would take Alinor to a place of safety. If the challenge he had left upon Jean-Pierre's bed did not goad him to meet him in honest combat—He would torment the man until he had no choice but to meet Wulfgar or to admit his cowardice.

Chapter Five

Alinor did not know what to think of the fact that Wulfgar had not abandoned her as she had fully expected he would. Truthfully, it didn't even occur to her to wonder at first, for she'd been so certain when he came at her with his sword that he would slay her that she had not been able to think of anything for quite some time afterward. By the time it did cross her mind, she was far too weary from the arduous pace he set to be in any state to consider it with any logic.

He headed north when he was satisfied he'd thrown off pursuit. After a time—Alinor had no idea of how many days had passed—they began to move westward. They came at last to a homestead in a green valley, but Alinor had passed her limit long since. When Wulfgar dismounted, she simply fell off, unconscious.

Before Alinor was even fully conscious, she sensed blissful comfort; softness beneath her; the scent of freshly aired linens; warmth; stillness. It felt so good

211

that she was reluctant to give it up. She merely stretched, winced when her muscles complained and snuggled deeper. She would've drifted away again, but her movements seemed to set off a chain reaction of movements. Someone nearby gasped—a woman— then spoke to her in a language she didn't recognize. She opened her eyes to peer around cautiously just as a door banged closed.

She stared at the door for several moments and finally allowed her gaze to wander from the door to the room around her, striving for a sense of recognition. Alarm touched her when she neither recognized the room where she found herself, nor could track any memory of having gotten where she was.

With an effort, she pushed herself upright and explored the room further, but it didn't become more familiar. Vaguely, she began to recall little snatches of things, however—of being pushed and pulled as someone removed her clothing, of being bathed—fed. She must have been ill, she decided, but she couldn't remember feeling ill. She couldn't remember anything except being tired to the point that she was beyond caring whether or not she fell off the horse.

A heavy tread outside the door distracted her at that moment—the tread of a man, coming closer.

She gasped as the door was abruptly thrown open, staring blankly, and with more than a little alarm at the strange man who filled the doorway. Slowly, recognition dawned.

"Wulfgar?"

He looked her over searchingly. "You are well?"

"I was sick?" Alinor countered in surprise.

He frowned, nodded, slowly closing the door behind him.

Alinor thought it over, but found she still couldn't remember being ill. "Where are we?"

"Wales—the home of my mother's brother."

That explained the strange speech. It didn't explain that Wulfgar had suddenly developed the ability to speak to her in French. His accent was difficult, his speech halting, as one who had to think many moments to find the words—or one who was mentally translating from his own language into another—but plainly he had some knowledge of her native tongue.

He had seen her as his enemy and had refused to reveal his knowledge before. Did that mean he no longer saw her as his enemy? Or simply that he had brought her to a place where he felt he wouldn't have to watch his back?

It seemed absurd that he could have seen her as any threat at all. She would not have been a match, or any threat, to a much smaller man that Wulfgar … and there were few men of his stature, or breadth or strength in all of France, or even in England that she had seen. She was further disadvantaged now, huddled in someone else's nightclothes, so weak it was an effort even to hold herself upright, among strangers in a strange land. The brief intimacy they had shared seemed to belong to another lifetime—someone else.

"What happened?" she finally asked, as much because she had little memory of it as because she felt the need to distract him from looking at her so piercingly.

His face hardened immediately with anger. "I issued a challenge to your betrothed that he can not ignore unless he wishes to be known as a coward."

It was said accusingly, thrown down at her as a challenge—as if she were responsible for Jean-Pierre's honor, or lack of it! She felt color wash into her cheeks. "It was not by my choice that I was betrothed to him," she said angrily. "I wanted none of him!"

His eyes narrowed. "And yet I saw no sign that you were held captive."

Alinor gaped at him, but she felt her anger rise a notch higher. "I suppose you think I should have killed myself rather than yield to my parents' wishes?"

"Freda took her own life because he had sullied her!" he said harshly.

"She took her life because she loved you and feared you would hate her otherwise!" Alinor snapped angrily. She was almost immediately sorry she'd allowed her tongue to get away from her, for she saw that she had struck bone deep with her sharp retort.

He moved away from the door, pacing. "You know nothing of it—you did not know Freda," he snarled, but his disclaimer lacked conviction.

"I know the way of the world. I know what it is to be a woman."

He snorted. "You are a child yet!"

If he had slapped her, it could not have stung more. All the doubts she'd so carefully submerged and dismissed swarmed into her mind and she voiced the first thought that surfaced without considering whether there was truth to it or not, or how it might be received. "I am woman enough to carry your child!" she said tightly.

His gaze snapped immediately to her belly, the color draining from his face. He looked away. "If that was truth … it resides there no longer."

Alinor was still grappling with the realization that she must, subconsciously, have known that she was carrying his child, for she had not had her menses since Wulfgar had taken her and her courses were far too late for it to be anything else. It took her several moments to assimilate what he had said and for the implications to sink in. Behind that a lump of sadness swelled in her chest. It was unreasonable to feel grief

214

for what she had lost when she had never even acknowl-edged the child that grew in her belly—when she was unwed and the child fathered by the man who had taken her prisoner—However unreasonable, though, she couldn't deny that she felt a terrible sense of loss. She looked down at her hands. "God in his infinite mercy …."

"Your god has no mercy," Wulfgar snapped harshly.

Alinor glanced up at him in shock. She was of no mind to argue religion with him, however, particularly when she could see, from his own words, that he was an unbeliever. Her own belief, though she would never have admitted it for fear of damnation, was not as strong as it should have been, which hardly qualified her to take a position as defender of the faith.

Unfortunately, she could think of no retort at all. Hugging her knees to herself, she studied her toes, which just peeked from beneath the voluminous gown she wore. "What will you do now?"

He did not answer for so long that she finally looked up at him.

"Jean-Pierre has accepted my challenge—at last. I await word of when and where he will meet me."

Alinor felt as if a hand had squeezed her heart. "He can not be trusted," she said a little breathlessly.

"I am well aware of that!" Wulfgar snarled.

"Nay! You think because he has accepted the chal-lenge that he will fight you fairly. He will not! If you go, you will be slain!"

Wulfgar's eyed narrowed. "I am accounted a good man with a sword," he said stiffly.

Alinor came up on her knees. "Good enough to dis-patch a dozen men or more!" she exclaimed. "He will not meet you in single combat! He will lay a trap for you and they will all fall upon you if you meet him! If they capture you alive he will have you tortured until

215

you will beg for death! Can you not be content with the victory you have taken?"

"He took all from me! ALL! I will not be content until I have deprived him of breath!" Wulfgar growled angrily.

"You can not get your beloved Freda back! If you pursue this, you can only join her!"

"So be it! At least I will not have to live with the knowledge that I left her to his tender mercies!" he snarled, pacing the room like a caged beast.

A mixture of emotions washed through her as she watched him; sympathy for his pain and guilt that he'd failed the woman he cared so much for; envy that the woman had held his heart; and anger, too, that he seemed to account her of no worth. She knew she was no great beauty, but neither was she ugly or disfigured and her dowry had made her a prize in her own land that many men had considered worth pursuing.

The thought of her dowry prompted another thought and, typically, she spoke impulsively. "You have another means of revenge if you would but look upon it!"

He stopped abruptly, turning to look at her in surprise. She blushed, but she was not timid. The thought would not have occurred to her if her heart had not voiced it. "I am no dowerless bride! I bring an estate of some note—in a fertile valley that produces well and supports a goodly number of livestock. It is not of great wealth, but 'tis certainly equal to what you …uh … what was taken."

Wulfgar scowled at her. "I am no landless fortune seeker!"

"You took that which was meant for my husband and none other! You are honor bound to right the wrong you have done me! For I have not offended thee and it was wrong to punish me for something of which I had no knowledge of or hand in!"

His look of affront vanished. For several moments, he looked at her with a mixture of discomfort and surprise. Finally, all gave way to a hint of humor. "You are petitioning for my hand?"

Alinor cringed inwardly. Put like that it made her sound brazen indeed. "I merely point out," she said stiffly, "that there would be justice for all concerned if you … if I …." Mortification overcame her and she found she could not continue.

He looked her over as if he were sizing up a mare brought round for him to consider for purchase. She misliked the look, well aware that she must look far from her best. He said nothing, however. After a few moments, he moved to the hearth. A small piece of wood had burned in half and rolled beyond the reach of the flames and he nudged it back with the toe of his boot.

Alinor studied him for several moments, angry, inexplicably hurt. She didn't know why it distressed her so much to think of him dying to defend another woman's honor—or that he so obviously did not want to consider her as a wife. She had thought, when he had come back for her—What had she thought? Perhaps he was right. Perhaps she was still a silly, heedless child—because she had thought she must mean something more to him than just the means to an end.

It had been simple minded to believe, just because he had not brutalized her—because he had been sweet and gentle—that it had meant something to him when he had coupled with her, that she had meant something to him. She should have known that it was merely his way—or, perhaps, he had thought that would be a revenge in itself? To treat her gently so that she could only compare her husband unfavorably when Jean-

217

Pierre took her into the marriage bed?

"Why did you come back for me?" she asked quietly.

He glanced at her sharply, his face hard, unyielding.

Because he was not done with her, she realized.

Alinor's chest tightened with disappointment. "Go then!" she said angrily, flopping back on the bed and turning away from him. "Avenge your precious Freda by allowing Jean-Pierre to lift your head from your shoulders! You are a pig headed man and —I do not care!"

She heard him stride across the room. Expecting to hear the door slam as he left, she was startled when she looked up to see him standing beside the bed, looking down at her speculatively. "You have been at great pains to convince me to forswear my vow. What is it you hope to gain, I wonder? Was all of this to protect him?"

Alinor gaped at him, but sat up to face him angrily. "You accuse me of deceit?"

"For whom 'do you not care'? Me? Or your precious Jean-Pierre?" he growled, catching her upper arms in a bruising grip and dragging her to him.

Alinor was still gaping at him in dismay when his mouth came down to cover hers in an angry, possessive kiss that threw her into instant turmoil.

CONQUERED

Chapter Six

Shamefully, her body reacted with gladness and pleasure to his touch, though her mind screamed that it
was for punishment only, that he meant to wound, not
caress—and still a moan of pleasure escaped her. She
clutched his tunic as weakness washed through her,
parting her lips even as his mouth opened over hers,
welcoming his plundering caress as he explored her
mouth thoroughly, aggressively with his tongue. His
taste and scent washed through her in a pleasurable tide
that laid waste to the last bastions of her pride, sending heat and expectancy pounding through her body,
making her femininity feel hot and achy for his possession. She could not think at all beyond the thrill
that raced through her veins, the breathless anticipation that invaded her.

He broke the kiss almost before he'd begun, thrusting her away from him as roughly as he'd pulled her to
him. Still clutching his tunic for support, Alinor opened
her eyes with an effort, keeping her expression care

fully neutral as she looked up at him, but she could not steady her thundering heartbeat. She could not seem to catch her breath. She wanted him. She wanted him to show her what he'd given her only a taste of before.

Grasping her hands, he pulled them free, his expression hard, unyielding, though his gaze was hot, tumultuous. For several moments he seemed to wage battle within himself. In the next, he pushed her down onto the pillows and followed her, crushing her beneath his weight as he thrust a hand roughly down the neck of her gown, squeezing her breast almost painfully. With his other hand, he jerked her gown up to her waist. Alinor gasped, arching her back as he covered the peak of one breast with the hot moisture of his mouth, flicking her nipple with tongue. The muscles in her belly clenched as his other hand skimmed it, then cupped the mound of her femininity. She drew her knee up to allow easier access, begging for his touch. When he slipped on finger through the petals of flesh of her femininity, she was wet for him. Gasping at the bolt of pleasure that went through her as he pushed his finger inside of her, she grasped his shoulders, digging her fingers into his flesh.

Her reaction seemed to catch him off guard. He lifted his head, hesitated for a fraction of a second and then it was as if a dam broke upon his restraint. His mouth and hands were everywhere at once, stroking her, suckling, teasing, tasting. On a mindless tide of exquisite sensation, Alinor returned each caress with one of her own, tearing at the lacing of his tunic until she could feel the hard flesh of his chest against her cheek, taste the saltiness and feel the smoothness of his skin on her tongue.

He growled, low in his chest as she nipped at him with her teeth, pulled away long enough to snatch his tunic off over his head and then tossed it aside and descended upon her again, closing his mouth over hers. Alinor arched up to meet him, brushing her breasts against his chest, relishing the sensation of bare skin against bare skin, so caught up in the feel of his body on hers and his tongue as it stroked and caressed her own that she was barely aware of her restless movements against him. When he withdrew his tongue to break the kiss, she followed him, dancing her tongue along his, tasting him, learning his mouth as he had hers, exploring his body with her hands.

A groan rumbled from his throat and he pushed her thighs apart, insinuating one knee between them and then the other until he was nestled between her thighs. Alinor arched her hips, rubbing her femininity against the hard bulge in his breeches when he removed his hand, kneading that tiny bud of flesh hidden in the petals of her femininity that so desired contact with him that she could think of nothing beyond the escalating throbs of pleasure emanating from it with each thrust of her hips.

She was gasping for breath when he broke the kiss at last, near to sobbing with need, helping and hindering at once as he struggled with the lacings of his breeches and she fought to grasp his heated flesh in her hand. When he freed his cock at last from his breeches, she arched her hips, grinding her femininity against its length, desperate to feel him inside of her.

He ground his teeth, shaking with the effort to control himself as he grasped his cock in one hand and finally aligned it with her body, nudging, thrusting, then finally parting her flesh, sinking slowly through the passage that contracted around his distended flesh, grasping him tightly and impeding his progress.

Digging her fingers into his shoulders, she rocked her hips upward to meet his downward thrust, moaning dizzily as she felt him sink to her core and slowly with draw until only the rounded head of his cock remained inside her. Pleasurable tremors began inside her belly with his full possession, building in intensity each time he withdrew and thrust again, sinking deeply inside her.

She felt a growing tension inside of her, knew her body was struggling to reach a threshold of sensation. Focusing every part of her being on reaching that un-defined goal, she moved with him, countered each ca-ressing stroke of his cock along the exquisitely sensi-tive recesses of her body ... and still it eluded her, re-mained just beyond her grasp as she struggled toward it, digging her heels into the mattress to meet each jarring plunge of his cock. She felt it within her reach when he stiffened, went still for several heartbeats and then began to thrust hard and fast. A thrill went through her, the knowledge that he had found pleasure in her body as she had his and that quiver of excitement sent her over the edge onto a plane of such wondrous rap-ture she cried out, unable to hold it inside of her, float-ing downward finally into a near oblivion of supreme, boneless bliss.

Wulfgar lay limply upon her for many moments, his breath harsh. Finally, he gathered himself and moved away, sitting on the edge of the bed for some time. Slowly, as she stared at his back, Alinor's contentment ebbed and a sense of foreboding replaced it.

He seemed so aloof, as if he was determined to dis-tance himself from her both emotionally as well as physically.

Finally, without a word, he rose and adjusted his clothing, donned his tunic once more, tightening the lacings in sharp, jerky motions that told her his anger had not completely abated. Not once did he so much as glance in her direction and Alinor felt a resurgence of her own anger, and guilt. It had been a mistake, she realized now, to give herself with such abandon. He could only think the worst of her. It made no difference at all that she had been a maiden when he had taken her. He must think she had the heart and soul of a whore to have so thoroughly enjoyed their coupling.

Shivering as the chill of the room skated across her sweat dampened skin, she pulled the covers up and turned away from him as she saw him turn to leave. He paused for many moments at the door, studying her, she sensed, and finally left.

When he had gone, she lay for many minutes fighting the urge to weep, trying to understand how something that had felt so wonderful—something she knew they had shared, could have ended so coldly.

She had had little enough experience in the arts of flirtation and courtship. They were far from court, where such things were practiced almost to an art form, and she had only been to court once before in her life. There had been no true courtship—in fact very little conversation—between her and the men who had petitioned her father for her hand. Perhaps, if her father had not settled upon Jean-Pierre, she would have had the opportunity to begin to understand the workings of a man's mind better, but he had and she had been very glad that she had not had to endure much of Jean-Pierre's brand of courtship.

In truth, until she had met Wulfgar, it had never occurred to her to have an interest in trying to win the attention or admiration of a man at all. She had known she would have no choice in the selection of a husband and had not met one who interested her more than another. Now that it mattered, she had no idea of what she might have done wrong.

He had been angry about Jean-Pierre. She understood that much, and also that he thought—must think—that she was somehow trying to dupe him—toying with him, perhaps? She couldn't quite see, however, what he thought she had to gain by it beyond trying to protect herself.

Mayhap that was it? He realized that she had been careful, most of the time anyway, not to arouse his wrath? In the beginning she had only thought that if she was too much trouble, he might begin to wonder if she was really worth ransoming—might decide to simply unburden himself. She had had no clear plan, however. She had only wanted to survive, had hoped that she would not be returned too swiftly to Jean-Pierre.

It occurred to her after a while to wonder if, perhaps, he was angry because he had not wanted to desire her and he did. She examined that thought for some time, trying to decide whether it was merely wishful thinking, or if it had merit.

Perhaps he thought of it as some sort of betrayal of the woman he had loved?

That did not fit, however, unless he cared for her, or thought he might come to care for her. Men eased themselves on any female handy. She knew that much at least, for she had heard the maids complain of it endlessly—sometimes angrily. He would not feel that he was betraying Freda if he were merely easing his needs upon her.

A seed of hope sprang from that thought, one she was almost afraid to feed, but it occurred to her finally that she could not quell it once it sprang into her mind. If there was any chance at all that he thought coupling with her might lead to a growing fondness, then it was certainly worth the effort of enticing him into her bed. If he became fond of her, perhaps he would decide her suggestion had merit and would wed her and take her home!

She discovered the following day, however, that he had deprived her of any opportunity of putting her plan

224

into motion, for, by the time she had nerved herself to ask for him of the maids, he had already gone to meet Jean-Pierre.

* * * *

Wulfgar found as he rode west and south that he could not dismiss Alinor's remarks from his mind. He hated Jean-Pierre with a rage that had blinded him to anything beyond the need for revenge. In all the time that he had plotted his revenge he was well aware that he could not so much as conjure the man's name in his mind and still think clearly. He knew nothing at all about his enemy. In truth, he had not made an effort to learn him as a man, only to follow his movements, looking, always, for the perfect opportunity to exact his revenge.

He could not bring Freda back or ease her suffering. He could not regain the lands the new king had settled upon his man, Jean-Pierre. He could only plot to give Jean-Pierre a taste of the suffering he, himself, had endured before he ended his life.

He could not fathom why it was that it had not occurred to him that he could not make Jean-Pierre suffer over the loss of his bride unless Jean-Pierre loved Alinor as he had loved Freda. A love match was a rare thing among the upper class. He had not expected that his own would be such, but he had been smitten the moment he had set eyes upon his future wife, had barely been able to contain himself until the knot was firmly tied. They had not even been wed a se'nnight when he had been called to meet the Norman invasion. He had not seen her alive again.

When he had learned that the Norman had sent for his betrothed, he had not been able to see beyond the fact that it so closely mirrored his own situation that it was as if the gods had handed him his means of revenge. Perhaps that was why had had looked no further?

He did not trust the Norman female. He could think of no reason why he should and many why he should not. He had been both surprised and relieved when he had found that she gave him no trouble at all, either when he took her, or later when he had had to stay on the move to stay ahead of Jean-Pierre. At first he had thought she was just too frightened to try anything. Finally, he had decided that it was simply her manner of ensuring her survival—to the point that she almost had not survived at all. He hadn't realized until he had reached his uncle's home that he had pushed her so far beyond her endurance that she was nigh death. If they had not arrived when they had, she most likely would have died, for she had slept straight through three days not even rousing to full consciousness when the maids had shaken her to force food and water down her.

He frowned at that thought, wondering if it was possible he had gotten her with child—he knew it was possible, but was it likely? There had been dried blood on her clothing when the maids removed them. He had assumed it was from her monthly cycle, or perhaps even from breaching her maidenhead—surely if she had miscarried there would have been more blood?

He shook the thought. Either way, it made no difference now—except that it heaped more guilt upon his head when he was already carrying so much it felt like a great boulder upon his shoulders. It made very little difference that he had not intended to cause her harm. He had done so, and possibly killed his own child in the process.

He tried to shrug it off. He had lived with so much guilt for so long that it was like a throbbing tooth— never far from his mind, but he had no choice but to gone on with his life, hoping he would eventually find something he could do that would bring surcease from the pain.

Which brought him back to the question of whether or not he could trust the word of a known enemy. Finally, he decided that it could do no harm to use caution and reconnoiter the area before he went to meet Jean-Pierre.

Chapter Seven

She had been allowed the freedom of the manor house and the immediate area around it, but Alinor had been left in no doubt that she was a prisoner, for she was always under watch. They had not been kindly or friendly, but then neither had they been abusive.

None spoke to her. She had no idea whether it was simply because they did not know her language or if it was a precaution because she was a prisoner. She listened carefully to everything that they said, however, and managed to pick up a word here and there, though she could not be completely certain of the meaning.

The day Wulfgar had left, an old crone had come into her room with several maids, who had proceeded to hold her down so that the horrible old crone could poke and probe at her. At first, she had been so mortified she had not been able even to imagine what reason might lie behind it, but it had dawned upon her finally that the old woman was undoubtedly a midwife, sent to verify her lie.

Wulfgar had been gone a week and half of another before a rider was spotted, and Alinor had spent the better part of a week wondering what was to become of her, certain that Wulfgar would not return at all. When a guard came to report sighting a rider, however, everyone began to gather in the yard to watch his approach. Alinor was not sure what the messenger had related until that moment, but the gathering was enough in itself to alert her to the fact that someone was approaching.

She recognized him the moment he came into view and her heart leapt in her throat—She was relieved, she told herself, that he had come back because, surely now, she would find out what was to become of her.

He sat stiffly in the saddle, as if he was holding himself erect with an effort. Noticing, Alinor began to move toward him. Someone—one of the maids set to watch her—caught her arm, preventing her unconscious urge to go to him. She turned to the woman. "He is wounded."

The woman merely looked at her blankly.

Alinor turned to look at Wulfgar again just as he swayed in the saddle.

"He is hurt!" she repeated angrily, jerking her arm free and running toward Wulfgar even as he began to slide off his horse. She caught him, but he was far too heavy for her even if he had not been barely conscious and she succeeded only in breaking his fall with her body. She hit the ground so hard she was too stunned to move—wondering for several moments if the horse had fallen upon her as well as Wulfgar. Before she could recover sufficiently to check him for signs of life, they were surrounded and Wulfgar lifted up and carried away. The maid who had tried to restrain Alinor, seized her wrist, yanked her to her feet and led her back to the manor.

She was not allowed to accompany Wulfgar. Instead, in spite of all she could do to fight her way free, she was dragged to the room she had occupied since her arrival and locked in. She beat on the door for a while, demanding to be allowed to see him, but finally had to accept that they would continue to ignore her.

Days passed in an agony of worry. Alinor paced the room like a caged animal, going to the door whenever she heard footsteps and pressing her ear to it to see if she could hear anything that might give her a clue as to whether or not Wulfgar still lived. Near the end of the fourth day Alinor's guard unlocked the door and summoned her.

Alinor looked the woman over doubtfully, not at all certain she wished to know what the woman had in mind. If she had retained any doubt of it before, however, she was quickly disabused of the notion that what she wanted was of any consequence at all. The maid simply marched across the room, seized her by one wrist and dragged her from the room. Leading her down the hallway to another room, she opened the door and shoved Alinor inside.

Alinor stared at the door in consternation for several moments after it was slammed behind her before she turned to survey the room. It was another bed chamber, she realized immediately, and although it was still full light outside, the shutters had been closed and lit candles surrounded the bed.

A priest stood beside the bed, examining her through narrowed, condemning eyes.

Alinor scarcely noticed him, however, for her gaze had been drawn to the figure in the bed.

He was so pale and drawn as to be almost unrecognizable, and his condition, the priest and the candles clicked together almost instantaneously and her mind shouted 'last rites'. She clapped a hand to her mouth to stifle a gasp of horror, felt as she had the day Wulfgar had fallen upon her, as if she had been body slammed against an immovable object and all the air crushed from her lungs. She couldn't move. For several moments, she felt like she was going to faint and fall into a dead heap on the floor.

She noticed finally that Wulfgar was watching her. He lifted a hand, held it out to her. His image swam before her eyes as tears flooded them. She blinked, trying to banish them, trying desperately to summon a smile, but it was a ghoulish imitation of a smile at best and fell flat almost at once.

She wanted to go to him, but she could not seem to command her legs to move until his hand dropped tiredly to the mattress. She forced herself to take a step and then another, moving stiffly, with tremendous effort. When she finally reached the side of the bed, she sank weakly to her knees, grasping his hand in both of her own and bringing it to her cheek. She thought she wouldn't be able to speak at all, but from no where the angry, accusing words spilled forth. "You have satisfied your honor? Avenged your beloved Freda? Look was has come of this mad scheme of yours!"

She turned to glare at the priest. "Go away, you! He does not need you! He will be well and strong again!"

Wulfgar made a coughing sound and her head whipped around. He was frowning, holding his chest with one hand. Her heart seemed to stand still as she watched his struggle. Finally, it subsided and he grinned at her. "I will be well."

Alinor burst into tears. It was only by an effort that she refrained from throwing herself upon his chest, but she feared she would cause him pain.

"This is the woman you are to wed?"

Alinor broke off mid-wail. "What?"

"You have fornicated with this man and conceived a child?"

Alinor looked at him as if he'd lost his mind. It hardly seemed the time to start chastising her for her transgressions, and, in any case, even if she had conceived, that was no longer the case.

"I raped her," Wulfgar growled. "I have confessed as much. Do what you were summoned to do and leave."

Alinor glanced from the priest to Wulfgar. "He was not brought to perform the last rites?"

Wulfgar looked at her in surprise. "What made you think that?"

Grinding her teeth in impotent fury, Alinor leapt to her feet, balling her hands into fists. "You allowed me to believe you were dying!"

Wulfgar frowned, but looked away guiltily. He might not have intended that she think she had been summoned to his death bed, but he had known from the way she behaved that that was what she believed. She felt like punching something, preferably him. "Do you know what you put me through, you … you pig!"

"What?"

Alinor gaped at him, feeling the blood rush into her cheeks. She had been devastated. He had to know that, had to have seen it in her face, but she wasn't about to give him the satisfaction of saying it to him. "I thought I was to be a prisoner here forever!" she snapped.

His expression closed and she immediately regretted the impulsive words her pride and anger had summoned. They could not be taken back now, however, and she was still too angry to find caution. "I will not wed this man!" she said to the priest. "I want to be returned to my family. They will pay ransom for my return."

232

The priest frowned. Alinor didn't so much as glance in Wulfgar's direction.

"It matters not whether you were willing or not. You have fornicated. You carry this man's child. You can not condemn the innocent to eternal damnation because of your pride."

Alinor flushed. "I am not with child."

The priest frowned, turning to Wulfgar. "Is this true?"

"As far as she knows, perhaps. But the mid-wife examined her and assures me she still carries my child."

It was one shock too many. Alinor felt her knees buckle. Slowly, she wilted to the floor, covering her face with her hands, trying to fight the blackness that threatened to engulf her.

Someone helped her to her feet. In a daze, she heard the priest recite the marriage lines. When prodded, she repeated the vows as told. Finally, she was led back to her room and left alone. Still feeling more than a little faint, and ill, she crawled into the bed and lay with her eyes closed, trying to make sense of what had just happened.

She had wed Wulfgar. It seemed he had decided, after all, that her suggestion of how he might obtain his revenge would be the easiest road to take.

Chapter Eight

Alinor had almost an entire week to worry about her wedding night. Naturally, she had no fear of coupling, but she was deeply troubled about the situation that had resulted in her marriage and not at all certain how best to handle it.

There was no doubt in her mind that she had grown deeply attached to Wulfgar. She very much feared that there was little doubt in his mind either, considering her behavior, but she had no desire to be an object of pity or the butt of jokes by displaying her feelings when it was painfully obvious to her that she had no place in Wulfgar's heart. Moreover, she was uncertain of whether she had a chance to make a place for herself. If she did, she wanted it. She didn't want to keep him at arm's length just to protect her pride and lose all chance of gaining what she wanted.

She could not help being eager for his caresses. She had to acknowledge that there was very little chance of hiding that much—some, mayhap, but not much.

When Wulfgar had recovered sufficiently to be up and moving about, his uncle arranged a wedding feast for them. To Alinor's relief, this was confined to those residing in and near the manor. It was uncomfortable enough as it was to go through the motions of celebrating their marriage among people well aware of their situation, but fairly familiar. To be gawked at and whispered about by strangers would have been pure misery.

Thankfully, they were also spared the bedding ceremony. There could be no doubt that she was virginal no longer, or that Wulfgar had accepted her as she was and vice versa. The wedding guests merely escorted Wulfgar to their room, therefore, and left them.

The maids had groomed Alinor to look her best for the wedding, washing her hair and combing it until it gleamed with health and life; bathing her in scented water; scrubbing the dry, rough skin from her body and kneading oils into her skin to soften it; and when they prepared her to receive her husband, they had used equal care.

Despite everything that had passed between them, or perhaps because of it, Alinor's heart leapt suffocatingly in her chest when Wulfgar entered the room, closing the door behind him. His gaze was immediately drawn to her where she sat propped up in bed on the pillows with her hair flowing around her, wearing her beribboned gown, like some confection that had been offered up to tempt him. A blush crept up her chest and neck to her cheeks under his scrutiny and, following the red tide, his gaze came to rest upon hers at last.

His expression was impossible to read. As he moved toward the bed and halted beside it, however, she saw that his eyes were dark with the promise of forbidden pleasures. Her nerves went taut, a flush of anticipation running through her that made her skin prickle with heightened awareness. Without taking his gaze from hers, he shrugged the robe he wore from his shoulders, allowing it to drop to the floor at his feet.

New, reddened scars and much older ones, now white, marred the once smooth flesh of his body, but Alinor was enthralled by his sheer magnificence, for, despite his recent brush with death and the pallor from it, his arms, chest and shoulders were massive with hard, bulging, ropy muscle, each clearly delineated by the skin stretched over it. His torso was a washboard of ridged muscle, his belly flat and hard. His cock, protruding from a nest of dark hair low on his belly caught her attention and held it.

She had not seen his manroot before. Now she found herself both fascinated and shocked by the look of it. It was an obscene shaft, veined and topped by a knob slightly larger in circumference than the shaft. It was stunning to think that her body would—had accommodated such a thing without causing her great pain, for it looked huge to her—small wonder, for there was no part of him that did not look huge to her.

She looked up at his face uneasily when he moved toward her.

Grasping her arms, he urged her to come up upon her knees and lifted her nightgown. Pulling if off over her head and then tossing it aside, he caught her wrists, holding her arms out while he studied her as she had studied him. A shiver went through her that seemed equal parts excitement and nervousness. Despite her best efforts to quell the thought, it bounded into her mind to taunt her—Was he comparing her to Freda? And worse, did he find her lacking?

She had the uncomfortable feeling that he must. He'd accused her of being a child yet and she wasn't certain if he had meant her figure was not womanly enough to suit him or if he meant he considered her behavior childish.

In truth, though she had eaten well since she had been at the manor of his uncle she was well aware that she was still far too thin from the many weeks that she had traveled so hard and eaten so little.

Shame filled her and she tried to wrest her hands free to cover herself. He released her, but when she snatched the bed linens up to cover herself he took them from her, tossing them toward the foot of the bed. "Don't," he murmured huskily as he placed a knee upon the bed and climbed into it so that they were kneeling face to face. "You are beautiful to my eyes."

Alinor blushed, searching his face to see if the words had only been spoken to spare her feelings, but there was nothing there to tell her of anything beyond his needs. Grasping her shoulders, he leaned down, rubbing his cheek along hers, breathing in her scent as he caressed her gently, as if he saw and understood her nervousness and was determined to move slowly and allow her time to relax. His heated breath brushed her ear, raising a cascade of goose bumps that rushed down her neck and along her arm. She shivered, lifting her arms and pressing her palms against his chest as he moved lower, nuzzling her neck, placing light kisses there that made her breasts and belly tighten with need. Her nipples stood erect, pouting, demanding attention.

His gentle caresses seem to seep through her pores like strong wine and ran through her blood, intoxicating, demolishing her reserves as it sent a flash of heat and tension to the core of her womanhood. She slipped her palms up his chest to his shoulders, digging her fingers into his taut flesh and when he lifted his head, she pressed her lips to his, glided them across his hard mouth in a light caress, then, with the tip of her tongue, traced the seam where his lips met.

He sucked in a sharp breath. Sliding his arms around her, he caught her hips and pulled her onto his lap as he sat back on his heels, spreading her thighs so that she was astride him, a knee on either side of his hips. Her buttocks slipped along his hair roughened thighs, sending enticing ripples of sensation through her. Grasping her hips, he pulled her snugly against him, his cock slipping between the petals of her femininity teasingly, nudging the tiny, sensitive bud that was the center of her delight as he slid the hard, distended flesh of his cock back and forth along her moist cleft. A shudder of gratification ran through her, bathing her core in a hot tide of moisture and flooding her passage to ease the way of his possession, sending a dizzying lethargy throughout her body. A small, unconscious sound of pleasure vibrated from her throat and she slipped her hands from his shoulders, locking her arms around his neck to hold herself closer to him as she plucked at his lips with her own, teasing him with the tip of her tongue until at last he opened his mouth over hers, plunging his tongue into the moist, sensitive inner recesses of her mouth.

The hot tide rose, and she began to move restlessly against him, luxuriating in the tingles of delight that raced along her flesh, burrowing deeply inside of her and building the exquisite tension with each brush of her bare flesh against his.

Her movements seemed to break his restraint. His kiss became more heated, his breath harsh as he caught her hips, guiding her as she rocked her moist cleft along his hardened cock, stroking him. Lifting her slightly, he positioned his cock so that the head nudged her cleft, seeking the entrance to her passage. Eagerly, her heart pounding with anticipation, Alinor moved to align her body with his, breaking their kiss on a gasp as she felt his cock head enter her. Lifting her head, she stared deeply into his eyes as she bore down upon him, felt his shaft sinking slowly inside of her, felt the muscles of her belly adjusting to his girth, until she was impaled to the hilt.

For several thundering heartbeats they gazed at each other once they were fully joined, holding themselves still as they relished the thrilling sensations rushing through them. Wulfgar slid one hand up her back to cup her head, threading is fingers through her hair and pulled her close, nibbling a trail of kisses down her throat and finally opening his mouth over one distended nipple. Her heart clenched almost painfully as his mouth closed around the sensitive peak, pleasure like fire rolling through her and the muscles of her passage responded of their own accord by clenching around him. He groaned as if in agony, catching her hips in both hands once more and lifting so that his cock moved through her in a downward stroke, and then pushing down on her hips and thrusting at the same time so that he sank deeply inside her once more.

Catching the rhythm, she began to move as he'd shown her, rotating her hips as she discovered a place inside of her that quaked with intense pleasure each time he stroked it, moving faster, then slower, until she found the angle and rhythm that brought her the most pleasure, that sent her racing along the path of repletion. And though she felt the building tension, felt herself rising rapidly toward her goal, felt her pleasure mounting higher, faster, more intensely, the magnitude of it caught her so unaware, so blindingly with its intensity that she cried out, groaning as if she were dying.

The pleasure was still jolting through her in waves

when he tossed her onto her back on the mattress and began pumping in and out of her in deep, swift strokes until his own climax burst upon him, his hot seed pouring into her in a scalding fountain that bathed the quivering flesh of her womb and passage and sent aftershocks of pleasure and an intense sense of completion through her.

Trembling with the effort, he pushed himself off of her, collapsing on the other side of the bed.

The sense of completion vanished as abruptly as his withdrawal. A cooling breath of air wafted over her, sending a shiver of discomfort through her, but that was nothing compared to the sense of abandonment that crept insidiously through her as he lay unmoving beside her, staring pensively at the canopy above the bed.

A sense of betrayal followed upon the heels of that and Alinor strove to nudge a spark of anger to life … anger directed mostly at herself. What had she expected, after all, fool that she was? That he would profess undying love for her only because he enjoyed easing his body upon her? Just because it was the most wondrous experience in her life, it did not necessarily follow that it was so for him. Very likely his experience was no different with her than with any other woman he had lain with.

She had overheard men talk of coupling with women. The vessel they used to sheath their sword was unimportant so long as they found their ease—and they always did.

She would not cry over it, though she longed to release her pain and anger in tears. It would do nothing but irritate Wulfgar if she wept each time they coupled as if she were wounded and he would soon be looking for a woman who left him in peace afterward.

Sitting up, she pulled the covers up over herself and

turned on her side away from him. She would've liked to have found her gown, as well, but cringed at the thought of drawing his attention to her nakedness.

He had said she was beautiful. How stupid of her to take it to heart. It could have been nothing more than the sweet words men were prone to use to ease their passage. She knew she wasn't beautiful, even in the first blush of health—and she was less than that now. What an absurd piece of self-deception that had allowed her to believe he truly meant it!

With an effort, she pushed the thoughts aside as she heard the deep, even breaths that told her he slept and composed her own mind to seek rest. She had gotten herself into a miserable mess, so caught up in her own infatuation that it had not occurred to her that having that which one wants most only allows one to suffer daily, and endlessly, over the realization that one does not really have it at all.

Chapter Nine

Within the week, Wulfgar, Alinor and a small escort set off to the nearest port to take ship for France. Men joined them along the way, seasoned soldiers that Alinor finally decided must be the remains of the army Lord Wulfgar had once commanded in the days before his lands were taken.

Alinor found she did not feel at all well throughout much of the trip, though Wulfgar did not set the killing pace that he had when they were eluding Jean-Pierre's troops. Bouts of nausea plagued her. At first she feared she had contracted some strange malady, but she did not worsen and finally she realized that the old crone who had examined her and reported to Wulfgar had been right. She was with child.

She knew she should be elated. Women were supposed to be thrilled at the prospect of bearing there husband's child. Somehow, though, she could not seem to feel anything at all beyond a sense of disbelief and finally she simply put it from her mind altogether, unable to focus on anything beyond her physical misery.

The crossing was no better, nor any worse that she could tell, than her previous crossing, beyond the fact that she was far more than vaguely nauseated. They had barely left port when she emptied the contents of her stomach over the side of the rail and she clung there throughout the crossing, continuing to gag long after she had ceased to have anything at all in her stomach.

She was so weak by the time they arrived that she was barely even aware of being carried through the crashing surf. When Wulfgar settled her on the sand beyond the reach of the waves, she wilted gratefully onto the damp sand, her eyes closed as she tried to fight off the dizzying sensation of movement that continued to plague her.

She yearned, desperately, for the comfort of her own bed—her own room. Until she had set foot once more on French soil, she had not realized how terribly she had missed all that she'd left behind—or perhaps she had and had simply refused to acknowledge it because she had known it was pointless even to think of it. Now, however, it filled her mind with a fever of impatience and she struggled up as she heard the men unloading the fear crazed horses.

"We will camp here for the night at least," Wulfgar said shortly when he saw her moving toward the horse that had been brought for her use.

She turned to look at him in dismay. "But … we are only a few days' ride from Arrus. I am well enough to go on."

"The horses are too crazed to attempt it now. You would not be able to handle it."

Alinor gaped at him for several moments and finally turned to study the frenzied dance of the horse.

She knew he was right. She was no horsewoman and could barely stay on the back of a calm horse, but disappointment flooded her all the same. Her shoulders slumped. Nodding, she lifted her skirts and moved to the packs that had been piled on the beach, trying to decide whether there was any point, really, in unpacking anything when they would probably be leaving at first light.

The very thought of food made her feel distinctly ill, but no one else seemed to have suffered the effects of the crossing quiet as much as she had. They had not eaten since they had broken their fast at dawn. She should see what she could find to cook over the campfire several of Wulfgar's men had built of driftwood they had collected.

She yelped, dropping the pot she'd unearthed when Wulfgar swooped down upon her. Snatching her off her feet, he swept her into his arms, carried her to a spot near the fire and deposited her. "Sit!" he growled impatiently.

Alinor blinked at him in surprise, but he said nothing more, merely turning upon his heel and stalking off. She watched him for several moments as he and his men moved about the beach, setting up camp, but looked away when she realized his men kept throwing curious glances at first her and then Wulfgar. Pulling her knees up beneath her gown, she hugged them to her and propped her cheek on her knees, staring at the fire thereafter and doing her best to ignore everything going on around her. She must have dozed, for she awoke to the aroma of cooking food. At once, her belly was of two minds, the one clamoring for something to fill the empty void and the other rebelling.

She squeezed her eyes tightly, fighting the wave of nausea while she tried to decide whether to yield to the hunger and appease it or if her belly was merely playing a trick upon her and would immediately reject any attempt to swallow.

She opened her eyes when Wulfgar sat beside her. He was holding out a trencher filled with huntsman's stew—that manmade concoction whereupon they threw whatever was at hand into it so that it never tasted quiet the same any two times it was cooked and as often as not was completely unpalatable. Alinor forced a smile, but shook her head. "Merci, but I am not 'ungry."

He frowned. "I insist."

Alinor's smile fell flat. "I do not think I can eat it."

His lips tightened with annoyance. "You will try, however. You have my child in your belly."

She sent him a sullen glance but took the trencher, staring down at it in revulsion for several moments. He speared a chunk of meat with his eating knife and held it to her lips. Alinor shuddered, squeezed her eyes tightly and opened her mouth. To her surprise and relief, it tasted quiet good. She chewed it experimentally and finally swallowed. Her stomach protested immediately, but quieted after a moment and she took another bite. She had managed only a little when she became quite certain that she could eat no more if she was to have any chance of holding what she'd already eaten. She set the trencher aside.

Wulfgar frowned. "You have barely touched it. You will be no more than breath and bones if you refuse to eat."

Alinor glared at him, tempted to inform him that she did not care if he found her bones unappealing or not. No doubt his precious Freda had been buxom and well rounded for his pleasure. He could stab himself to death on her bones for all she cared! In any case, it was not she who refused, but her belly … not that she trusted herself even to speak that much. The more tense she became, the more determined her stomach seemed to reject the pitiful offering.

He picked up the trencher and held it out to her again. "Only a little more and I will leave you in peace."

Alinor stared down at the congealing food and lost her battle. Clapping a hand over her mouth, she thrust his hand away, leapt to her feet and dashed up the beach. She didn't notice Wulfgar had followed her until he nudged her shoulder and handed her a skin of water. Accepting it gratefully, she rinsed her mouth and spat before she sat back. Uncomfortable now that the bout had passed, she glanced at him. Even in the dim light of approaching night she could see that he looked nearly as pale and shaky as she felt.

"I could not help it!" she snapped. "If it makes you feel ill, then go away."

Something flickered in his eyes, but Alinor was far too distressed to take not of it, or even to try to understand it. His lips tightened. "You are an ill tempered wench!"

Alinor glared at him. "I am not 'a wench'!" she snarled. "I am your wife."

"Then obey me," he snarled back at her. "Your parents will be wroth with me if I arrive at their door with you nigh dead!"

Alinor gaped at him, outraged. "You think I did this on purpose?"

He stared at her a long moment and then looked away. "Nay. But you must try harder. If you continue this you will not be able to eat at all and you will not have the strength you need for the babe in your belly."

"I am a brood mare then? I must suppose that is better that being of no consequence at all!" Alinor said hotly, well aware that she was goading Wulfgar into anger, but uncaring.

He flushed. "An heiress is always of importance," he said tightly.

CONQUERED

Alinor flinched at the comment. She had forced him to admit his reason for wedding her and she should be fiercely glad. She was. It was completely unreasonable that she also felt a desire to burst into tears. She fought a round with her wayward emotions and finally subdued the urge. "I think I will rest now," she said finally, rising with an effort and making her way back to the tent that had been set up for her use.

She was asleep when Wulfgar crawled beneath the furs with her sometime later, but roused sufficiently to move closer to his warmth. Slipping an arm beneath her head, he snuggled her tightly against his length. Alinor murmured sleepily, lifting her head to nuzzle his neck. He stroked her hair and along her back and she felt a stirring of desire. Gliding her hand downward, she pressed her palm against the hard ridge that had been nudging her belly. He groaned, but caught her hand, and placed it firmly on his waist. "Be still, love. There will be time enough for that when you are well."

Alinor frowned, vaguely disappointed, but finally decided she was too comfortable and too sleepy anyway.

To her surprise, she woke the following morning as Wulfgar entered the tent. Settling beside her, he wordlessly handed her a portion of bread and a skin filled, she discovered, with warm milk. She looked up at him in surprise as she sat up and accepted them. "Angus says his woman finds this easier to eat when she is breeding," he said gruffly. "Eat it slowly and do not get up until you do not feel ill."

Alinor stared at the tent flap when he departed as abruptly as he'd entered. Slowly, a smile curled her lips and warmth suffused her. It was a thoughtful gesture. She decided to accept it and enjoy it, refusing to allow her fertile mind to suspect his motives.

247

To her relief, she found that Angus' wife had been right. The goats' milk and dried bread went down easily and barely gave her a quiver of doubt that it would remain.

Regardless, she ate sparingly. It would be better to keep only a little than to keep none at all by trying to eat more than she felt like eating. She lay still for a time after she'd eaten, listening to the men as they broke camp and began loading the horses. Finally, she rose and dressed, rolled the furs and tied them and dragged the bundle outside.

Wulfgar, she discovered, was waiting outside. Handing him the bundle, she went in search of privacy for her needs. When she returned, the tent had been struck and loaded and the men were already mounted and ready to depart. Wulfgar studied her searchingly for several moments and finally lifted her onto her mount, waiting until he was certain she was firmly seated and had her mare in hand before he mounted his own horse.

"We will go first to the home of your father," Wulfgar said as he pulled his horse along side her own.

Alinor nodded, feeling at once a surge of both happiness and dread. Her father was not going to be pleased that she returned home with a far different husband than the one he had arranged for her.

"Your father is more like to disown you than negotiate peace," Wulfgar murmured, as if to himself.

"He will not like it," Alinor said. "But he will accept it."

Wulfgar's look was dubious, but he did not argue the matter.

Chapter Ten

"What!" Chrétien d'Arrus bellowed furiously.

Alinor set her jaw belligerently. Beside her, she felt Wulfgar tense. She stepped in front of him. She was fairly certain he would not come to blows with her father, and he had disarmed when he entered the keep, but there was no sense in taking the chance.

She was glad they had a private audience—courtesy of her mother, who had insisted that they go to her solar for refreshment.

"He is my husband," she said tightly. "My choice."

Her father glared at her. "You were betrothed to Jean-Pierre! As good as wed—or my word is nothing! The contracts have been signed and witnessed!"

Alinor shrugged. "I wed Lord Wulfgar of my own free will, before a priest, father. It can not now be undone."

"Indeed it can!"

Alinor's heart skipped a beat. She had not antici-pated that her father would refuse to see the inevita bility of the situation. "Indeed it can not! I am with child! Wulfgar's child. The church would not grant an annulment and I would not ask for it."

Her father gaped at her as if she had lost her mind. "A captive bride, wed against her will! I will petition for an annulment. Under the circumstances…."

Claire d'Arrus laid a hand on her husband's arm. "Think of the child, Chrétien," she said quietly. "Jean-Pierre would not welcome the child of his enemy, even if you succeeded in having your way. We must accept this and make the best of it. Jean-Pierre is not unreasonable. We can make some sort of restitution for the loss."

Chrétien glared at her. "Mind your needle, woman, and leave business to men!"

"My daughter is my business!" Claire snapped. "I told you she was not happy with your choice and no good would come of it. I have no doubt she did it to spite us."

"I did no such thing, mother!"

"I took her captive! She had no choice in the matter!" Wulfgar said tightly.

Alinor gave him a look. "I could have refused to say my vows!"

"I would have wed you anyway! You would not have been the first bride to take her vows bound and gagged." Wulfgar snarled.

"Mayhap, but you did not have to!"

"Peace!" Chrétien d'Arrus demanded. "I know nothing of this man."

"I am Wulfgar, late of Chittenhold—Saxon," Wulfgar said stiffly.

Chrétien's lips tightened. "Landless—and so you seized an heiress to replace the lands you lost."

Wulfgar's eyes narrowed. It went against the grain to explain his actions to any man, but he was obliged

250

to consider the rights of a father. "I seized the bride of my enemy, Jean-Pierre, in retaliation for … what was taken from me."

"My daughter!" Chrétien growled, glaring back at him. "You made war upon my daughter—you should have challenged Jean-Pierre like a gentleman."

Wulfgar gritted his teeth. "I did challenge Jean-Pierre … to single combat, to settle the issue."

Chrétien was taken aback. "You're saying you bested Jean-Pierre?"

Wulfgar flushed. "He did not meet me. He sent a dozen knights to take me prisoner."

"And yet, you are here."

"Your daughter warned me that he was not a man of his word and would lay a trap for me. Because I was warned, I was able to win free."

Chrétien glanced from Wulfgar to Alinor and back again. Finally, he sat and gestured for Wulfgar and Alinor to sit, as well. "He speaks the truth, daughter?"

Wulfgar ground his teeth. He was not accustomed to having his word questioned by any man. Father or not, he was of more than half a mind to return to England at once. He might be landless now, but he was no beggar.

Alinor laid a hand on his arm. "He is my husband, father, and a man of honor. He brought me here only because I begged him to. I … told him my dower lands would be my husband's and that he would have his revenge upon Jean-Pierre if he married me. He refused them … until he learned that I carried his child.

"Where is the difference? You can not tell me Jean-Pierre would have wed me without the dower lands!"

Her father frowned at her. "If you can not understand the difference, child, then I will not try to explain it."

"I do not understand the difference because there is

none! If he had come to ask for me before the Duke of Normandy invaded his lands, he would have been as eligible as any other … more so that some others. If we had been wed, and then he had lost his holdings in England, we would still only have had the dower lands!"

Chrétien stared at her a long moment and finally looked at Wulfgar. "Women have no logic."

Wulfgar's eyes gleamed. "They do not."

Alinor looked from one to the other indignantly, but her mother caught her eye. "Come, Alinor. Sit closer to the fire with me. I feel a bit of a chill."

Chrétien turned a piercing eye upon her. "You are not ill?"

Claire smiled at him. "No, my love. But I was certain that you and Wulfgar would have more important things to discuss and I wish to speak to my daughter about woman things."

Chrétien nodded and flicked a hand dismissively toward her and Claire gave her daughter an amused look. Alinor glanced at Wulfgar a little anxiously, not at all certain that she wished to leave him with her father, but her father had engaged him in conversation and he did not look her way. Claire slipped an arm around her waist. "You have not been well," she murmured consolingly. "It is the babe?"

Wulfgar glanced toward the two women as they settled near the hearth. At a little distance, they were as two peas in a pod, of much the same height and build, the same dark hair, the same large, brown eyes that gave them a look of wide eyed innocence, whatever mischief they might be about. Alinor's mother could have as easily been thought to be her sister, for she still retained a youthful look about her.

"She was of much the same age as Alinor is now when Alinor was born. I'd hoped for a son, of course, but I have not been displeased with Alinor."

Wulfgar dragged his gaze from them with an effort. "Alinor has never spoken of brothers or sisters."

Chrétien sighed. "Because there are none. Claire bore three sons for me and two daughters besides Alinor, but none lived more than a few years. One never drew his first breath, a second died within a few days. The others were carried off by fever.

"This is why it was important to me to settle Alinor well—with a strong warrior, capable of defending her and her holdings. I do not have great wealth, but the lands I hold are fertile enough to tempt our neighbors. I would not have been against a love match if Alinor's heart had settled upon someone suitable, but she favored none above the rest and Jean-Pierre, whose land marches with her dower lands, is widely known as a warrior of merit." He looked Wulfgar over with a slightly more favorable gaze. "You look to me as if you have a good sword arm."

"I am accounted capable."

Chrétien shrugged. "We'll know soon enough."

Wulfgar's brows rose questioningly.

"Jean-Pierre placed a man on Alinor's holdings before he left to join Duke William. Like as not the man will not yield willingly."

Wulfgar's eyes gleamed. "T'would be a pity if he did."

Chrétien frowned, but in a moment a chuckle escaped him. "You were hoping for as much."

Wulfgar eyed him speculatively for several moments. "Aye. There is more than one way to draw a serpent from his hole."

Chrétien grunted. "You will need more men that what you have brought with you."

Wulfgar shrugged. "I have faith in my men. They

253

have fought many battles beside me."

"Hmmm. All the same, you and I will have to consider this matter carefully before we leave. I'd just as soon take the land with as little damage as possible. If Jean-Pierre has no notion of what you are about, then he will not have sent word to warn them."

"I make no doubt Jean-Pierre believes me dead," Wulfgar said grimly. "For I was sorely wounded 'ere I won free of the trap he'd set for me."

"But you are fit for fighting now?"

Wulfgar shrugged. "Well enough."

"There is no great rush, surely? If he thinks you dead then that is to our advantage. We can bide awhile, give you time to heal as you should and regain your strength."

Wulfgar frowned, turning to look at Alinor. "Alinor is not well. I would like to settle things and have her comfortable in her own home as soon as possible."

Chrétien said nothing for so long that Wulfgar became aware of the prolonged silence and glanced at him.

"Is that the way of it, then?"

Wulfgar flushed uncomfortably. He could see what was in the man's mind and his first impulse was to deny it, but it occurred to him quite suddenly that the denial would be a lie. "Aye. That is the way of it."

* * * *

Alinor had been in bed for quite some time before Wulfgar joined her.

Her mother had arranged a small celebration in honor of her marriage and they had feasted long into the night. She had not wanted to leave when her mother had suggested that they retire for the evening, but she was weary from the travel and the events of the day. In any case, she had thought Wulfgar would surely follow her when he saw that she was going to their apart ments.

They had not coupled since they had begun the journey and Alinor had taken great pains to prepare herself for him. She had been anxious that he would come before she had had time to complete her preparations, but when the maids had left at last he still had not come. Finally, she had settled herself in bed to await him.

In the end, she had dozed despite her determination to wait for him. Despite her exhaustion, however, or perhaps because of her determination, she had woken when he had come in at long last.

Two things were immediately apparent.

He thought that she was asleep and was taking great pains not to disturb her; and he was drunk, as she had never seen him before.

He undressed himself with an effort. Watching him, the temptation grew strong to giggle. She quelled it, not certain that he would take it well in his present state. By the time he had finished, however, all desire to laugh had fled. He was, she decided, quite beautiful to behold. Warmth and excitement flooded her as she studied him and thought of how wonderful it felt when their bodies joined.

Finally, he doused the candles and climbed into bed beside her, lying stiffly on one side, staring up at the ceiling. Alinor lay still, as well, waiting for him to reach for her. When he did not, irritation surfaced. She was of half a mind to simply turn her back upon him and go to sleep. It occurred to her, however, that he had not sought to ease himself on her for many days and he would be in need.

She didn't at all care for the way the maids had eyed him, all a flutter with excited giggles whenever he strode through the hall.

She scooted across the bed and cuddled against his

side, placing her hand on his chest. He stiffened, but after a moment, he slipped an arm under her head and held her close. When he made no effort to do more, Alinor stroked his chest caressingly.

He caught her hand, held it a moment and finally released it.

Alinor lay fuming for a while, but she was not about to leave him ripe for the maids' suggestive glances.

Pushing herself up on one elbow, she leaned over him and began to kiss her way down his chest to his belly. He sucked in a harsh breath, slipping his hand up her back to her shoulders in a gesture, she knew, was not intended as encouragement, but rather the opposite. She ignored it, reaching down with one hand in search of his cock as she continued to nibble a teasing trail of kisses down his belly. He jerked reflexively when her fingers closed around his engorged member.

Alinor smiled against his belly in satisfaction. He might pretend he had no interest in coupling with her—and perhaps he did not—but his cock had a mind of its own.

Leaning down, Alinor kissed the rounded head. His cock jerked in her hand. A harsh groan rumbled through his chest. Alinor took his cock into her mouth.

Chapter Eleven

Wulfgar bolted upright, his fingers tangling in her hair, clutching and releasing, as if he couldn't quite decide whether to hold her there or pull her away.

Lifting her head, Alinor gave him a look of innocence. "Did you not like it?"

Wulfgar stared at her a long moment, his heart thundering in his chest as if it would beat its way out, unable for several moments even to catch his breath to speak. "This is ... not right."

Alinor studied him for a long moment, but there was nothing to suggest that he was repelled by what she had done and much to suggest otherwise. "You are my husband. It is right that we pleasure each other in whatever manner we wish."

When he did not contradict her, she lowered her head once more. Covering the head of his cock with her mouth, she sucked it. Groaning as if he were dying, Wulfgar fell back against the bed, digging his fingers into the bed linens. Entirely satisfied with his

257

reaction, Alinor slipped his cock deeper into her mouth and then lifted her head, moving his turgid flesh in and out of her mouth as he moved inside of her when they coupled, trying to find a rhythm that would give him the most pleasure.

Every muscle in his body seemed tensed, as if he were struggling to resist the pleasure she gave him, and yet he could not be still as she held him tightly in her mouth, stroking him. Abruptly, she felt a change in him, a new restless, a new desperation and she realized that he was nearing his crisis. Heat rushed through her, pooling like liquid fire low in her belly. She renewed her efforts, moving faster, thrusting his hands away when he tried to push her away.

Sitting bolt upright with a growl, Wulfgar pulled her free and shoved her down on the mattress on her back. Alinor was too stunned to do more than gape at him when he grasped her legs, lifting her hips from the bed as he pulled her thighs apart and buried his face between them. When his mouth opened over her femininity, she cried out in surprise as an intense shaft of pleasure stabbed through her, making the muscles in her belly tighten almost painfully in response. She clutched his head as he stroked the sensitive petals of flesh with his tongue, the heat of his mouth, the slightly rough texture of his tongue sending lightening forks of ecstasy sizzling through her until she was thrashing mindlessly, moaning incessantly.

Within moments, she felt herself rushing toward her crisis. It burst upon her like a rupturing melting pot, so intensely she cried out. He lifted his head, a gleam of triumph and desire lighting his eyes as he dragged her toward him and impaled her on his distended flesh, thrusting hard, burying himself deeply and pulling away quickly to thrust again. Alinor lay spent, gasping at the

waves of pleasure that rocked her with each deep pen-
etration. Within seconds she felt her body gathering
toward release once more. It caught her up in a more
intense explosion even than before as she felt his cock
jerk as he spilled his seed inside of her.

Bracing his hands on the bed on either side of her,
he hovered above her for several moments, struggling
to catch his breath and finally simply dropped sideways onto the bed beside her and lay unmoving except
for the harsh breaths that continued to saw in and out
of his chest.

Too weak to move, Alinor remained where she was
for several moments, but the night air across her heated
skin sent a shiver through her. With an effort, she
moved closer to Wulfgar. Snuggling against his side,
she draped an arm across his heaving chest, stroking
him in appreciation.

He caught her hand after a moment. "Do not," he
said through gritted teeth.

Alinor stiffened, felt hurt wash through her.

"I will die if you begin that again," he muttered irritably.

As his meaning sank in, Alinor tried, unsuccessfully,
to stifle a giggle.

"The thought of murdering your husband amuses
you?" he asked stiffly.

Alinor nipped him teasingly and chuckled. "Surely
it would be a pleasurable way to die?"

Growling, he rolled onto his side and shoved her
onto her back. His expression was serious, but there
was a teasing gleam in his eyes. "You are a wicked
temptress, Alinor. You make no allowance for an aged
husband."

Alinor gazed up at him for several moments and finally lifted a hand and caressed his lean cheek. "Rest

then. I am weary also. I just … wanted to be sure you did not find someone else to assuage your needs."

He frowned, withdrawing. "I am no monk, Alinor."

Alinor came up on one arm, glaring at him. "You had best consider taking the vows. I will never deny you, but neither will I look the other way while you find sport elsewhere."

"You are my wife," Wulfgar growled. "Not my confessor."

"Yes! Your wife! You vowed to honor me, not to dishonor me by taking other women into your bed!"

"You are too young to understand the ways of the world," Wulfgar said with determined patience. "A man has needs."

"A woman also," Alinor responded tightly. "And, you are wrong, I do know the ways of the world, but I know also that my father has always been faithful to my mother. Would you not care if I were to look about for another stallion to ride?"

Wulfgar caught her arms in a bruising grip. "Has one caught your eye?" he growled furiously. "Only point him out to me and I will see to it that he is stallion no more, but gelding."

Alinor looked down, satisfied with his answer. "There is one ….It would be a great shame to geld so magnificent a beast, however."

His fingers tightened on her arms. "Name him."

Alinor looked up at him and realized immediately that it had been a mistake to tease him. There was murder in his eyes. Her heart skipped a beat. "A Saxon lord by the name of Wulfgar."

He didn't believe her. She saw that at once.

"I will not hurt you, Alinor. But know this, your touch means death to any man who strikes your fancy. You are mine," he said through clenched teeth, "and I will not look away while you comport yourself like the ladies of loose morals and choose lovers at whim."

Alinor sighed impatiently. "On my honor, I desire no one but you."

He studied her a long moment and finally released her. "Women have no honor."

She glared at him angrily for several moments and finally lay back in a huff, turning her back to him.

He remained as he was, staring up at the canopy for so long that Alinor thought he might have gone to sleep. Finally, he rolled to face her, studied her rigid back for a moment and then pulled her back against him, wrapping an arm around her. "I have satisfied your needs?" he asked stiffly.

Alinor bit her lip, knowing he would be outraged if she laughed. "Very well, my lord," she responded finally, keeping her voice level with an effort.

* * * *

Claire d'Arrus was torn between shock, amusement and irritation when Alinor confessed what she had done. "Child! I despair that you will live long enough to learn to mind your tongue! What possessed you to sew a seed of doubt in the man's mind? Men are simple creatures. They see only black and white and can not detect the fine shadings between. Next he will begin to doubt the child in your belly is his."

Alinor felt the blood rush from her face. "What have I done!"

Claire studied her angrily for several moments, but finally her face softened. "Nothing that can not be mended ... if you will mind that wicked tongue of yours! When he has had time to assure himself that you are not looking around for someone with which to cuckold him, he will begin to trust again ... it will be best if providence provides you with a child in his image that he can not deny .... If you have learned a lesson from it, then some good will have come of it."

GOLDIE MCBRIDE

Alinor looked at her doubtfully. "I am not at all certain that I will remember it the next time something pops into my mind. I do try …. But he had not touched me since we left England and I have seen the way the maids titter over him. I was afraid that he would turn from me altogether."

Sympathy filled her mother's eyes. "It is a terrible thing to love someone so much. It does tend to lead to poor judgment, and, alas, yours was not as it should have been even before."

A blush crept up Alinor's cheeks. "It is that obvious then?"

"To me, yes. To that great lout you married, obviously not, else he would not have been so quick to suppose you would look around for another … uh … stallion."

Vaguely relieved, Alinor was still not terribly happy. It occurred to her, however, that if she was jealous because she loved Wulfgar, that, surely, his implied a similar attachment. Unfortunately, her mother disabused her of the notion.

"It is a common mistake to judge others upon yourself. You must understand that no one else feels, or thinks, or looks upon things in quite the same way that you do. They are not motivated by the same things that you are, nor will they react the same. In any case, men are territorial animals. They will growl over a bone they do not even want, only because it is theirs."

"Oh," Alinor said in dismay. "You think, then, that he was only angry because I am his wife?"

Claire shrugged. "He has been kind to you, despite the circumstances. It is not impossible that he has developed an affection for you. Particularly since he lost his wife so tragically and claimed to love her. He would have a void that needed filling."

Alinor supposed that was said to make her feel bet

262

ter. Somehow it didn't. "If ... father died, do you think that you would love another?"

Claire looked pained. "I would not look for another to take his place, for no one could." She noticed Alinor looked near tears and could have bitten her tongue. Small wonder her daughter spoke so thoughtlessly! "I already pointed out that we are not all the same, Alinor. In any case, I never said that I could not love another, only that I would not look."

"That is the same thing!"

Claire sighed with exasperation. "Then you should simply give up now. There is no point in trying to win his heart, I am sure, for it is in the grave."

Alinor's jaw set belligerently. "You always told me that men liked their comfort and a woman who could assure that could also be assured of earning their man's affection."

"You will not make him comfortable if you treat him to tears and rages of jealousy."

"Then I will not."

Claire looked at her dubiously.

"I will not!" Alinor repeated more forcefully, wondering even as she said it if she would be able to control her impulse to speak, or act, first and mourn the consequences later.

To her surprise, although Wulfgar made it clear that he remained displeased with her, he watched her every movement whenever she was within sight, like a predatory cat watched its prey. It was unnerving, and yet she could not help but be elated that he never so much as glanced in the direction of any of the maids who made sheep's eyes at him—He was far too busy watching her to notice the invitation in their eyes. Moreover, he slept in her bed each night, coupling with her each night before he would allow her to sleep.

Alinor didn't know whether to be gratified or disturbed by the results of their argument but by the time Wulfgar left with her father to reclaim their holdings, she was almost relieved at the opportunity it would afford her to rest.

She would have been happier if she had not been anxious about the outcome of the excursion, for she very quickly discovered that broken rest due to coupling was far preferable to the anxiety that kept her wakeful and restless once he had gone.

Chapter Twelve

Chrétien d'Arrus sent word ahead of his intentions to inspect his daughter's dower property. Wulfgar was opposed to the notion, but bowed to Chrétien's position. When they topped a rise and looked upon the stronghold that guarded the property's northern boundary, he understood why Chrétien had decided it would be best to approach openly.

Unlike the Saxons, the Europeans favored walled fortresses. Maison de Vardon was surrounded by a sheer stone wall that looked to be between twenty and thirty feet high. Above its ramparts, Wulfgar could see the pointed spires and steep slate covered roof of the mansion itself, but nothing else beyond the guards stationed along the top of the wall.

The mansion was aptly named, for it stood upon a knoll that even now, after first frost, showed specks of green. The land that stretched out around it in every direction was still in cultivation this late in the growing season and Wulfgar had no doubt that the forest that had been cut back into the distance was equally fecund. Alinor had not exaggerated when she had told him of it.

A mixture of emotions filled him as he surreptitiously surveyed the lands that would be his home and Alinor's; pleasure in the sheer beauty of it; gratitude that he would once again have an estate to manage and a hearth of his own; humility that Alinor and her family had accepted him when he was no more, now, than any other landless knight; and homesickness.

He had not allowed himself to think of living in a foreign land. In truth, he had hardly given any thought to the land at all beyond the certainty that taking it would goad Jean-Pierre as nothing else had. Now, although he looked forward to claiming it with hope and a sense of renewed purpose, he also realized that he would never truly feel as if he belonged. The lands Jean-Pierre now held had been in his family for generations. He had been born there as his father before him and every inch of it was as familiar to him as his own body.

This place was Alinor's.

As if Chrétien had read his mind, he spoke just then. "This part of the property comes to Alinor from Claire. The mansion was built for her mother, but has been well kept and added to several times over the years. There is a much smaller keep on the southern end of her property … not much to it at all, but the land is as fertile. I purchased it after my second daughter was born, but …." He allowed the sentence to trail off and after a moment Wulfgar realized that he was thinking of the children he had lost. There had been no point in enlarging his holdings when he had seen he would have no other heirs.

A knot tightened in Wulfgar's belly. He had seen himself how much Alinor was like her mother.

"We shall see soon enough if Raul Dubois has a

notion of what we are about," Chrétien muttered under his breath as he signaled for the troops to halt before the gate of the keep … which had not opened to greet them as Chrétien had expected it would. They waited, becoming uneasy as time passed. Finally, the creak and groan of chain rang out as the portcullis slowly began to open.

Wulfgar glanced at Chrétien. "It's a trap," he muttered, tossing one corner of his cape back so that he could reach his weapons without hindrance. A ripple went through the men behind him as they noticed his posture.

The gate was little more than halfway open when he dug his heels into his destrier's sides and yelled the battle cry.

If Chrétien's men had not been as well trained as his own, they would very likely have been doomed, for less than half their men managed to make it through before the portcullis was slammed closed once more. Those who'd entered were well versed with the layout of the keep, however, and leapt from their horses immediately and charged the walls to capture control of the portcullis. Once they were inside, the battle lasted little more than an hour, for the mansion itself was not fortified.

Raul Dubois had had no word from Jean-Pierre they discovered after they'd questioned him, beyond having been informed that the heiress had been killed and that he was not to allow Chrétien the chance to retake the keep.

Chrétien had to be restrained from killing the man on the spot, but Wulfgar had other plans for him. "No! We will send him to Jean-Pierre. Obviously, he was devastated at the thought of Alinor's death. He can take Jean-Pierre word that she lives."

Chrétien studied him for several moments and finally moved away from the man they had been questioning. "You are certain you wish to issue this challenge?"

"Soon, or late, Jean-Pierre will come to make certain his holdings are secure. If we send his man to him, he will come soon and we can be ready for him."

Chrétien thought it over and finally shrugged. "Likely, you are right."

Wulfgar nodded and moved back to the man. "The message you will take to Jean-Pierre is this: Your bride is now mine and thus her lands, as well."

The man glared at Wulfgar sullenly. "Who am I to tell him sends this message?"

Wulfgar leaned down until he was almost nose to nose with the man. "The Saxon who's bride he slew and who's lands he now calls his own. I am Wulfgar."

Three men were allowed to leave with him. Wulfgar sent a dozen men with them to see them to the coast and aboard a ship bound for England—to lessen the chance that they might decide discretion was the better part of valor for messengers bearing ill tidings.

Most of the soldiers were mercenaries and given the choice of accepting a new overlord or seeking their fortunes elsewhere. Some chose to leave and were escorted to the boundaries of Alinor's lands. The men who remained Wulfgar divided up and absorbed into his own troops, who were under orders to put them to the sword if they so much as hesitated to follow a command.

Taking a troop of men, Wulfgar set out to retrieve his wife while Chrétien stayed behind to oversee repairs from the battle.

* * * *

'We have taken my lady Alinor's keep.' Alinor had been both relieved and terrified when the messenger

268

had arrived and brought word to her and her mother—terrified, quite naturally because until the messenger had related the message she and her mother had been under the amiable impression that Chrétien expected to take the keep peacefully. Her father had certainly been at great pains to create that impression. Wulfgar had been his usual uncommunicative self and given her no clue at all of what his thoughts were on the matter, of course, which had caused her some uneasiness. She had decided, though, that her father was probably right—it was her dower property and there was no reason to think Jean-Pierre would be suspicious of her father inspecting it—and Wulfgar's caution was just that.

She supposed, to Wulfgar's mind, the message he had sent was expected to reassure her and her mother that all was well. Unfortunately, he had left out the tiny details of whether he and her father were well—or wounded in battle—and when another week passed with no sign of Wulfgar Alinor became convinced that he had been injured, might be even now hovering between life and death.

Her mother did her best to reassure her, but since she was equally convinced that Chrétien had been mortally wounded, neither believed the other's reassurances and they did not comfort each other much.

When word came at last that a troop was spotted approaching the keep, both Alinor and Claire raced to the window of the solar and threw it open, jostling each other for a better position to see who it was that had come. By that time, the troop had already entered the keep, however, and neither of them could see the men at all.

They were still debating whether to meet the men in the courtyard or wait in the solar when Wulfgar strode into the room. Alinor and her mother both paled.

"You are well?" she asked, examining his face for any sign of weakness or pain. "You were not wounded?"

"Where is Chrétien?"

"He stayed at the keep to oversee repairs," Wulfgar said curiously.

"He was not wounded?"

"No more than I—a scratch or two—I sent word. Did the messenger not tell you?"

With her arm wrapped comfortingly around her mother, Alinor glared at him. "You have frightened … me … my mother half out of her wits. You might at least have thought to add that no one was greatly hurt. We could tell nothing at all about the message beyond the fact that there had been a battle for possession when we had not expected one."

Wulfgar's eyes narrowed as he looked from one woman to the other. "You did not expect me to return? I am sorry to disappoint you." With that, he turned and stalked from the room, only pausing in the doorway long enough to tell Alinor she should make ready to travel to Maison de Vardon.

When he had gone Alinor and her mother exchanged a dumbfounded look. "What is it that he thinks we have done?" Alinor asked in a quaky voice, afraid she knew already.

If possible, Claire had turned even more pale than before. "I am not at all certain," she said evasively.

Alinor's face crumpled. "He thinks you have plotted to rid me of my husband and I was a party to it!"

"Do not look at me so accusingly! You know very well we did not! It is not my fault that he looks for plots under every bush! You should have told him we were only anxious that they had been harmed. You were not used to be so careful to hide your feelings! Why did you hold yourself back instead of going to him?"

"He is Saxon, not French! They are very reticent, and suspicious or repulsed by displays of emotion!" Alinor moved to a chair and sat, covering her face with her hands. "I always say or do the wrong thing, no matter how I try! He is convinced that I am his enemy. That is why he turns everything I say over and examines it for a different meaning! I do not know how I might go about convincing him that I care for him."

Claire moved to her and patted her bowed head. "Pride can lead to your downfall, Alinor. Be yourself. Eventually, he will realize that subterfuge is not your strong suit and you are more like to say and do exactly what you think and feel."

Chapter Thirteen

"You were wrong to believe that I hoped ill would befall you, or that my parents had conspired to make it so. My parents are not pleased by the circumstances of my marriage, but they have accepted you because they know it is what I want …. I was glad that you returned safely," Alinor said tentatively when she had recovered sufficiently from their bout of lovemaking to think clearly once more.

Wulfgar grunted, but said nothing.

It was amazing, Alinor thought that one could convey so much without saying anything at all. For herself, she could have talked for an hour and still not have conveyed the depth of skepticism Wulfgar had with only a grunt. She was torn between despair and irritation.

"We might as easily have suspected you had done something to my father … if we were devious enough of mind to consider everyone else so!"

"You accuse me of being devious?" Wulfgar de

272

manded tightly.

A shiver went through Alinor. They were lying as they generally did, with her back tucked tightly against his belly. It was dark in the room in any case, which would have made it impossible to read his expression even if she had been facing him.

There was no doubt, however, that he was angry still.

"Mother says that people only suspect you of doing things that they would do."

He merely grunted this time.

"I think she is right—mostly—but, of course, that does not take into consideration the things one learns of other people."

He didn't even grunt that time and Alinor wondered if he had fallen asleep.

"I was worried for your safety," she said in a small voice.

"This is why you bit my head off when you saw that I was not hurt?"

Alinor bit her lip. She supposed, from his point of view, she could see where it might seem to contradict an assertion of concern. "No. That was because you had allowed me to spend a week worrying when you were perfectly all right."

Wulfgar caught her jaw, forcing her to tip her head toward him. He studied her for several moments and finally covered her mouth in a scalding, but disappointingly brief, kiss. "Sleep. We leave at first light."

* * * *

The household goods that had been purchased for Alinor upon her betrothal had been sent behind her when she had left for England and, not surprisingly, had not been returned when she had failed to arrive. Therefore, she had had nothing with which to set up a household when she returned home with Wulfgar.

273

Alinor's mother had set about remedying the situation when Chrétien and Wulfgar had left to secure the property, however, and Wulfgar was plainly appalled at their efforts. He took one look at the baggage train that had been assembled and stopped dead in his tracks for several moments. Finally, looking like a thundercloud, he helped Alinor and her mother to mount, climbed upon his own horse and they rode out.

The Maison de Vardon was not far distant from Arrus—as the crow flew. They could have reached it cross country within a couple of hours. By road, in they had not had the baggage train, they would have made it in little more than half a day. The oxen pulling the baggage carts, however, had been bred for strength and stamina, not speed. Moreover, due to the weather, the road they had to travel was not in very good condition.

All things considered, Alinor thought they made good time, for they arrived at Vardon before nightfall the same day that they had set out.

Her parents stayed only a week. Wulfgar and Chrétien spent their days preparing for battle, and their evenings discussing strategy. It was finally decided that Chrétien and Claire would return to the Chateaux, where Chrétien would prepare his own keep—either for siege if Jean-Pierre attacked Arrus first, or to come to Wulfgar's aid if Vardon was attacked first.

Wulfgar did not believe they would wait long before Jean-Pierre made his move. Once he had seen to the defense of the keep, he concentrated on gathering together supplies to ensure the protection of Vardon and its people in the likelihood that Jean-Pierre would try to destroy all that he did not seize to feed his troops.

Wulfgar wasn't particularly comfortable with the method of warfare necessary to defend a keep. He was accustomed to battling in the open, with room to maneuver, to retreat or attack as necessary. Chrétien's advice, he knew, was sound and the majority of the men under him were accustomed to the European practices even if the men who had come with him were not.

He did not like the notion of skulking behind stone walls and pitching battle with his enemy, however, and more than that, he did not care for the fact that Alinor would be in the midst of the fighting. He was almost certain that Jean-Pierre would head straight for Vardon and he was tempted to send Alinor with her parents. It was the 'not quite' that prevented him from doing so, for he felt better to defend Alinor himself than to leave her defense to anyone else, even her father.

Alinor found the entire situation unnerving. If she had thought of it at all, she would have been convinced that Jean-Pierre would not come so far only to make war to gain more land—but he had gone to England to gain land, when he had already believed that he had hers and his own French estate, and she was obliged to admit that Wulfgar might be right.

If the circumstances had been different, she would have welcomed the distraction. She was fairly certain she and Wulfgar had not resolved the little misunderstanding that she had inadvertently created, but he was too caught up in preparing for war to spare much time for her.

To make matters worse, she was afraid she had a new problem.

She wasn't at all certain she was with child, for she could see no sign of change in her body that would reassure her. She had not had her menses since before Wulfgar had taken her. The old crone had, apparently, assured Wulfgar that she was with child, even though there had been some question that she had miscarried, but her belly was as flat as before. Surely, in all the time that had passed, she should at least have a little pooch?

She was certain she must be with child by now, even if she had not been before. The problem was that the child had been one of the reasons Wulfgar had decided to wed her. She had berated him for getting her with child and refusing to marry her.

He would remember that.

If she had the child a year or more after they had first met then he would know she could not have been with child when she claimed to be. To his mind it would be a lie, and he hated deceit in any form, big or small.

The worst of it was that he had begun to caress her belly at night, as if he were thinking of the child—anticipating its arrival.

If he had not been so distracted, she felt sure he would already have noticed, perhaps even questioned her about it, for she was—should be—nearly four months gone, nearly upon the time when she should feel the quickening.

She would have been willing to lie to prevent yet another barrier from being erected between them, but, because she had been so stupid as to put it into his mind that she might have a roving eye, he coupled with her far too often for her to complain of her woman's time, to claim miscarriage—to claim anything at all, and she was fairly certain she was not up to feigning a miscarriage even if not for the fact that it was too late to do so.

Briefly, she entertained the wild idea of flinging herself from the tower, just so she would not have to face the inevitable confrontation with Wulfgar—She rather liked the notion of him weeping over her broken corpse, but it lost its luster when she realized she would not be there to enjoy it and she could not convince herself that he would be devastated anyway.

Moreover, she was not at all certain that the fall was high enough to kill her outright and the idea of lingering for days, weeks, months or even years after she had mutilated her body past mending had no appeal at all.

She was fairly convinced, then, that she must be with child for she was not generally prone to such insane urges and her mother had told her it was not uncommon for women who were with child to 'not be themselves'. She liked to think that might also account for some of the more bizarre things that she had said and done since she had met Wulfgar. It gave her hope that, once the babe was born, she might then be able to win his affection instead of steadily driving him further away.

She was finally able to put her fears to the back of her mind when she awoke one morning to the news that an army had crossed onto their southern boundary and sacked the small keep at Coyne. The standard they carried was the boar's head. Jean-Pierre had come. Wulfgar assembled his men and went out to meet him.

* * * *

"In matters of war a woman's opinion is never welcome. Any expression of concern will, at best, earn a woman a pat on the head and advise to attend to women's matters. At worst, it will result in an argument that could endanger your man's life, for they can not afford distractions of any kind when they are about the business of trying to hack each other to death," Claire had told her daughter more than once over the years.

Alinor was certain it was sage advice. She was just as certain that there could be no one worse than she when it came to handling a matter diplomatically. She merely watched Wulfgar's preparations to leave in tense silence, therefore, her tongue firmly between her teeth, although she was in an agony of dread. She was still trying to decide what expression she should be wearing if Wulfgar chanced to glance at her when he did.

He frowned and she decided the petrified look probably wasn't the least provocative expression she could have come up with. "You will be safe here."

Alinor nodded, although it hadn't crossed her mind to be fearful for herself. It should have. She had an unpleasant certainty of what Jean-Pierre was capable of, and knew that, if he could, he would make her a widow first and a bride shortly behind that.

She could not presently think beyond the possibility of becoming a widow, however.

"I shall leave half the men here to hold the keep."

Alinor gaped at him in horrified dismay. It was bad enough to think of him meeting Jean-Pierre on an open field when he would have been far safer behind the walls of Vardon. She saw no reason for him to expose himself to more danger by leaving so many to hold the keep. "You will not need them?" she asked faintly, before she had time to think better of it.

"I can not afford to leave the keep virtually unprotected. If he should outflank me ... I want enough men here to hold it until your father can come to your aid."

Alinor blanched. Was he expecting to die? Hoping to join his beloved Freda? She wondered a little wildly. "Must you go out to meet him?"

He studied her for several moments and finally strode toward her, enfolding her in a tight embrace. "You will be safe. I swear it. I can not sit idly here and wait for him to ravage all that lies between here and Coyne."

They could burn it all to the ground for all she cared,

but, as frightened as she was for his safety, she realized Wulfgar would be insulted if she suggested he could not best Jean-Pierre. In truth, she had no reason at all to believe he was not equal to or far superior a warrior than Jean-Pierre. She clung to him tightly. "You will take care? You will not expose yourself foo—needlessly?" She said anxiously.

"Nay, love. I have no death wish," he said soothingly, stroking her hair. He pulled a little away from her and placed a palm on her belly. "I have a wish to see my son come into this world."

Alinor summoned a wavery smile. If he had said anything but that! Now she would be worrying herself sick that the child in her belly was a female!

It occurred to her that, perhaps, it was the opening she had hoped for. She should seize this moment to tell him that it might be many months more than they had anticipated before that day arrived, but before she could summon the courage to do so, he kissed her briefly on the lips, released her and strode from the solar.

Chapter Fourteen

When she heard the troop ride out, Alinor left the solar, crossed the courtyard and climbed the stairs to the walk at the top of the keep walls, moving to a position where she could watch Wulfgar until he and his men disappeared from sight. When she turned away at last, she saw that the captain of the guard had come to stand nearby. "Did my lord send word to my father that he would go out to meet Jean-Pierre's army?"

He glanced at her and frowned. "Nay, my lady. He said nothing of it to me."

Alinor nodded and turned to stare into the distance. "I should think my father would wish to know."

"Should I send a messenger then, my lady?"

Alinor turned and smiled at him. "That is an excellent idea, Captain!"

She felt somewhat better after that. Very likely her father would do as Wulfgar had, take no more than half his men if even that many, but it could only improve the odds in Wulfgar's favor to have more men with

280

him.

She had nothing to do then but wait—a thing that was not nearly as easy to do as one might think. She did her best to direct her mind toward the business of keeping her household running smoothly, but no matter how hard she worked it was difficult to keep her anxieties at bay.

Finally, a messenger came with the news that Wulfgar and her father had managed to rout Jean-Pierre's forces. He had not managed to capture Jean-Pierre, however, and meant to pursue him to the coast to make certain they returned to England.

Alinor was both disappointed and uneasy when the messenger departed. Wulfgar had never made it a habit to elaborate on his messages. She couldn't decide whether there was censure in the mention of her father or not for her interference in the matter. It seemed significant that he did not return at once.

She finally decided she must be imagining Wulfgar's displeasure, however. He had made it clear that nothing would satisfy him short of killing Jean-Pierre. He had not gone to make certain that Jean-Pierre had returned to England. He had gone to make certain Jean-Pierre did not.

A week dragged by and then another. The first snow had fallen the day Wulfgar had left and it had snowed many times since. She had no doubt that the weather was making things difficult for Wulfgar, but worry gave way to anger long before she finally had word of him again.

Wulfgar returned for supplies, carrying the news that, instead of returning to England, Jean-Pierre had circled round and was now hold up at his French estate.

* * * *

As soon as he was spotted, Alinor sent the maids scurrying to build up the fire in their apartments, to heat water for a bath, and bring food. Wulfgar found her there overseeing their efforts with a critical eye. It was several moments before she realized he had come into the room and, as he stood watching her, he realized that the sense of homecoming that had flooded him the moment Vardon came into view had nothing to do with place, and everything to do with Alinor. He frowned at the realization, wondering what moment in time had marked the transition from captor, to lover, to loving husband, but he could not seem to recall a time when he had not felt contentment only from the knowledge that he was with her and she was his.

Nor could he mark the time when his pursuit of Jean-Pierre had ceased to be driven by the need for revenge and become a determination to protect Alinor from the animosity that raged between them.

He was certain, however, that he loved Alinor as he had never loved Freda. He had never known Freda as he knew Alinor. Freda had been a fire in his blood from the moment he set eyes upon her. He had never been able to think beyond the need to possess her, or his rage that she had been taken from him before he had even become accustomed to the fact that she was his.

It was different with Alinor. His desire for her was just as intense, perhaps even more so, and yet it was more than that. He had missed sleeping with her curled next to him, hearing her voice, seeing her face—he had even missed her unruly tongue and her sometimes amusing, sometimes infuriating, efforts to mend her unthinking remarks.

She noticed him just then and looked up, surprise, pleasure and doubt chasing across her features.

The doubt bothered him. It was always in her eyes when she looked at him, evidence that she did not completely trust him and because of that, she always tried to hide her feelings from him.

He thought that was the way of it, in any case. He could never be sure. She was always so open in every other way that he could not be certain that she cared, but held herself back because she did not trust, or if she only seemed to be holding herself back because she did not care for him as he did her.

It mattered. It should not have. She was his wife, regardless, but he wanted more. He wanted all.

"My lord! There was such a clatter I did not hear you come in! Come. Sit by the fire and warm yourself." Turning away, Alinor shooed the maids out and closed the door.

When she looked around again, she saw that Wulfgar had not moved, but still stood as he had before, watching her. He looked weary to the point of sleeping on his feet. Grasping his hand, she tugged him toward the hearth, leading him to the chair she had positioned their for his comfort and pushing at him until he sat. "You are nigh frozen," she fussed, chafing his hands for several moments and finally kneeling to pull his boots off.

"I've had the maids prepare a hot bath for you. Would you rather bathe first? Or eat?"

Wulfgar's eyes gleamed. "That depends."

Alinor lifted her brows questioningly.

"On what you are offering me to eat."

Alinor stared at him a long moment in incomprehension, then, slowly, a blush rose all the way to her hairline. "I can not think that that would appease your hunger."

"It is that hunger I am most in need of assuaging—

283

but as I suspect I smell like a mountain goat, I suppose I should brave the bath first."

He stood up to undress and Alinor stepped back, examining him surreptitiously for signs of injury. To her relief, although she saw a number of small cuts, none appeared in need of attention. When she realized that he had noticed her inspection, she busied herself collecting his soiled clothing, crossing the room to pile it outside their door for the maids to collect for the laundress as he climbed into the tub.

The tub had not been designed for anyone quite as large as Wulfgar she saw when she turned. She bit her lip to contain her amusement, knowing the tub could not be at all comfortable for him. Despite the hot water, he shivered as he lathered his arms, chest and shoulders. Her amusement vanished and she moved quickly to kneel behind him and help him with his bath, lathering his hair and scrubbing his scalp and then pouring warm water from the pitcher slowly over his head to rinse it. When she was certain she had rinsed the soap from his hair, she urged him to lean forward and scrubbed his back. He groaned with pleasure as she rubbed his back and she continued for some moments after she had finished washing, and then rinsing, the soap from him.

"You could join me," he suggested in a thick voice when she finally stopped and moved around the tub to pick up the length of linen that had been warming by the fire.

She chuckled. "There is barely enough room for you."

He studied her speculatively for several moments and finally rose from the water. Alinor held the linen up for him. When he stepped out, she stood on her tiptoes, wrapping it around him and drying him briskly. "I have a robe for you."

As she moved toward it, however, he caught her around the waist. Dragging her back against him, he caught her jaw and bent to kiss her long and lingeringly. Alinor felt a rush of heat. He had trapped her arms between them, however, and she struggled to free them. He broke the kiss, moving slightly away to look at her questioningly, but she didn't notice the look. The moment he released her she slipped her palms up his chest and locked her arms behind his head, pressing herself fully against him.

A tremor went through him as she lifted her lips for his kiss. His arms tightened almost crushingly as he captured her lips one more, kissing her hungrily, his mouth and tongue near scorching as he caressed her mouth with his own.

Alinor was so caught up in the heat raging through her veins that many moments passed before she became aware of the tremors running through him. Reluctantly, she broke the kiss and pulled away. "You are cold."

His eyes were glazed, almost feverish, his skin flushed. Alarm ran through her. Small wonder he had seemed to be behaving strangely. "You are fevered," she said in dismay.

"Aye," he said, scooping her into his arms and striding across the room to the bed. He climbed upon the mattress with her still in his arms, falling upon her like a man starved as he settled her against the bedding. Alinor gasped with a mixture of surprise and excitement as his mouth and hands moved over her, thrusting her clothing aside so that he could touch her bare skin. Struggling, she finally managed to push him away enough to fumble with the lacings of her gown. He brushed her fingers away impatiently, tugging her clothing off and tossing each article in first one direction and then another until she lay naked beneath him.

He seemed seized by a sort of madness, nipping her flesh with his teeth, sucking upon it, massaging, tracing every inch of her body. Within moments, Alinor felt as if she were seized with it, as well, descending into an abyss where she was aware of nothing but the feel of him against her and his caresses. His breathing was harsh, ragged. She could not seem to catch her breath.

Grasping her wrists, he pinned them to the bed on either side of her head, suckling upon the sensitive tips of her breasts until her entire body was awash with a fevered tension, and she writhed beneath him, moaning endlessly. She wasn't even aware of when he ceased to hold her captive for his caresses until he kissed a burning path up her throat and opened his mouth over hers.

She slipped her arms around his neck as he thrust his tongue into her mouth to taste and explore the sensitive inner surfaces, threading her fingers through his silky hair, stroking his shoulders, his back as far as she could reach.

He moved away impatiently after only a moment, breaking the kiss to move his mouth down her throat once more, kissing her breasts, her belly. When he reached her thighs, he pushed them apart, kissing the exquisitely sensitive flesh near the apex of her thighs. She cried out as his heated mouth settled over her femininity, sucking, lathing with his tongue. Within moments, her body convulsed in an explosion of pleasure.

She was still caught up in the aftershocks when he moved over her once more, nudging her femininity with the head of his cock and finally seating himself and thrusting inside of her in a desperate rhythm that strummed her body, taking her quickly to culmination a second time that was far more intense than the first.

He came with her that time, explosively, crying out hoarsely before he collapsed in a boneless heap half on top of her. Alinor drifted to sleep with the feel of Wulfgar stroking her belly gently.

When she woke, Wulfgar had already ridden out once more.

Chapter Fifteen

Wulfgar had told her that he had only come for supplies and that he would return once more to Jean-Pierre's holdings to make certain that he was settled for the winter before he relaxed his vigilance. She had not expected that he would leave again immediately, however, and certainly not while she lay sleeping.

She was peeved that he had left without even bidding her farewell, but not greatly disturbed—at first. In the beginning, she had not been able to recall anything about the night before except their lovemaking. Later, she recalled that he had murmured something about her belly as he lay stroking it. It was then that dismay filled her, and the anxiety that he had realized that she had deceived him and was angry about it.

It was ironic that he had only seemed to notice now, when her belly had begun to take on a roundness that reassured her that she was with child, when she had finally become certain that the tiny flutters she had been feeling were the movements of the child and not nervous stomach.

A messenger arrived from Arrus the day Wulfgar departed. Her parents had invited her and Wulfgar to join them in the festivities they had planned for Christmas. Excitement flooded her, but was immediately dashed when she realized that Wulfgar might not return before then.

As disappointing as that was, it was far more upsetting that she would miss the opportunity to speak with her mother about all the things that had been worrying her. She thought Wulfgar would probably take her when he returned, unless the weather turned particularly nasty, but that could be weeks yet.

She thought it was possible that she had blown everything all out of proportion, but she wanted her mother's reassurances that much of the problem was no more than pure imagination and the rest of little or no consequence. Of equal importance, she did not understand the changes in her body. By her count, her child would be born late winter or early spring, but that did not seem right when her belly was yet so small. If she had been a buxom woman, she could have understood it, but she was not. It would almost have been easier to accept that she had not conceived when she thought, even if she then had to face Wulfgar with her deceit. At least then she would not be so worried that the child would be too small to survive.

The more she thought about it, the more certain she became that she needed her mother to advise her and that she could not wait weeks for the reassurances she needed. The following morning, she packed for a short stay and arranged for an escort. The man Wulfgar had left in charge of the keep's defense was not happy with her decision, but she pointed out that her parents had sent for her. Wulfgar had not left orders that she was not to leave. Wulfgar had said that Jean-Pierre was far away, in his own keep, and it was not far to her parents' keep in any case.

They debated next over the size of her escort. Alinor considered three men more than enough. He wanted to send a dozen. Finally, after she had pointed out that there was no sense in weakening the security of the keep by sending so many, they settled upon a half a dozen men and Alinor set out.

Alinor was uneasy about her decision almost the moment the gates closed behind them. At any other time, she might have simply said that she had thought better of it and changed her mind. Everyone had already begun to look at her as if they suspected she was afflicted with a touch of madness, however, so she firmly ignored the sense of danger that assailed her the moment she found herself exposed.

She had committed herself to the trip. She needed to see her mother. It could not take long to travel to Arrus and once she was there, she would know it had been nothing but her imagination.

The snow was deep. They decided that it would take less time to take the road, even though it would have been a shorter distance to simply cut across country.

To Alinor's dismay, the uneasiness did not abate. Instead, the further they traveled from Vardon, the deeper her conviction became that something simply did not feel 'right'. It did not help one whit that she noticed her escort was looking distinctly uneasy, as well.

They reached the halfway point, however, without incident. Alinor was just beginning to feel that she had worried needlessly when a group of riders emerged from the trees ahead of them. Alinor's hand jerked reflexively on the reigns and her horse skittered, toss-ing its head and dancing sideways. As one, they halted. The man to her right muttered under his breath. "There are only four of them to our six."

The leader, who was riding to her left, shifted in his saddle, glancing all around them. "This has the feel of a trap to me—and Lord Wulfgar will have our ballocks for endangering his lady. Jacques, Piers, Frayne and Claude—hold them. Christophe and I will return with Lady Alinor to Vardon." Leaning down, he grasped the reigns of Alinor's mount. "Back. Now!" he yelled, even as he urged the two horses around, kicking his own into a gallop.

It would have worked had Jean not been right, but they had not gone far when another group of riders flooded from the woods, again blocking their path. Instead of skidding their horses to a halt, Jean changed directions abruptly, heading cross country.

Alinor's mount, much smaller than the war horses, floundered, pitching her from her precarious perch and into the snow. She lay stunned for many moments, fighting to catch her breath. Around her, she was vaguely aware of the clash of swords. Shaking herself, she got to her feet with an effort, glanced around and headed for the only cover available, the trees. The snow was loose, however, and deep. It was like trying to wade through waist high surf, only worse, for the snow offered no buoyancy, only resistance. She had man-aged to cover no more than a few yards when a rider swooped down upon her. Leaning from his saddle, he caught her around the waist and dragged her up onto the saddle before him.

Alinor screamed, clawing ineffectually at his armor. Abruptly, something hard caught her across the jaw. Pain exploded inside her head and she slumped against the man, dazed, barely conscious. The sounds of fight ing ceased even as her captor turned his mount and kicked it into motion once more.

"I see my little bride has missed me," the man muttered with a sneer.

Alinor shuddered as Jean-Pierre's voice washed over her, giving up the fight to cling to consciousness.

* * * *

It was some time before Alinor realized that they were heading for the coast. That seemed almost as insane as capturing her to begin with. It would have made more sense, surely, to return to his holdings in France than to return to England? Why bother with her now anyway? She was not such a great heiress at to be worth so much effort, and, in any case, she was obviously with child now. Was it because she carried Wulfgar's heir? How would he even find anyone willing to make the crossing in the dead of winter?

Alinor shook those thoughts off. It did not matter why she had been taken or even where she was being taken. The only thing of any importance was how she might get herself out of her fix. She had no notion when the party that had sent for her would be missed, but it occurred to her forcefully that the only way Jean-Pierre would have been able to set his trap for her was if he had a spy within Vardon—or if he had sent the messenger himself.

The messenger should have been questioned more carefully. She should have been more suspicious— but hindsight was of no use to her either, beyond trying to estimate how long it would be before it was known that she was missing, and, if her parents had not sent the messenger it seemed probable that Jean-Pierre would have her in England before anyone even realized she had been captured.

They had slain her escort and left their bodies lying where they fell, but it had snowed almost continuously since and few people would be traveling now. They might lie their for days before anyone stumbled upon the bodies and reported it. The men had made no plans to return to Vardon immediately and would not be expected back—her parents, she realized now, would not be expecting her.

She would have to try to escape, for if Jean-Pierre managed to get her to England Wulfgar would need to bring an army to free her and Duke William would not ignore an army. Wulfgar would draw attack from every side if he tried—perhaps that was why Jean-Pierre had thought it was better to take her there?

Jean-Pierre gave her no opportunity to escape, however. When she woke, she found herself bound hand and foot. She had expected as much, had known she would have to free herself of her bonds before she had a chance of escaping, but she did not even have the opportunity for that. Except to rest the horses and to relieve themselves, they did not stop at all, even eating in the saddle. Regardless, their pace was slowed by the weather and it took far longer to reach the coast than it had when she had traveled it before. She was so exhausted by the time they reached the coast that even her fear did not lend her the strength she knew she would need to escape.

She was too weary even for the crossing to terrify her and so ill from being tossed around by the churning water that death would have been welcome. She managed to rouse herself sufficiently, however, once they had crossed the channel to realize that escape was not much of a possibility and that she had far worse things to consider.

Jean-Pierre had not touched her. He had not even spoken to her once he discovered that she refused to respond to his taunts, but he had made it perfectly clear that he intended to ravish her the moment the opportunity arose. She could not allow that, although she was well aware that fighting him off was not an option.

If she had not been carrying Wulfgar's child, she might have considered that enduring was worth it if it insured life, but she was, and enduring would not insure her life or the child's—for she didn't delude herself for a moment that he would be gentle with her even if she gave him no resistance.

She had to protect her babe—the question was, how?

Desperation and a fertile mind supplied a note of hope when she was allowed to go into the woods to relieve herself. She had squatted near a plant that she had previously had a very unpleasant encounter with. She was about to move away from it when the idea sprang into her mind. Glancing toward the man set to watch her, she wrapped her hand in the folds of her skirt and pulled the plant up, rubbing it against her bare thighs and belly before she could lose her nerve.

Her skin immediately began to sting but she resisted the urge to press a handful of snow against it.

It occurred to her, afterwards, that she might only have made herself miserable for no reason at all, or that the poisons in the plant might hurt the babe—but she had no other choices that she could see.

By the time they reached Jean-Pierre's English holdings, Alinor was nearly mindless with the itch from the rash and all else paled by comparison.

Jean-Pierre cut the bonds around her ankles before he pulled her from the horse, but Alinor's knees buckled the moment her feet touched the ground. With an impatient oath, Jean-Pierre swung her into his arms and carried her inside. Instead of stopping in the great room, as she had hoped, he climbed the stairs to his apartment. When they reached his bed chamber, he slammed the door behind them, strode across the room and tossed her onto the bed.

Alinor immediately scrambled away, but she was not quick enough for him. He caught the fabric of her gown. Hearing a distinct ripping sound, Alinor fought harder to crawl away from him. As if the sound itself had spurred him on, however, Jean-Pierre leapt upon her, grasping her gown and ripping it from her in a frenzy until no more than tatters hung about her.

She fought him. Despite her resolve to acquiesce for the sake of her child, she was so terrorized she lost all sense of logic and fought him purely on instinct. After slapping her several times with no appreciable effect, he finally slammed him fist against her jaw.

Stunned, Alinor went limp, trying to fight the blackness that threatened to descend, leaving her completely helpless and at his mercy.

She was relieved, momentarily, when he rolled off of her, until it finally clicked in her mind that he had only left her to discard his own clothing. He halted abruptly, however, cursing.

"What, by all that's holy, is wrong with you?"

With an effort, Alinor lifted her head to look at him. Following the direction of his gaze, she looked down at herself. Her mind went perfectly blank for several moments. Finally, however, she recalled her desperate ruse. "It is nothing. A rash only," she muttered somewhat drunkenly, so dizzy from the blow that she could hardly gather her wits about her. "My lover said I was not to concern myself over it. It would go away."

Jean-Pierre looked at her in revulsion for several moments. "Your lover?"

Alinor nodded with an effort. "The captain of the guard—he said it would surely be gone before Wulfgar returned."

Jean-Pierre's eyes narrowed and Alinor's heart squeezed painfully while she waited, wondering if he would believe her lie—wondering if her ruse would work as she had hoped. Finally, he stepped to the door and bellowed for one of his men to fetch the old Saxon witch woman.

He paced the room while they waited. Slowly, the dizziness receded sufficiently that fear curled around Alinor's innards.

Finally, they heard a shuffle outside the door. Jean-Pierre strode to the door and snatched it open. Grasping the old woman who stood there by one arm, he dragged her into the room and shoved her toward the bed. "Attend her."

The woman stumbled but managed to right herself and shuffled nearer. Alinor dragged her gaze from Jean-Pierre and looked at the woman, wishing Jean-Pierre had left and given her the opportunity to speak with the woman alone. The woman leaned forward, looking at the angry, reddened skin that covered Alinor from her waist almost to her knees. Her glance flicked briefly to Alinor's face.

"It is the rot, my lord. Her man's done got it off some whore and given it to her."

Jean-Pierre cuffed her. "You lie, witch!"

The woman cringed, scurrying away. "'Tis the truth," she whined. "Your cock will rot off if you touch her."

"You can cure this?"

"Nay, my lord. There is no cure."

Jean-Pierre ground his teeth in impotent fury. "If you value your life, old woman, you will find a cure."

When he had slammed out of the room, the old woman glanced at her. To Alinor's amazement, her eyes were alight with both amusement and, strangely, respect. "There's a nasty rash ye've got yerself. Ye should have used the leaves more sparingly."

Chapter Sixteen

Wulfgar's anger grew the closer he came to Arrus. He had been looking forward to returning to Vardon with an impatience that had grown impossible to ignore after nearly a week of shivering in a miserable tent. When he had seen the activity in Jean-Pierre's keep increase as they began making preparations for a feast, he had been convinced that Jean-Pierre had indeed settled in for the winter and had, with relief, ordered his men to strike camp and head for home, anxious to return to Alinor.

He had been stunned when he returned and found her gone. Disappointment had very quickly turned to irritation, however. He had been more than a little inclined to sulk at Vardon and send word to Arrus demanding that Alinor return immediately, but, after wandering the halls miserable for several days, had decided instead to go after her.

His mood was foul when he arrived at Arrus and it did not improve when he was shown into the great hall and saw no sign of Alinor. "Where is my lady?" he growled when Chrétien and Claire greeted him.

They exchanged a glance. "She is at Vardon," Claire said a little breathlessly even as Chrétien jumped to his feet.

"She is not with you?" Chrétien demanded.

Wulfgar stared at them for several moments. "I was told a messenger had been sent inviting her here for the festivities nigh two weeks ago."

"Oh," Claire gasped, pressing a hand to her heart.

Chrétien paled. "We sent no messenger."

Wulfgar's heart sank, but he had no need to question her parents further. He could see from their faces that they were as stunned and frightened as he was. Whirling on his heel without another word, he strode from the keep. Chrétien, bellowing for his cloak, followed him.

Wulfgar found once he had ridden out that he was seized by an unaccustomed indecisiveness. It immediately leapt to mind that Jean-Pierre had somehow taken her, but he could not decide whether it was logical to assume so or not. He had tracked Jean-Pierre and his men back to his keep. He was certain of that. There had been only one window of opportunity for Jean-Pierre to leave without his knowing it—when he had returned to Vardon for supplies.

Jean-Pierre must have followed him, waiting until he'd left again to set his trap.

The question was, would he have taken her back to his keep at Merrill? Or would he have considered that that was too easy and have taken her to England? Wulfgar frowned. The channel was treacherous most any time, but far more so at this time of year.

After a moment, he kicked his horse into motion and struck off along the road to Vardon. He'd ridden cross country before. Most likely, Alinor's escort would have taken the road.

He found the men purely by chance when his horse stumbled over one of the bodies hidden in the snow. Dismounting, he pushed the snow aside and studied the man he'd discovered. Recognizing the man, he pulled his sword from its scabbard and began to poke around until he found several others.

Chrétien rode up with a troop of men while he was examining the corpses. He dismounted, joining Wulfgar.

"Her escort?"

Wulfgar nodded grimly. "Thomas said he sent six men with her. I have found only three." He glanced around at the woods. "Wolves might have dragged the others off," he added thoughtfully.

Chrétien dropped to one knee in the snow. "Alinor?"

Wulfgar glanced at him sharply. "He would not have killed her."

"You think this is Jean-Pierre's doing?"

"Thieves would not have fallen upon six well armed men."

Chrétien nodded, looking around at the woods. Finally, he motioned to the men still mounted and had them search for bodies. They found a fourth man a little away from the others and Chrétien sent a man back to Arrus to bring a cart for the dead.

Wulfgar stood up. "They came out of the woods here. These men would have been ordered to guard their back while the other two tried to escape with Alinor."

Briefly, hope flickered across Chrétien's countenance before he realized Alinor had not escaped or she would have been returned to Vardon.

"I will take Merrill apart stone by stone if need be," Wulfgar said through gritted teeth.

Chrétien stood abruptly. "I will gather my men and meet you at Vardon."

* * * *

When their army had gathered at the gates of Merrill, Chrétien and Wulfgar rode forward, demanding to speak with Jean-Pierre. The captain of the guard laughed. "He can not come, Monsieur. He is busy entertaining his lady."

Wulfgar made an abortive moment, as if he would charge the gates that moment, but Chrétien grasped his arm. "He thinks to taunt you into riding within his archers' range. You are no good to Alinor dead!"

Pulling his horse around, Wulfgar rode back toward his men. Chrétien brought his horse even. "We must settle in for a siege. We can not use the trebuchets when Alinor is held within without risking her life. At any other time, I would suggest we dig under the walls, but the ground is frozen now. The keep might well fall from siege before we could dig a tunnel to bring the walls down."

Wulfgar nodded grimly, but he was of no mind to wait to starve them out. Alinor would starve as well as everyone else and she was far too thin already, and well gone with child. The risk was too great that she would be among the first to starve. After studying the walls for some time, Wulfgar ordered the trebuchet brought forward and carefully positioned so that the stones it lobbed against the keep struck the outer wall itself, low so as to weaken it. There was still a danger to Alinor if any of the stones went wild, but far less so than lining it up to strike the men along the crenalations or firing wildly into the keep itself.

The men who held the keep jeered when the first stones began to strike the walls. When cracks began to form along the walls, however, and the stones of the wall itself began to crumble, they brought men up with long bows to fire at those manning the trebuchet. It was out of range, but occasionally a spent arrow would strike one of his men and pandemonium would briefly ensue.

Wulfgar had begun to have the uneasy feeling that he had been tricked long before the walls finally collapsed, for, in all the time that they had battered at Merrill Jean-Pierre had not once been spotted. In the beginning, he had been certain that Jean-Pierre would not have taken her all the way back to England. The more he thought of it, however, the more he saw the advantage to Jean-Pierre in doing so.

His holdings in England had no stone walls to protect it, but Wulfgar would not be allowed to bring an army into England—or indeed any number of men of sufficient strength to overcome Jean-Pierre.

Impatient to know for certain, Wulfgar set his men to building another trebuchet. In only a few weeks, they had two firing steadily at the walls. In little more than a month, holes began to form and finally, one large section of the keep walls collapsed and the combined armies of Wulfgar and Chrétien stormed the breech. Within a day, the men defending Merrill lay down their arms and were rounded up. Every inch of the keep was searched, but Wulfgar knew long before the searchers reported back that Alinor was not there.

Selecting the highest ranking officers, Wulfgar had them questioned. When they proved reluctant, they were tortured until he had the information he sought.

Chrétien felt they should petition Duke William for Alinor's return. He had never met the man, but from what he knew of William, he felt that William would do his best assure her safe return. Wulfgar was of no mind to wait so long. It could take many months to free her using diplomatic channels and he had no confidence that Alinor could survive Jean-Pierre's tender mercies so long—if she still lived even now.

Taking only the men who had come with him from England, he set out with the determination to finish the war between himself and Jean-Pierre.

* * * *

Alinor had begun to despair that Wulfgar would come for her. Try though she might to reassure herself, it crept through her mind, unbidden, that Wulfgar need not take the risk. He had been acknowledged as her husband and heir. If she were dead, all that had been hers would be his and he would be free to wed another more to his taste.

She knew Wulfgar was a man who valued his honor, and that he was not of an avaricious nature—he was bull headed and sometimes quick tempered, but he was no fool. He must know that it would be nearly impossible to rescue her. Perhaps, even though it had never been his intention to profit from her death, he had realized the futility of trying to get her back? Perhaps, even though it was not her fault, he could not stomach the notion of taking her back when he must believe that Jean-Pierre had made her his whore?

He might yet if Wulfgar did not come for her. Despite Jean-Pierre's fear of disease, he had been suspicious from the first and she was not certain he still believed the rash she had perpetuated with judicious applications of the poisonous plant was in truth the disease of whores.

Moreover, she was growing increasingly unnerved about the old Saxon healer's involvement in her deception. It would mean her life if she was discovered. She had assured Alinor that she did not count the cost to herself so long as she protected Lord Wulfgar's child, for she was well past the age where life had a great deal of meaning, but she deserved the peaceful death of a long life, not the death that Jean-Pierre would deal her if he discovered her deception.

Then, one evening when the healer came, her eyes were alight with excitement. At the first opportunity, she leaned close and whispered, "Wulfgar has come for you. Be ready, for we must move quickly when the time comes."

Alinor was at once thrilled and terrified. Two days passed in an agony of suspense. Even the healer, Hilda did not come. Then, in the afternoon, she slipped into Alinor's room. "Do not eat tonight," she said quickly and turned to leave. "I will come for you an hour past supper."

"You will take me to Wulfgar?" Alinor whispered urgently.

The woman paused and looked back at her. "He comes here. I am to take you down to the great hall to meet him."

Alinor paced the room when she had gone, pausing by the window from time to time to watch the sun as it sank toward the horizon, listening to the manor around her, though she wasn't certain what she listened for. It seemed certain Hilda had arranged to poison the food, but she closed her mind to that unimaginable horror. If it would insure the safety of Wulfgar ....

She was standing by the window, listening to the sounds below that told her the men had gathered to eat when her door was flung open. Jean-Pierre stood upon the threshold.

"I see you are better today," he said coolly.

Alinor stared at him in apprehension. She had feigned illness to match her rash and spent much of her time in bed, but Jean-Pierre had not even been into her room in weeks and she had relaxed her guard. She saw now that that had been a serious error in judgment.

"You will be joining me tonight. Make yourself presentable."

Chapter Seventeen

Alinor discovered she had no need to feign illness as she was seated beside Jean-Pierre at the head table. She was ill with terror, but well aware that she could not behave in any suspicious manner or she risked unraveling the entire plot that Hilda and Wulfgar had hatched.

She could not bring herself to eat the food. She had no idea of what Hilda had given the cooks to lace into the food—if it would merely cause illness, or death—nor if all of the food had been poisoned or only some dishes. To her relief, one of the young serving maids appeared beside her shortly after she was seated, placing a trencher in front of her. "Hilda prepared this especially for you, knowing the difficulty you have had in holding your food," the girl murmured.

Alinor forced a smile, refusing to allow Jean-Pierre to catch her eye. In truth, even the certainty that the food was not tainted did nothing for her appetite for she could not help but notice that Jean-Pierre ate little himself. Her belly felt as if it had tied itself into knots. With an effort, she managed to eat a few bites, chewing her food slowly.

"We will wed when you have dropped that bastard you carry in your belly."

Startled, Alinor glanced at Jean-Pierre. "My marriage to Wulfgar is legally binding," she retorted. "It can not be annulled, whatever you may think."

Jean-Pierre shrugged. "I must arrange to make you a widow. I've no objection to doing so—Of course that entails laying my hands upon that sniveling coward you wed."

Alinor flushed. "My husband is no coward—nor a fool, as you thought. Meet him in single combat as he has asked—without your army at your back," she said tightly.

Jean-Pierre uttered an unconvincing laugh, but a flush of annoyance mounted his cheeks. "I am no fool either. I went to meet him before." He shrugged. "He slipped up behind the men who had accompanied me to the meeting and attacked. That is not the actions of a man of courage and honor."

Alinor glared at him. "He did not fall into your trap, you mean! If he has ever been a fool at all it was in believing you to be a man of honor."

Jean-Pierre's eyes narrowed. "And yet, you have taken a lover already and not wed to him even a full year."

Alinor felt the blood rush from her cheeks. She looked down at her hands. "It was a moment of foolish pride," she said slowly. "I was angry that he paid me no mind and thought to make him jealous. I did not intend that it go so far."

"I will make certain that I give you my undivided attention," Jean-Pierre murmured as he leaned close.

Alinor leaned away, eyeing him distastefully. "Hilda

says the disease can not be cured."

"And yet you seem healthy enough to me."

Before Alinor could think of a suitable retort, Jean-Pierre's face contorted, as if a pain had lanced through him. His gaze went instantly to his trencher. Abruptly, he stood up, looking around the hall. Alinor glanced around fearfully, as well, noticing at last that the hall was rapidly emptying, that some had fallen to the floor, writhing in agony. Clutching one hand to her stomach and the other to her mouth, Alinor rose abruptly. "I do not feel at all well," she announced in a voice muffled by her hand.

"Poison!" Jean-Pierre rasped. "We have been poisoned."

Turning away, he put his finger down his throat and promptly began puking. Alinor thought for several moments that she would lose the little she had eaten, but the opportunity she had been awaiting had arrived. Giving Jean-Pierre a shove, she rushed past him. Hilda appeared in the doorway leading to the kitchens and grasped her arm, hurrying her toward the great oaken doors that fronted the manor. Before they had made their way halfway down the hall, a battering came at the doors, causing them to shudder. Again and again, something battered at the door. Abruptly flew open.

Men on horseback dropped the log they had used as a battering ram and charged into the hall, upending tables and benches, trampling the men who were rolling around on the floor. Alinor's heart leapt. "Wulfgar!"

His head jerked in her direction. He forced his horse through the melee, leaning low, one arm outstretched. Alinor ran to him, holding her arms up to him. Scooping her up, he settled her on the saddle before him. Alinor wrapped her arms around his waist, clinging tightly to him, bunching herself into a tight ball to allow him room to fight, for, despite their illness, Jean-Pierre's men had begun to rally, grabbing their weapons and racing to defend the manor.

Wulfgar's glance went to Jean-Pierre, his eyes narrowing. After a moment, he uttered an oath and turned away, fighting his way free of the great hall. They rode hard until they reached the tree line, but, once there, Wulfgar signaled for the men to halt. Urging his horse alongside Thomas, he grasped Alinor's arms, breaking her grip.

"What are you doing?" Alinor gasped. "We must hurry."

Wulfgar caught her jaw, kissing her briefly. "Take her, Thomas. If I am not there by the time you are ready to leave, take her to her father."

"No!" Alinor cried. "Come with me! Please, Wulfgar!"

"I must end this now. I can not let him live when he has dared to touch you."

Alinor clutched his arm. "He did not! I swear he did not!"

Wulfgar's lips crooked up at one corner. "Aye, not in that way, I know. Hilda told me of your clever ruse. But I will take no more chances with your life. While he lives, he will always be a threat."

Despite her efforts to cling to him, he handed her to Thomas, who gripped her tightly. "Yes," she said a little desperately, "but not here! Not now! You are out numbered. If you care for me at all, please do not make me a widow!"

Wulfgar leaned toward her, touching her cheek briefly. "I care for you with all my heart, Alinor. This is why I must protect you—with my last breath, if necessary."

Alinor wasn't even aware that she was crying until she felt the dampness drip from her jaw. Twisting around, she looked up at the grim faced man who held her. "Leave me and go back."

"I can not," he said tightly. "My lord bade me to take care of his lady."

"But … he is outnumbered! There's no need for three men to accompany me when he has greater need of you than I have!"

He said nothing for several moments. Finally, he looked down at her coldly. "Six men died defending you because you were so willful that you left the keep—and would not have a whole troop accompany you—Lord Wulfgar would more likely lob the head from my shoulders than welcome me if I abandoned you to go to his aid—though I will tell you truly, I would far rather die by his side than live, knowing I left him for your sake."

Alinor was effectively silenced. In truth, she could think of nothing to say in her defense. What could she say, after all? She had not intended that they die? She had not expected that there would be danger? It was true, and yet hardly an excuse when it had cost the men their lives.

Much, if not all, that had happened since she had been betrothed to Jean-Pierre had been because of her, and yet she could not think what she might have done differently—knew that it had been out of her hands even before she had known of Wulfgar. She found, though, that it made her feel no better, no less guilty, no less saddened, to realize that it would have happened no matter what she had done.

* * * *

A sense of exhilaration and purpose filled Wulfgar as he rode once more toward the place that had once been his, the place that his grandfather had built in his time. He did not think of that, however. His entire being was focused upon the men riding toward him, more specifically the one who led them.

The two groups clashed with the clang of steel, the growling bellows of men and the scream of horses midway between the forest and the manor. Despite the ruse Hilda had used to even the odds, Wulfgar's men were outnumbered almost three to one. Wulfgar felt the battle madness descend upon him as he waded through the writhing throng of battling men and horses, hacking and thrusting at anyone who crossed his path, focused upon reaching Jean-Pierre.

Abruptly, the melee seemed to part, leaving the opening Wulfgar had waited for. He charged forward with a roar, swinging his great sword at Jean-Pierre's head. He met steel instead of the satisfying crunch of bone and flesh as Jean-Pierre brought his own sword up to parry the blow. Their swords scraped together until the hilts met, throwing off sparks. For several moments, the two men swayed, each trying to overcome the other by strength alone.

It was no contest, for Wulfgar was by far the strongest of the two. Jean-Pierre fell from his horse, rolled, trying to come to his feet. Wulfgar leapt from his own saddle, swinging even as Jean-Pierre managed to right himself. Again Jean-Pierre blocked a blow that would have cleaved his head from his shoulders. Their blades locked, held. With gritted teeth, they swayed, shoving against one another. Finally, Wulfgar gave Jean-Pierre a heave that sent him stumbling backward.

Again, they advanced upon each other, Wulfgar bringing his blade down again and again, hacking away at Jean-Pierre's strength and confidence as each blow sent a jarring pain through his arm.

"Quarter!" Jean-Pierre finally managed between gritted teeth.

"No quarter!" Wulfgar growled. "You gave none to Alinor."

Jean-Pierre lurched toward Wulfgar in a lightening strike, slicing through the leather armor that covered his thigh, cutting deeply, but he found no advantage. The move exposed his left side completely and Wulfgar did not hesitate. With a roar of triumph, he brought his blade down, severing Jean-Pierre's head from his shoulders. It hit the ground, rolling, a grimace of surprise etched on his features.

Breathing heavily, Wulfgar turned to survey the battle waging around him. His men, he saw, were holding their own, but even as he raced to take his horse and mount once more, he saw more men pouring from the half finished walls surrounding the manor.

"Finish it and be quick about it!" he yelled to his men, falling upon the soldier nearest him and cleaving him almost in half, then whirling toward the next, his focus now on winning free of the men that had first met them before they were joined by reinforcements.

Winning free at last, Wulfgar spurred his horse into a gallop, hurrying to join Alinor and the men he'd sent to escort her home.

He would have far preferred to lead the soldiers away from her, but he doubted they'd fall for the ruse and, without him and his men, she was virtually unguarded.

* * * *

They had been riding for perhaps an hour when the thunder of approaching riders reached them. Thomas glanced at the man beside him. "Wulfgar, you think?"

The man glanced over his shoulder. The moon had risen, but it was still far too dark to see more than a few yards in any direction. "I think I'm not of a mind to wait here and find out."

They had not gone far before they realized that they could not outrun whoever it was, friend or foe, who was thundering down upon them. Thomas slowed, looking around for cover. With relief, Alinor heard Wulfgar call out to them.

With an audible sigh of thankfulness, Thomas dragged on the reins, pulling his horse to a halt. Within moments, Wulfgar and his men rode into view. They skidded to a halt when they came abreast of Alinor's party. "Half the garrison is behind is," Wulfgar said breathlessly reaching for Alinor and pulling her onto the front of his horse once more.

"Are you hurt?" Alinor gasped, tightening her arms around his waist.

"Not as badly as I will be if they catch up to us," he said shortly. "How far, do you think, Thomas?"

Thomas shook his head. "A good hour and a half, maybe two. We'll be lucky to make it in that in the dark."

"We'll not make it at all if we don't ride hard," Wulfgar said grimly. He spared a look down at Alinor. "Are you up to it, love?"

Alinor nodded. "Yes. Let us go."

They rode, endlessly it seemed to Alinor. Behind them, dimly, they heard the sounds of pursuit, but Alinor found very quickly that she could focus upon nothing but the fact that her babe had chosen this night, of all nights, to fight his way into the world.

Chapter Eighteen

The pain rapidly became intolerable. Try though she might, Alinor found she could not be still. Every position she chose only seemed to make her hurt worse. Gritting her teeth against it, she prayed it was no more than the jolting of the horse that was causing her such pain. She knew it could not be time for the babe. If she had it now, it would not survive even if she did… and it seemed unlikely that she would. They could not stop, however, or all were doomed. Finally, she reached a point where she was so enveloped in pain that she ceased to be aware of anything else.

"What ails you, Alinor?" Wulfgar demanded.

"Nothing," Alinor said breathlessly.

"It is not nothing," Wulfgar growled. "What is it?"

Alinor gasped, clutching her belly as a particularly hard contraction hit her.

Wulfgar paled, a look of pure terror washing over his features as he placed his hand on her belly, feeling

CONQUERED

it grow rock hard beneath his palm. "Jesus Christ! You can not!—Not now!"

"No. I will be fine when I can get off this horse," she assured him a little breathlessly.

Wulfgar glanced helplessly at Thomas, who had pulled alongside them when he saw Wulfgar slow his steed. "She is having the babe."

"Now?" Thomas demanded. "Christ! I have never seen a woman who was not more trouble than she was worth!"

Wulfgar glared at him. "You speak of my wife?" he growled threateningly.

Thomas glanced at him in alarm. "Nay, my lord! But—we are not even a dozen all together, and most are wounded! We can not hope to hold that hoard off that pursues us!"

"I know of a cave in the cliffs not far ahead," one of the men near enough to hear them volunteered.

"A cave!" Wulfgar roared furiously.

The man looked taken aback, but shrugged. "I only thought it might be better than trying to birth her babe in a rocking boat—assuming we reach the beach."

Wulfgar considered it for only a moment. "You will show me. Loose the horses, take the boat and row out into the water. With any luck they will think they have lost us and turn back."

Alinor clutched at Wulfgar. "Nay. Let us go with them. It is too soon for the babe. Likely the pains will cease if I could but lie still for a bit."

Wulfgar shook his head. "Mayhap they will, but not in a boat. You will be jounced as much or more if we get you into the boat. We will go to the cave and rest a bit. When you are feeling better, we will signal for them to come back for us."

Alinor found she simply didn't have the strength to argue and she had ceased to care about anything beyond the hope of escaping her pain. She said nothing more, trying only to close her mind to the blinding pain. It was the with the greatest relief that she heard the sound of pounding waves not long afterward and knew they were nearing the beach—though she had never thought to be glad to hear that sound.

It took precious minutes to locate the cave, but they discovered it at last and Wulfgar carried her inside, laying her carefully on the cold stone floor. "Attend your lady," Thomas said. "I will keep watch at the entrance."

Wulfgar shook his head. "You have done enough, old friend. Far more than many a man would. Go with the others."

Thomas' jaw set stubbornly. "I have never questioned any order you gave me, Lord Wulfgar, but I will not leave you and your lady alone."

Wulfgar studied him a long moment and finally nodded. Turning away from the cave entrance, he made his way carefully through the dark interior, kneeling when he saw Alinor's dim outline. She was curled into a tight ball. Pulling his cloak from his shoulders, he spread it on the floor of the cave and lifted Alinor onto it, wrapping it around her. "Better, love?"

Alinor groaned in spite of all she could do. "Yes," she lied.

"Quiet!" Thomas whispered harshly. "They are almost upon us."

Time lost all meaning to Alinor after that. She was vaguely aware of movements around her, whispered conversations, but she had ceased to exist. Her belly was on fire with pain and she could find no relief from it. In the beginning, there had been some respite, no more than a few minutes, but even that would have been welcome after a time, for she had none at all.

She became aware at one point that there was light in the cave and glanced around to discover a small fire had been built near where she lay. "They will see the light. You must put it out."

"They have gone—satisfied that they chased us into the sea. You are safe, love."

Alinor clutched Wulfgar's hand when he would have moved away. "I am so sorry."

Wulfgar frowned. "For what?"

"Everything … for being so much trouble."

Wulfgar stroked her cheek soothingly. "You are no trouble to me."

It was kind of him to say so, though she knew it was a lie, but the pain consumed her again and she forgot everything else. She began to wonder after a while how much time had passed.

"Where is Hilda?" she asked fretfully.

"She escaped into the woods. Do not worry about her. She has gone to live with her son. She will be fine."

"Jean-Pierre knows. He will kill her."

"Jean-Pierre is dead and no longer a threat to anyone," Wulfgar said harshly.

"You have avenged her then?"

"What?"

"Freda. You have found peace?"

Wulfgar said nothing for so long that she began to wonder if she had only thought, and not said, the words. "Aye. When I found you."

Alinor frowned, but she wasn't certain what he meant by that, for he had had no peace since he had found her.

"How long have we been here? Are they not coming back for us?"

Wulfgar glanced at Thomas. "They have returned. We will leave as soon as you are better."

"Am I dying?"

"Nay!" Wulfgar said harshly. "Do not talk of such! It has only been a little while. It only seems long because you are in pain."

Despair filled Alinor. "Not long? Wulfgar, I do not think I can endure this if it is to take much longer."

Wulfgar looked at Thomas and nodded toward the mouth of the cave. Rising, he followed him. "What think you?"

Thomas shook his head. "I've helped a mare with her foal, and a sow with her piglets, but I've no notion of birthing a babe. We should look for a woman to help her."

"Look where?" Wulfgar said sharply. "Likely if we could find one it would be too late to be of use to her."

"My mother told me it took her three days to birth me," one of the men outside volunteered.

Wulfgar glanced at the man. It was Kavan, the man who'd told them of the cave. "I have doubt that Alinor can last two more. She is nigh exhausted now."

The man shrugged. "There's never any telling how long these things will take. When my mother birthed her last, that took no more than a matter of hours."

Everyone, including Wulfgar, looked him over curiously. "You have knowledge of this? First hand?"

He blushed. "I've no sisters. My mother needed someone to help and none of the others could stomach it."

Wulfgar grasped the man by his tunic and hauled him to his feet. "You will help Alinor, then."

Startled, Kavan flicked an uncomfortable glance at him. "I am willing enough, my lord, but if there is ought wrong, I do not have the skills to help her."

"You've more knowledge than the rest of us. At least have a look. If you think it will wait a while, mayhap it would be best to try to get her across the channel and find a woman to help her."

When Kavan had examined her, however, he shook his head. "I can see the child's head. If we move her now we're likely to kill them both."

He leaned down and caught Alinor's face, shaking her slightly. Alinor had been drifting on a haze, but the movement roused her. "You must push."

Alinor frowned at the stranger uncomprehendingly.

Catching her hand, he placed it on her belly. "When your belly grows tight again, suck in a deep breath and hold it while you push."

She tried, encouraged by his calm words and reassuring touch, certain that it meant her trial was almost over. After a while, however, she found it was harder and harder to focus on what he was saying and to do as he told her.

Kavan sat back, frowning. "She is too weak. She will never push the babe out at this rate." He thought about it for several moments and finally directed Wulfgar to sit behind her, holding her up. Taking Wulfgar's cloak, he folded it and placed it beneath her. "This way the child's weight should help. Place your hands on her belly and each time it hardens, push downward … not too hard. Just help her."

Within moments, Alinor felt her legs begin to shake from the effort. Each time she reached the point of giving up, however, the stranger would speak sharply, or encouragingly, to her, always distracting her from the urge to simply give up the effort and slip to the floor.

"Almost there. Just push a little more. Hold only a moment. Now. Push."

Abruptly, something heavy slipped away and the pain ceased as abruptly as if it had been sliced from her body. Alinor wilted weakly against Wulfgar's chest, barely conscious.

A moment passed and then another. Alinor had just realized something was not right when she heard a choking noise followed by an angry wail. A sob of relief escaped her.

"He is alive?"

"Aye," Wulfgar murmured against her cheek. "He is."

Kavan frowned. "Hold her only a few more moments."

"Is something wrong?" Alinor asked fearfully.

Kavan glanced at her. "Nay. Small wonder this fellow gave you such a time. He's a strapping lad. But first I must tie this off when the blood ceases to flow." He paused, tearing a strip from Alinor's gown. "And see that the after birth has passed."

He nodded at Wulfgar finally and Wulfgar helped her to lay down beside the squalling infant. Tired as she was, Alinor gathered him close to her heart, laughing and crying at the same time. "He is so tiny!"

Kavan exchanged a look with Wulfgar. "You are not used to seeing infants. He is a good sized lad, I give you my word."

Alinor tugged the cloak back so that she could study the baby's face and finally looked up at Wulfgar, smiling. "He is beautiful, is he not?"

Wulfgar looked down at the bloody, red faced, wrinkled thing she held in her arms. "Aye," he agreed weakly.

Chapter Nineteen

Alinor had just settled into her bath when a maid rushed into the room to tell her that Wulfgar had returned. A thrill of excitement went through her, but also exasperation and dread. She had not expected him quite so soon. She had spent the past hour preparing her bath, anxious to look her best for him when he returned since it would be the first time since his son's birth that she would be able to receive him as a wife. After a moment, she sent the maids to tell him she would be down shortly and rushed the maids through washing her hair.

The door to their bed chamber burst open, slamming against the wall just as the maid was finished rinsing her hair. Startled, the maid squeaked in surprise, dropping the pitcher. Alinor's head whipped toward the door.

Wulfgar stood in the doorway, his expression dark with anger. As his gaze settled upon her in the tub, however, a curious mixture of surprise and desire abruptly replaced the anger. He pointed at the maids. "Out!"

The maids looked at Alinor questioningly and she nodded. "Have someone bring up the food I asked to be prepared for my lord."

"Later," Wulfgar said shortly as the maids scurried from the room. Closing the door behind them, he strode across the room to the hearth, placing his back to it and staring down at her.

"You are cross," Alinor observed coolly.

Wulfgar stared at her a long moment and finally scrubbed his hand along his jaw and turned away. "I was ... not pleased to be told upon my arrival that my wife was detained—when I have been gone for weeks."

Alinor studied his rigid back for several moments before it occurred to her that he had suspected she was 'detained' because she was entertaining. Anger washed through her, but after a moment it occurred to her that it was entirely her own fault that he had jumped to such a nasty conclusion. Her mother had told her she would live to regret having sown that seed of doubt, and indeed she did, for trust, she saw, would be slow in coming, particularly after the lie she had told to dissuade Jean-Pierre's attentions.

She had been revolted at the very thought of accusing her own husband of bringing her a disease from a whore, though.

Unfortunately, that was the one part of the story she had fabricated that had mightily displeased Wulfgar. When coupled with her previous remark about her own needs, it had proven to be fodder for jealousy.

Sighing deeply, Alinor returned her attention to finishing her bath before the water grew cold. After a few moments, she realized that Wulfgar had turned to watch her. She pretended she had not noticed, but the desire in his eyes was a goad to tease him—in part because of his unpalatable suspicions, in part because it thrilled her to see the hunger in his gaze as he watched her. "Would you care to bathe while the water is still hot, my lord?"

Without a word, Wulfgar began shedding his garments, though his gaze never left her. When she rose and swiped the excess water from her body, he went perfectly still, his gaze locked upon her as she stepped from the tub and wrapped a length of linen around herself. The linen clung damply to her skin, nearly transparent. After a moment, Wulfgar seemed to shake his stupor. Tugging off his boots and breeches, he climbed into the tub, grabbed the sponge that she had been bathing with and began to scrub himself quickly. When he dropped the sponge and leaned forward to splash water over his face, Alinor knelt and took the sponge, then felt around in the tub for the soap he'd dropped. He sat back abruptly as her hand grazed his thigh, but Alinor pretended she hadn't noticed, concentrating on rubbing the soap into the sponge. Setting the soap aside, she moved behind him and scrubbed his back, then lathered his hair before retrieving the pitcher to rinse the suds from his hair.

She was still trying to rinse the soap from his hair when Wulfgar twisted around abruptly, grasped her around the waist and dragged her across his lap. She gaped at him in surprise.

"Woman—'tis a dangerous game you play."

Alinor dropped the pitcher to the floor and draped her arms around his neck. "Is it?"

His eyes narrowed.

Leaning toward him, Alinor grazed the line of his jaw with a nibbling kiss. "What will happen if I do?" she whispered in his ear before tracing the swirls of his ear with the tip of her tongue.

A shudder went through him. Gripping her tightly, he rose straight up from the tub, glanced speculatively toward the bed and finally stepped from the tub. Kneeling, he laid her upon the rug before the hearth, capturing her lips in a heated kiss as he followed her down, covering her body with his own.

Alinor found her hunger equaled his. Murmuring an approval into his mouth, she wound her arms tightly around his neck, entwining her legs with his. It was all the encouragement he needed. Leaning away, he dragged the wet linen from between them and tossed it away. Their wet bodies clung, slipped, drove them both over the edge as they rolled on the rug, seeking to position themselves.

Despite her readiness, a twinge of discomfort suffused her as he slipped his engorged flesh inside of her, driving deeply, but the discomfort passed quickly as he began to thrust, haphazardly at first, pausing and pulling away so that he could suckle her breasts, kiss her shoulder and neck, her lips. Finally, feeling the desperate need descend upon her, she locked her legs around his waist, arching to meet his thrusts, demanding a rhythm that would take her to culmination. He fell into a rhythm then that pleased them both, thrusting and retreating smoothly, deeply.

Within moments, Alinor reached her crisis, crying out in bliss as her body convulsed around his engorged flesh. The clenching of her body around his cock sent him over the edge, as well. They lay gasping and sated in the aftermath, still entwined, their bodies still joined.

After a moment, Wulfgar gathered her tightly in his arms and rolled to his back. Alinor lay limply atop him, her cheek pressed to his chest. A sense of peace settled over her. Turning her head slightly, she placed a light kiss in the center of his chest, above his pounding heart. "I desire no one save you, Wulfgar."

He stiffened, pushed her away so that he could look at her.

She smiled wryly. "I have an unruly tongue. Many times I have spoken without judicious thought and then found that what I have said did not come out just as I meant it to. I could not bear to think that you might do this with anyone else. I only meant to make you understand how it would make me feel if I found that you had—not to place doubt in your mind about me."

Wulfgar frowned thoughtfully, stroking her back, but he said nothing.

She reached up, placing her palm on his cheek so that he looked at her. "I love you, Wulfgar, with all my heart. I desire no other."

Wulfgar's eyes lit, but after a moment he looked away, frowning. "A proper courtship would not have left us vulnerable to so many doubts," he said slowly. "I spoke thoughtlessly myself ... many times."

Alinor chuckled, drawing his attention. "You will think me strange, but ... I thought it thrilling that you stole me away."

Wulfgar's lip quirked upward. Rolling onto his side, he faced her. "I terrified you."

Alinor bit her lip. "Mayhap a little—but I was far more terrified that you would decide to take me back ... and disappointed that you seemed so disinterested in ravishing me."

Wulfgar chuckled, but sobered almost at once. "I was not disinterested. I could think of little else, but I could not bring myself to force you and watch the innocence in your eyes die."

"Oh." Alinor frowned and then blushed. "I thought ... I thought it was because you ... feared that you might come to care for me, at least a little."

"I am so easily read, then?"

Alinor shrugged. "Apparently not."

Wulfgar tucked his fingers beneath her chin. "I can not honestly say what I felt then … beyond confusion. All I do know is that from the moment you looked up at me and I saw fear, and innocence, and trust in your eyes I was torn between the desire to protect you and … the desire to have you. There is no doubt in my mind that I love you, Alinor—as I have never loved anyone else. Any doubts that remained in my own mind vanished when you were taken from me, and when I watched you struggling to bring our son into the world. All I could think of then was that there would be no life for me without you."

Alinor hugged him tightly, lifting her lips for a kiss to seal their vows. "I am so relieved little Wulfgar took no hurt from all of our adventuring," she said on a happy sigh when they parted at last.

"Aye," Wulfgar agreed.

"He is such a beautiful child! He looks just like his father."

Wulfgar looked torn between amusement and doubt. "Only a mother's eyes would see beauty in such a creature."

Alinor struck him playfully, but laughed. "I knew you were horrified when you first saw him! And no consideration made for what the poor babe had endured finding his way into this world. You should see him now. He is beautiful."

Wulfgar forestalled her, however, when she would have rushed away. Standing, he scooped her into his arms and strode to the bed. "Later. Just now I am far more interested in showing you how much I adore you and allowing you to show me how much you adore me."

Alinor wrapped her arms around his neck, smiling. "I would love to adore you … all over your body."

CONQUERED

Wulfgar gave her a heated gaze as he placed her atop the mattress and followed her down. "Me first," he growled huskily.

The End